**EVERY JARADA IN THE
ROOM WAS FIGHTING WITH
A SAVAGERY THAT TOOK
WORF ABACK . . .**

A Klingon warrior's greatest joy was in battle, but there was something unhealthy about this melee. The scene reminded Worf of sharks in a feeding frenzy, when the scent of blood sent them attacking anything, even one of their own. Those sharks were no more sane than these Jarada, and Worf knew he must report this to the captain immediately.

Suddenly, the insectoid aliens turned and charged Worf. The Jarada, Worf noted, outnumbered him forty to one. With odds like that, only a fool or a berserker would fight if he had any alternative. Worf decided to take the only sane option available.

He snatched the blankets from his bench and tangled them into the legs of the two leading Jarada. They went down and several others piled into them. While the mob was sorting itself out, Worf executed a high-speed evacuation in search of a less exposed position . . .

Star Trek: The Next Generation

STAR TREK®
THE NEXT GENERATION™

#22

IMBALANCE

V.E. MITCHELL

POCKET BOOKS

New York   London   Toronto   Sydney   Tokyo   Singapore

An *Original* Publication of POCKET BOOKS

POCKET BOOKS, a division of Simon & Schuster Inc.
1230 Avenue of the Americas, New York, NY 10020

STAR TREK is a Registered Trademark of Paramount Pictures.

This book is published by Pocket Books, a division of Simon & Schuster Inc., under exclusive license from Paramount Pictures.

ISBN: 0-671-77571-5

First Pocket Books printing June 1992

10 9 8 7 6 5 4 3 2 1

POCKET and colophon are registered trademarks of Simon & Schuster Inc.

Printed in the U.S.A.

To the crew of the "scoutship" IGS *Initiative*, for sharing the STAR TREK dream and for tolerating a "commanding officer" who is "out there" as often as she is "down here":

Lt. Cmdr. Loudon Stanford, who ignores all of us as much as he can

Lt. Ruth Vance, who *wishes* she could ignore what we do to the computers and tries to keep everyone else organized

Lt. JoAnn Long, who sees everything pass across her desk—over and over and over

Lt. Craig Hall, who put up with four years of this insanity before transferring to Starbase Houston

Lt. (j.g.) Mary Heuett, who picks up the pieces after the rest of us have turned them into chaos

Ensigns Noel Brevick and Jon Gustafson, for meritorious service in the face of monumental tedium and terrifying deadlines

and our commanding officer:

Capt. Earl Bennett, who finds new and fascinating ways for keeping space cadets off the unemployment lines

Chapter One

Captain's Log, Stardate 44839.2:

The *Enterprise* is en route to Beltaxiyan Minor, a Jaradan outpost in the Archimedes Sector. The Jarada, an exacting and reclusive race, have contacted the Federation with a request to negotiate an exchange of ambassadors. In addition, they *specifically* requested the services of the captain of the *Enterprise* as chief negotiator.

Personal Log, Continuing:

While I am only too happy to further peaceful relations between the Federation and its neighbors, the nature of this assignment is enough to give anyone pause. The Jaradan attitude toward protocol is as demanding as their isolationism is strict. One can't help but wonder if there is more to their request than a simple exchange of ambassadors.

"COMMENTS, ANYONE?" Captain Jean-Luc Picard glanced around the table in his ready room to see which of his officers wanted to add something to the briefing. Riker, Geordi, Troi, Crusher, and Worf all wore frowns of varying degrees, telegraphing their opinions as clearly as if they had spoken. Only Lieutenant Commander Data, his golden eyes alight with anticipation at the discoveries he had made about their assignment, seemed oblivious to the tension in the room. *So be it*, Picard thought, recognizing the signs of an imminent lecture. "Mr. Data, would you give us your report, please?"

"Certainly, Captain." The android cocked his head to one side, as if to better analyze his information as he reported it. "I have run searches on all available databases, including every classified system to which I could gain access in the time available. I have located fifteen references to the Jarada that have been recorded in the last five years. Unfortunately, the only report that is not based on second-hand or hearsay information is our own contact with the Jarada at Torona IV on Stardate 41997.7."

Commander William Riker leaned forward, his elbows on the table and the forefingers of his clasped hands pointed toward Data. The frown on his handsome face had deepened while Data had been speaking. "In other words, we know as much about this situation as anyone."

"I believe that would be a correct analysis, Commander. There is very little information to support any conclusions about the Jarada or their motives."

Dr. Beverly Crusher looked up from the dark polished surface of the table, brushing her red hair away from her face with an impatient flip of her hand. "The same goes for their biology and social structure. I've gone over everything I could find and I still don't know enough to draw any conclusions. We know they are insect*like*, but I can't even tell you what the appropriate model is. Is their society analogous to that of Earth's ants? Or bees? Or termites?" She shrugged, lifting her empty palms to emphasize the gesture. "Perhaps a model from a different planet would be more appropriate. I just don't know."

"Understood, Doctor." Picard's fingers tightened around his stylus, a concession to his frustration even though he had expected the negative reports. If the assignment had been easy, Starfleet would not have given it to the *Enterprise.* "Mr. La Forge, do you have anything to say?"

"About the orbit?" Lieutenant Commander Geordi La Forge looked up, breaking the intense concentration he had been giving his computer padd. As he moved his head, the room's lights danced off the gold and silver band of his VISOR. "It will be tricky, but nothing the ship can't handle. The orbital dynamics are fairly complicated because of the large number of objects in the Beltaxiyan system. Our biggest problems will come in the first few hours, while we collect enough information on the system to define our orbit and the orbits of everything in the area."

"Mr. La Forge is correct," Data glanced at the chief engineer before returning his attention to the captain. "The Beltaxiyan system has not been thoroughly explored by Federation researchers. Our information indicates that there are two planets within the star's habitable zone. Beltaxiyan Major is a gas giant with a mass approximately twice that of Jupiter. Beltaxiyan Minor follows a highly inclined orbit around the gas giant, with an orbital period of five Earth days. Beltaxiyan Minor's rotational period is locked into a three to two resonance with its orbital period. The system also contains a large number of smaller satellites and moonlets as well as several other planets in distant orbits, but we have insufficient information—"

"Thank you, Mr. Data. That will be all for now." In spite of his best intentions, Picard could not completely conceal his impatience with the android's lecture on orbital mechanics. The complexity of the Beltaxiyan system and the inadequacy of their knowl-

3

edge added to the difficulty of their mission, but only Data could find material for an hour's lecture on the subject. A flicker of amused affection passed through the captain's mind and his mood softened. The prospect of dealing with the Jarada had them all a little on edge.

Picard closed his eyes briefly, remembering their last encounter with the Jarada. He had spent days practicing the required fifteen-second greeting until his pronunciation and intonation had been perfect. Even now, the memory of that tense moment when they all waited to hear if he had passed the Jaradan test left his palms slick with nervous perspiration. No, this assignment would not be an easy one. That the Jarada had contacted the Federation suggested that they wanted something—and wanted it badly. It was his job—and the *Enterprise*'s—to discover what the Jarada wanted as quickly as possible, before prolonged contact gave them too many opportunities to unwittingly make a serious diplomatic faux pas. "Does anyone have something to add to the discussion?"

"Only that the away team cannot be too careful while they're on the planet." Riker rubbed his hand along his jaw, scraping it against his short, dark beard. "The mission profile contains very little information. Nothing there convinces me that the Jarada aren't playing a double game. We can't relax even the slightest bit until we know what they want."

"Agreed." Picard glanced at each of his senior officers, making sure that they understood the difficulties facing them. "If there are no further questions, meeting dismissed."

"Keiko sweetheart, I don't see why the captain insisted that you go on this mission." Transporter

Chief Miles O'Brien's face was creased with a worried frown as he watched his wife flip through the list of reference texts on her computer. She seemed so tiny, so fragile, and he didn't like to think of her facing the unknown risks of Beltaxiyan Minor.

For her part, Keiko was hunched over the screen as if to block out his concern with the intensity of her concentration. Frustrated by her lack of response, O'Brien looked for another way to get her attention. "This could be a dangerous mission, sweetheart. Don't you think someone else should be the one to go down to the planet? Someone better equipped to handle a bunch of overgrown locusts?"

"Dangerous?" Keiko finally looked up, grimacing at the taste of the word that had caught her attention. "Dangerous? A diplomatic mission?"

Taken aback by her tone, O'Brien could only stare at her for a moment. "Well, yes. We know so little about these people, and they're very touchy." He paused to regroup his thoughts. "Shouldn't the captain have assigned, maybe, Deyllar to go instead?"

"Deyllar? That big ox?" Keiko's tone shifted from anger to open contempt. "All he knows is how to catalog plants *after* someone tells him what they are." She drew in a deep breath, trying to curb her annoyance. "I *volunteered* for this assignment. I signed aboard the *Enterprise* to do field work, not sit in some office going over somebody else's specimens."

"But don't you think it would be better if you left this particular planet for someone else? Such as one of the officers who normally handles these assignments?"

Turning her chair to face him, Keiko planted her fists on her hips. Anger made her lovely face as dark as a thundercloud. "Miles, just because I married you doesn't mean I need you to tell me how to do my job."

Do I tell you how to fix the transporters? *I am the person best able to handle this assignment. I'm going and that's final.*" She spun her chair away from him, focusing her attention on the computer with intense concentration.

"But, sweetheart, what about our six-month anniversary? Don't you remember?" Frustration sharpened O'Brien's tone, which he fought to keep even. He had put a lot of care into planning the special private evening that would celebrate the anniversary of their first meeting.

"Our what?" Scowling, Keiko pulled herself away from her work again. Her forgetfulness sent a flare of anger through O'Brien, but before he could say anything, Keiko's expression shifted to exasperation. "Miles, that's three days from now. If you don't stop interrupting me, it will take me that long to get ready for this assignment!"

Before O'Brien could muster a new set of arguments, his communicator chirped. With a sigh he acknowledged the signal. Commander La Forge needed him in the transporter room to check the equipment calibrations against the incoming data for the Beltaxiyan system. The radiation readings, even this far from Bel-Major's magnetic field, exceeded the *Enterprise*'s normal operating range.

"You're concerned about the mission, Will." Deanna Troi's lilting voice was soft, pitched for Riker's ears only even though Ten-Forward was almost deserted. Later, there would be an influx of friends meeting for lunch, but for now, only one other table on the far side of the room was occupied. "Do you want to talk about it?"

Riker sighed and took a bite of his sandwich to delay his answer. Through the viewport beside their table, he could see the growing points of light that marked the Beltaxiyan system—the hot yellow-white disk of the sun, the bright spot that marked the gas giant Bel-Major, the dimmer pinpricks of Bel-Minor and the system's lesser satellites. This complex system would make a fascinating study if it weren't for the puzzle of the Jarada. "It's just that, the last time we had dealings with these people, they didn't want to speak with me. I was just a—I believe 'mere subordinate' was the term they used. Now they've invited me to their world as an honored guest. Do you wonder that I'm a bit jumpy about the situation?"

"Not at all." Troi smiled at the relief she sensed her words had given him. "In fact, I would be concerned if you *weren't* a little nervous. Facing the unknown with too much complacency has gotten more than a few men killed."

"You sure know how to reassure a person." He said the words deadpan, but after a moment his face cracked into a grin.

Troi chuckled with him. "It is my job, you know. Someone has to keep you command types grounded in reality."

"Touché," Riker turned his attention to his lunch, polishing it off quickly so he could get back to duty. He hadn't really been hungry, but he knew they would be too busy later for him to take a break. As it was, he finished ahead of Troi. While he waited for her, he allowed himself the luxury of admiring how the glow from the table painted golden highlights on her cheekbones and disappeared into the midnight cascade of her hair. Friends and once more than friends, the understanding between them was part of the teamwork that made the *Enterprise* such a special place for him. "Don't you have any doubts about this mission?" he asked as Troi finished her sandwich.

7

Briefly, she considered the question and her answer. "Of course I have doubts. We don't have enough information about the Jarada or their situation." She stood and started away from the table, flashing him a grin over her shoulder. "However, if we had more information, we would have to wonder how much of it was *wrong*. If you're after certainties in this universe, Will, you'll have to deal with something other than living beings."

Nodding to himself, Riker followed her from the room. As many times as he had seen her do it, as often as he reminded himself that it was her job, it still amazed him when she gave him the perfect response for a given mood and situation.

Lieutenant Commander Data watched the Bel-taxiyan system approach on the viewscreen, marveling at the variety of objects that orbited the Beltaxiyan star and the intricacy of their orbits. One part of his brain piloted the ship, monitoring their approach through the asteroid belts and outer planets, while other parts studied the orbits of Bel-Major's companions, logged four irregularly shaped moonlets circling Bel-Minor, correlated the wind-speed variations across Bel-Major's latitudinal belts, and cross-checked the radiation levels reported by their sensors with the most recent models for stellar processes in the yellow-white stars.

The readings for Beltaxiya were higher than expected, about two standard deviations above average, and finding an explanation for the discrepancy promised to be an intriguing problem for him to solve while the away team was on the planet's surface. He checked the radiation levels again to assure himself that they presented no danger to the *Enterprise* or its crew, but found no cause for alarm. The humans would have to remain on one of the smaller worldlets for several weeks before the radiation dosage would give them problems. On Bel-Minor, even though the background radiation was higher than recommended for permanent human settlement, the planet's magnetic field would provide sufficient protection for several months. The only problem the radiation might cause would be distortions of the sensor readings proportional to the radiation flux, but since they weren't planning to do any detailed planetary scans on this mission, he didn't need to worry about compensating for the variations.

Turning his attention to more immediate concerns, Data began refining his orbital calculations for the ship's approach to Bel-Minor. Unlike a normal planetary system, holding a "standard orbit" around Bel-Minor put the *Enterprise* into an extremely complicated cloverleaf orbit around Bel-Major. In addition, they had to avoid Bel-Minor's small moons, Bel-Major's mostly uncharted satellites, and the assorted asteroids that cluttered the resonance points of the various orbits. Someday, Data supposed, a mathematician would discover a general solution to describe the paths of multiple bodies orbiting the same primary, but until then the only way to solve the problem was by successive approximations. He excelled at such work, where his unique abilities could be used to their fullest. Clearly, he had gotten the best job out of this assignment, being left in command of the *Enterprise*, where he could study this complex and intriguing planetary system while the others beamed over to Bel-Minor. He supposed he should add diplomacy to his list of studies, but today it seemed far less interesting than the scientific puzzles that were spreading themselves across the viewscreen.

* * *

Worf watched Beltaxiyan Minor grow from a point to a disk on the main viewscreen, each minute bringing closer the moment when they would leave the ship to carry out their mission. He was not pleased with their orders, did not agree with Starfleet's decision which placed both the captain *and* the first officer at risk on the planet below. Commander Riker was correct—they could not afford to relax their vigilance for even a second.

Starfleet should not have required both senior officers as well as most of the command crew to be present for the negotiations. Worf did not like those orders. He did not like them *at all.* Diplomacy should be handled by diplomats, and the Federation should not have accepted the Jaradan terms which required the captain of the *Enterprise* to be the chief negotiator.

Calling up what little information the ship's computer had on the Jarada, Worf reviewed it for the fifth time since the briefing. He did not trust these beings, these insectlike creatures who provided so little information about themselves and yet expected everyone to meet them on the precise terms they dictated. Trust was a thing that must be earned, and the Jarada seemed to be going out of their way to irritate him. Everything Worf knew about them so far reminded him of Federation bureaucrats—their love of protocol and precedence, of precise timetables and schedules set without consulting the other party. He found it difficult to believe that such persnickety creatures had anything to offer the Federation.

At least the captain was taking a reasonable approach to security on this assignment. Worf had no real interest in meeting the Jarada and having them confirm his worst expectations about them, but he had even less desire to allow the captain out of his sight. As long as Worf was included on the away team, he knew that nothing would happen to Captain Picard.

The reason for that was very simple—he would not *allow* anything to happen.

A light started blinking on the console in front of him. He acknowledged the incoming message from the Jaradan Council of Elders and then summoned Picard from his ready room. Whether Worf liked it or not, the negotiations were about to begin.

"On screen," Picard ordered as he strode down the sloping ramp. He crossed the space in front of the command area and stopped between the forward stations, tugging the waist of his dress uniform jacket into place. The screen switched from a view of the approaching planets to a flickering gold and green pattern. After a moment this faded to show the torso of a being seated in a dimly lit room.

Picard gestured for Worf to adjust the controls, and the picture brightened. The triangular face was all planes and angles, making Picard think of an ebony mantis enlarged to human size. The Jarada had a narrow pointed snout and a hooked jaw with sharp, shearing teeth in the front. Interference patterns sent every color of the rainbow flickering across the flat central facet of the large compound eyes, and the Jarada's long, feathery antennae vibrated at the smallest sound. When the alien realized that Picard was watching, he began speaking.

"Captain Jean-Luc Picard of the Federation starship *Enterprise.* We of the Jarada greet you." The voice was reedy and sounded as if several people were speaking at once.

"Kk-hegg-ra'lesh bre-feg'ra leth c'fre!let ji!" Picard answered, hoping he had gotten the proper inflections into the nearly unpronounceable sentence. The pronunciation key that had come with this greeting— "We of the Federation are honored to serve"—had not been as detailed as the previous message he had

been required to deliver to the Jarada. For a moment after he finished speaking, Picard held his breath, waiting.

The Jarada lowered his head in acknowledgment, the light gleaming off the smooth black planes of his cranium. *Chitin* or *chitin-analog*, Picard thought, wondering if Beverly Crusher would get a chance to examine these creatures in detail. The Federation needed to learn so much about these people.

As if reading Picard's eagerness to begin their talks, the Jarada raised his head and responded to the greeting. "Your Federation honors us with your presence. We will be ready to begin our discussions in ten of your minutes, if you and your workmates can arrive at our Council Chambers then. We will consent to conduct the negotiations in your language if you prefer, because we have learned that the tonal values of our language are difficult for your race to reproduce."

"You honor us with your gesture." Picard was surprised, and more than a little puzzled, by the offer. After almost a century of making other beings dance to their tune, the concession was incredible. Either he had misunderstood the Jarada completely or the alien wanted something so desperately that he was willing to do anything to get it. Neither possibility boded well for the mission, but Picard had no way to choose the correct explanation as long as he remained on the *Enterprise.* The only way to find out was to beam over to the planet.

The Jarada bowed his head again, this time bending so far over that his face and antennae nearly touched the console in front of him. "The honor is ours entirely. We shall await your arrival."

The screen faded back to the green and gold pattern, and Picard turned back to his command crew. "You all know your assignments. Mr. Data, you have the conn. Away team, with me." He started for the turbolift without checking to see that Worf, Riker, and Troi fell in behind him. The doors closed on the sound of Data ordering Crusher and Keiko to report to the transporter room.

Chapter Two

PICARD AND THE REST of the away team—Riker, Troi, Crusher, Worf, and Keiko—materialized in a courtyard near the center of the Governance Complex. They were walled in by a dense grove of trees, the thick trunks and twisting branches making it impossible for them to see more than a few meters in any direction. The temperature was warmer than Picard had expected, with the building around the courtyard blocking off any breeze and the walls and brick walkways holding in the sun's heat. A heavy resiny scent, like a mixture of cedar and olive oil, wrapped itself around them.

Through gaps in the dense blue-green foliage, Picard caught glimpses of earth-toned walls, muted browns and reds and ochres that refused to coalesce into an organized pattern. Behind him something skittered against the rough bricks of the walkway. Worf whirled to face the sounds, reaching for his phaser before he remembered this was a diplomatic mission.

Riker was only a moment slower than the Klingon,

14

but relaxed almost immediately when he saw that the four Jarada approaching them were unarmed and wore ceremonial sashes of brightly colored, knotted cords across their thoraxes. By the time the rest of the away team had finished turning, the Jarada were crouched in a ritual greeting posture.

The insectoids had four pairs of limbs, with the lowermost set, the thick and sturdy strong-legs, used to support most of the body's weight and to provide the power they needed when they moved. Immediately above the strong-legs were the longer and more slender balance-legs, which served to steady their bodies after a long leap or to hold their torsos in a prescribed orientation, as now, when they were tucked close together beneath their abdomens in the formal crouch.

The Jarada had barrellike segmented torsos that gleamed with an almost metallic luster, as though each Jarada had polished its carapace until it glistened. Two sets of arms were attached to the upper end of their torsos, the lower pair larger and the top pair almost vestigial. The Jarada extended their larger true-arms toward their guests, holding their three-clawed hands facing upward, while crossing their tiny feeding-arms over their upper thoraxes.

Their heads, Picard noted again, were all planes and angles with narrow snouts and broad foreheads. Large compound eyes with broad central facets surrounded by smaller side facets were set on the sides of their heads, and their faces were framed by long, feathery antennae that quivered at every sound.

The largest Jarada, a space-black individual who wore a heavily ornamented sash and was about as tall as Keiko, took one step forward and repeated the formal crouch. Behind him, the other three Jarada bent their legs to bring their bodies still closer to the ground. "Greetings, Picard-Captain and esteemed guests. I am Zelfreetrollan, First Among Council for those of the People who dwell on this planet. Your presence honors our lowly Hive."

Picard bowed and extended his palms outward in the closest approximation he could make to the Jarada's gesture. From the corner of his eye he could see the rest of the away team copying his movements.

"First Among Council, your invitation honors my people, both those that accompany me on my vessel and those on the hundreds of worlds that belong to our Federation. It is our fondest hope that we can reach an agreement that will enable you to join us in a full partnership which will enrich all our people."

Zelfreetrollan flexed his legs, briefly dipping into a deeper crouch. "Our people, too, share that wish. We will conduct you now to a Meditation Chamber, where you can prepare yourselves for the beginning of our discussions. When you have recovered sufficiently from your journey, we will require that our Protocol Officer attend upon you and instruct you on the Way of our Hive." After another deep crouch he turned and started down the walk in the direction from which he had come. The other three Jarada, all smaller than Zelfreetrollan and with russet- or chestnut-colored exoskeletons, stepped aside until the away team had passed them.

A spicy odor, like cinnamon or nutmeg, hit Picard as the three Jarada fell in behind the away team as an honor guard. Suddenly he was seven years old again, watching his mother grate nutmeg for gnocchis, the shell-like dumplings she had made for family dinner every Sunday of his childhood.

Shaking off the memory, Picard focused his attention on the Jarada. Zelfreetrollan moved quickly in spite of his height, with his strong-legs reaching out in wide arcs that covered the ground more easily than a human's and his balance-legs catching his weight to extend his stride. His chitin-covered feet clicked against the bricks like the mechanical tapping of an intake controller putting its valves through a diagnostics sequence.

The thick trees opened out before broad, shallow stairs that led to the entrance of a building that seemed thrown together from a random collection of bulbous shapes, each a different color of earth-hued plaster. The upper stories sprouted from the lower at odd intervals, as if the structure were a vital entity with a will of its own, and the top level sprouted a central tower that could have been transplanted from Angkor Wat. The building's windows were round and had been placed without reference to any architectural theory that Picard had ever encountered. In fact, the captain thought as they approached the steps, the structure seemed more organic than constructed, almost as if it had grown from the seed of a building plant.

They entered the building and Zelfreetrollan turned left, leading them down a low, wide corridor that smelled strongly of spices—a mixture of cinnamon, cloves, and other things less identifiable. After the brightness of the courtyard, the dim lighting inside made the ceiling seem even lower than it was. Picard noticed that Riker, after bending to get through the doorway, kept ducking his head as though he were fighting against the feeling that he was about to strike his head against the rough plaster above him. In contrast to the uneven finish on the walls and ceiling, the floor was an exquisite mosaic of brightly colored tiles deeply set into mortar to give the floor an uneven surface.

Some of the designs were geometric, sharp outlines and precise shapes of saturated color so brilliant that even in the subdued light they seemed to glow with an inner radiance that made Picard's eyes water. Other

17

segments of the floor seemed to depict realistic scenes, possibly events in the history of the Jarada, but without more time he could not interpret what he was seeing.

When they passed one of the windows, Worf paused for a moment. The glass was set back on the interior edge of the wall, which was nearly half a meter thick. Decorative leading divided the window into small panes, each one a structurally isolated unit. Worf grunted and leaned forward to study the construction more closely. Behind him the skitter of the Jarada's claws against the tile floor reminded him of their mission. The Klingon straightened abruptly, almost banging his head against the ceiling. Half a dozen quick strides brought him even with the rest of the away team.

Picard lifted an eyebrow when Worf caught up with them, but the Klingon's only answer was a deepening of his normal scowl. The captain shrugged and turned his attention back to their course, trying to memorize the various branchings and turnings. Worf would tell them what he had seen when he was ready, and in the meantime, the random appearance of the building's exterior was carried through to the layout of its interior.

Although they were on a diplomatic mission where they should not need to worry about making rapid escapes from enemy territory, long-standing habits were hard to ignore. Away team leaders who became lost could get both themselves and their teams killed, and Picard had no intention of letting himself be caught in such a situation. He had chosen good people, and he was sure the rest of the team were also taking notes on where they were going, but Picard did not want to have to depend on someone else to guide him out of the maze of the Governance Complex.

This mission contained enough unknown dangers without inviting trouble by so obvious a mistake.

After several minutes of climbing and turning, Zelfreetrollan stopped before an ornately carved door. Two of the Jarada following the away team hurried forward, their claws clicking against the tiles. The odor of cinnamon grew stronger as they approached. Both Jarada crouched before Picard, then the smaller one opened the door for the away team.

"Refreshments await you inside, Picard-Captain, and a place to rest from your journey." Zelfreetrollan dipped his head in an abbreviated bow. "The honor guard will remain outside, if there is anything more that you require. Unless you request otherwise, our Protocol Officer will arrive in one-half of one of your hours, and our discussions will begin shortly thereafter."

Picard bowed in acknowledgment. "Your arrangements are most satisfactory, First Among Council."

"Then I will send an escort for you at the proper time." Zelfreetrollan crouched in response to Picard's bow. He held the position until the away team had filed through the door, each one bowing to him as he or she passed. Finally, the door swung shut, leaving the away team by themselves.

Worf pulled out his tricorder and began scanning the room, pausing every few steps to sweep the walls from floor to ceiling. Like the corridors, the walls were rough-finished plaster, a soft beige near the door that darkened to ochre on the outer wall near the windows. The color scheme made the room seem light and airy, even though the low ceiling had been designed to accommodate the shorter Jarada. Unlike the corridor, the air contained only a hint of spiciness, a memory of the much stronger smells outside.

The room was furnished with a long, narrow table,

19

two low couches, and several short, four-legged stools with padded, oddly shaped seats. Riker examined one of the stools, prodding the ribbed fabric to feel how the seat was built. From the shape and from the location of the padding, the stools appeared to have been designed to support a Jarada's abdomen while the insectoid rested one or both sets of feet.

"Not built with humans in mind, Number One?" Picard's voice held a trace of amusement. Given the Jarada's body form, the design was elegant and eminently practical.

"I'm afraid not." Riker continued his examination, as if the stool might tell him more about its creators. The legs were of a smooth dark wood, strongly braced and fastened with wooden pegs. In contrast to the room's door, the stool's legs were undecorated.

Picard lowered himself into the nearest couch, thinking how strange it was to seat himself on furniture that was barely off the floor. The honey-colored upholstery was smooth and cool to the touch, but the cushions were indented, the padding shaped to accommodate a Jarada's body form. Picard shifted position, feeling a bit like a schoolboy squirming at his desk, but after a moment he found a comfortable spot.

Crusher walked over to the table, which held a fluted pitcher and several flared glasses. She passed her tricorder over the pitcher and waited for the results. The device whirred and clicked to itself, taking so long to answer that a frown appeared on the doctor's face. She was reaching for Riker's tricorder to repeat the analysis when the readout appeared. The drink was a concentrated fruit nectar, almost as sweet as pure honey. "I wouldn't recommend drinking this stuff straight," Crusher told them. "But if anyone is thirsty, we can cut it with water to make a reasonable punch."

Picard glanced around, spotting a door on the far

wall which led to a small washroom. "Perhaps we should, Doctor. We would not want to offend our hosts by refusing their hospitality."

With Troi's help, Crusher diluted the fruit syrup and handed the glasses around. One by one the away team took seats on the couches. Worf was last to join them, coming to stand opposite the captain when he finished scanning the room.

"Comments, anyone?" Picard asked.

"There are no obvious listening devices." Worf's voice, like the grumble of distant thunder, was a warning of possible trouble ahead. "However, the acoustics of this room are such that the ventilation ducts could reflect our words to a detector that does not register on my tricorder."

Riker's eyebrow rose in surprise. He looked around the room again, his face showing new respect for the building's designers. "I assume you're suggesting that we act as though we are being monitored, then?"

"I assume that we *are* being monitored." Worf straightened to attention, his head brushing the ceiling. "An enemy commander will use all means at his disposal to learn our plans."

"This *is* a diplomatic mission, Mr. Worf." Despite the words, there was a twinkle in Picard's eye. The Klingon's adversarial approach to life underscored the potential for conflict that underlay any diplomatic mission, especially one where they had so little information about the beings with which they were dealing. While the *Enterprise* team would do everything possible to promote good relations with the Jarada, they could not ignore the possibility that the Jarada might have other ideas.

"Yes, Captain." Worf's tone conceded nothing.

"Counselor?"

Deanna Troi shifted position, a thoughtful look on her face. "I am having difficulties interpreting what I sense about the Jarada. Everything is very confused and—distorted. Almost as though something were blocking me."

"Do you mean—deliberately?" Crusher asked, looking up from her medical tricorder. Absently, she brushed a lock of her coppery hair away from her face and reached for her glass. Diluted, the fruit nectar was not bad, its flavor similar to a mixed fruit beverage available from the ship's food service.

Frowning in response to the doctor's question, Troi cocked her head to one side and tried to sort through her impressions. Finally, she shook her head. "I don't think so. But there is a lot of background noise, almost like static. Perhaps because the Jarada are so different from us, I am having difficulty sensing the patterns to their emotions."

"Doctor?"

"I got low-quality scans of all the Jarada who met us. It was the best I could do with the tricorder on automatic." Crusher flicked her gaze back at the tricorder's screen for a moment. "I will, of course, need a larger sample before I can make any definitive statements about Jaradan biology. However, they have at least three sexes and display a certain amount of sexual polymorphism."

"Three?" Riker's voice registered surprise. "I didn't see any obvious differences."

Crusher grinned at his reaction. "The tricorder is a little better at such things than the human eye. It reports that Zelfreetrollan is male, although the readings seem to indicate that he is sterile. The guards are neuter, with no sign that they were ever anything else. With the required females to produce offspring, that gives a minimum of three sexes."

"A minimum?" Picard asked. "Do you have reason to suspect there might be more?"

"Insect physiology is extremely complex, Captain,

even among the lower orders found on most planets. We have so few examples of intelligent insectoid races that it's almost impossible to draw a general conclusion. The most extreme case known is the Tal'rekswee of Nakslzray Four. They have six sexes—fertile and infertile males and females, plus neuters derived from each gender."

Keiko leaned forward, glancing briefly at the doctor's tricorder. "Most insect societies are extremely hierarchical, with the function of the individual determined by what is good for the society as a whole. This is particularly evident in the area of reproduction, where the capability of propagating the species is concentrated in a very few individuals. All the resources of the society are focused on protecting and providing for the few fertile members of the insect colony."

Pausing for breath, Keiko saw that her speech, on a subject so far outside her specialty, had caught the others off guard. She squared her shoulders, her posture challenging anyone to question her expertise. "Many species of plants are fertilized by insects. I became interested in how they functioned."

"Very good, Ms. Ishikawa." Picard glanced at each of his officers. "Does anyone have something besides speculation to contribute?"

"I do, Captain." Worf took a step forward. "This structure is built like a fortress. The walls are very thick and made of nonflammable materials. Also, the leading between the panes in the windows is structural, not decorative. The bars are sturdy and firmly anchored in the surrounding masonry."

"Indeed? That is useful to know." In his mind, Picard replayed their walk through the corridors, taking conscious note of details he had seen along the way. With its multiple levels and twisting corridors, the Governance Complex would make a formidable stronghold, almost impenetrable to anyone who did not have an accurate map. "Is such defensive architecture a recent development, or are we looking at a long-standing societal characteristic?"

"Impossible to say, Captain." Crusher gave him an apologetic smile. "The insectoid societies for which we have information are exceedingly traditional and maintain their cultural patterns for millennia when not perturbed by outside influences."

Riker rubbed his hand across the dark bristles of his beard. "In other words, we're going to have to study the Jarada in detail to learn what makes them tick."

Crusher nodded, a rueful smile spreading across her face. "I'm afraid so, Will. It's almost impossible to extrapolate anything about a conservative society. And since all the examples we have of insectoid races are highly conservative, we must assume that this is the appropriate model to use until we obtain contradictory information. Furthermore, we need to remember that in general, insectoid behavior is extremely formalized and incorporates a large number of ritualized behaviors."

"I hadn't noticed," Riker muttered under his breath. The volume was carefully gauged, loud enough for everyone to hear but soft enough for the captain to ignore.

Picard stood, bringing the discussion to a close. "In that case, we'll all have to keep our eyes and ears open for every possible bit of information. The more we know about the Jarada, the greater our chances of maintaining friendly relations with them."

As if in answer to Picard's words, someone rapped on the door. After a moment the intricately carved panel swung inward. A small copper-colored Jarada crouched to greet them, then said, "I am called Zelnixcanlon. If you are ready, I am assigned to you as Protocol Officer to counsel you in the Ways of our Hive. Is there any information you wish from me before I conduct you to the Council Chambers to begin the negotiations?"

Picard returned the Jarada's bow. "We thank you, Zelnixcanlon. Since we are new to your world, we would be honored if you would tell us exactly what to expect and how we should respond."

Zelnixcanlon's antennae fluttered like a pair of stalks in the wind, but the Jarada bent its legs until its abdomen touched the tiled floor. "This is my function, to instruct you in That-Which-Is-Needful." And for the next hour the Jarada did, describing in detail the ritual exchange of greetings and how the negotiations would proceed afterward.

The Jarada honor guard led them on an even more convoluted course to the Council Chambers than their original path to the Meditation Chamber had been. First the corridors led upward and twisted into the interior of the building, at one point passing through a gallery near the highest part of the structure. The small round windows looked down on the dense foliage that crowned the trees in the courtyard where they had beamed in.

At least Crusher assumed it was the same courtyard, although the perspective was so different from above that it could have been any of the five courtyards that their scans had told them were included within the complex. The combination of interconnected buildings and enclosed courtyards turned the Governance Complex into a convoluted maze.

From the upper gallery their path worked its way downward, through corridors and galleries that changed from lighter to darker colors and then back to lighter colors. The smells also changed, from the heavy spicy odor they had first noticed, to the sweet, fruity nectar of an orchard littered with windfall peaches, to a mixture of all the previous odors combined with other, less definable scents. Crusher, who was recording their journey with her tricorder, was the first to realize that the odors shifted near each major intersection.

She had noticed the scents much as she would another woman's perfume, but it wasn't until the third or fourth time her tricorder registered a major cross-corridor that she recognized the significance of her discovery. The Jarada used smells as markers for defining different areas within the building. Her tricorder gave her no clues to further explain the puzzle, but she resolved to keep her eyes open for anything that correlated with the variations in the odors. Instinct told her that the answer was important, but what it meant, she was not sure.

Crusher started to explain her theory to Troi, then changed her mind. Until they knew more, she might violate some Jaradan taboo by discussing the subject. It would be better to wait until she knew they could not be overheard. Deep in thought, she was surprised when the party reached the massive and ornately carved door that blocked the entrance to the Jaradan Council Chambers.

Chapter Three

THE DOOR TO THE Audience Chamber was a massive black object built to a scale that dwarfed everything else they had seen of Jaradan architecture. *Abandon hope, all ye who enter here,* Picard thought, acknowledging the irony. No matter how many times or on how many worlds he recognized the pattern, it never failed to amaze him that so many governments for so many diverse societies resorted to blatant displays of power when designing their state buildings. It was as if the rulers could not conceive of governing without intimidation, of authority without domination. Even in societies where the rulers were chosen by the consent of all members of the group, the oppressive architecture often persisted as a reminder that a few individuals exerted disproportionate control over the destinies of everyone.

As they approached the door, Picard got a better look at the ornate carvings incised into every square millimeter of the surface. Some sections were engraved with symbols, writing perhaps, and told the captain very little. Other panels were pictorial—

scenes of Jarada fighters in combat with other Jarada. The poses were highly formalized and the style reminded Picard of a pleasant week of shore leave many years earlier that he had spent exploring the ruins of al-Karnak in Egypt. The Jaradan carvings were similar to the stone reliefs that celebrated the triumphs of the pharaohs, and, once the thought occurred to him, Picard could not shake it.

The Egyptian civilization had been very structured, very regimented, very traditional—similar to the insectoid societies Troi had offered as possible analogs to the Jarada. Looking at the massive black door, Picard realized that they all had overlooked another word that described many such cultures—militaristic. He shivered from an unpleasant premonition, not at all happy with the thoughts conjured up by the scenes on the door.

At Picard's signal Keiko stepped forward with her tricorder and swept it across the carvings, recording them for later analysis. This door would tell them more about the Jarada than the total of everything the Federation had previously known. As if taking Keiko's action as their cue, two small copper-colored Jarada stepped to the center of the door and swung it open for the away team.

A broad aisle paved with brilliantly colored geometric mosaics opened before them. Stationed along the walkway at designated points was a ceremonial unit of mahogany-colored Jarada, each wearing a wide, heavily decorated sash across its thorax. Flickering torches provided the main illumination, giving the scene a timeless, barbaric atmosphere at odds with the technological sophistication displayed in other parts of the Jaradan complex. The arching barrel vault of the room soared overhead, its upper reaches lost in flickering shadows. The effect was deliberate, Picard thought, with the dim, uneven lighting calculated to make the room seem cavernous and any petitioner tiny and insignificant. It was another way of showing the governed their relative position in the scheme of things, and even though Picard understood how the psychology worked, he had to acknowledge that it was effective.

The away team advanced up the aisle. At the far end was a raised dais, its details obscured by the uneven light. The away team reached the first pair of guardians, who crossed both sets of arms over their thoraxes and lowered their torsos almost to the floor. A faint woody scent, like sandalwood or cedar, swirled around them. Picard paused, dipped his head in a marginal acknowledgment, and continued down the aisle. Behind him the others copied his actions, but inclined their heads slightly farther to establish their status relative to the captain's—as they had been instructed to do by the Jaradan protocol expert Zelnixcanlon.

The next pair of Jarada crouched deeply but remained upright, with their clawed hands extended outward toward Picard. The captain knelt, his arm sweeping forward and down in a chivalrous gesture reminiscent of the court of Louis XIV. Again, the rest of the away team mimicked his bow, although a hiss of indrawn breath from Worf told Picard that, for the Klingon, this part of the Jarada's mandatory ceremony went against his warrior's instincts.

As the Federation team continued up the aisle, each pair of Jarada in turn gave them a ritual greeting. Some postures were highly formal or extremely submissive, while others were just short of an arrogant dismissal of the away team's presence. After the fifth or sixth exchange, Picard felt the beginnings of a tension headache throbbing behind his eyes. He drew a deep, calming breath, pushing his anxiety—and the headache—away. This was just another gambit in the war of nerves the Jarada played with everyone outside their own hive. Picard's job was to prove that he was as adept at the game as any Jarada.

Two dozen sets of Jarada flanked the walkway as he knew they would from Zelnixcanlon's briefing, and each set required a different reaction. In some cases he was required to match the greeting with equal courtesy, while at other times the responses were asymmetrical, extreme formality paired against abrupt rudeness. Zelnixcanlon had told them that this precessional was a reenactment of historical events, but none of them, not even Troi, had been able to make much sense of the Jarada's explanation.

The ship's translation algorithm was consistently missing a few critical concepts, and Troi was still unable to decipher the emotional responses of the Jarada they met. Until they corrected those deficiencies in their knowledge, all Picard could do was to treat the ritual as another complex test of protocol. If he could remember all the responses in the proper order, the Federation would have completed yet another trial in their struggle to deal with the Jarada on equal terms.

The farther they proceeded down the aisle between the ranked Jarada, the warmer the room seemed to get. Sweat from the effort to keep everything straight beaded Picard's forehead and trickled down his back.

At times like this, confronting an almost unknown and decidedly touchy race, he wondered why he had accepted this last promotion. The captain of a Galaxy-class starship was more often a diplomat and a politician than anything else. Picard had been an explorer all his life, and he would have been happy to finish his career as he started, scouting beyond the edges of known space. It was a job he did superbly and he knew its value to the Federation.

His ego did not need the power and prestige that

came with the captaincy of the *Enterprise*, but he had found the challenge of commanding Starfleet's premiere starship irresistible. The scope and the potential of his current assignment were awe inspiring, and at times he still could not believe his good fortune at being chosen as captain of the *Enterprise*. Even so, when he was forced to admit it, he confessed that diplomatic assignments were his least favorite duty.

However, Starfleet had not asked him if he wanted to negotiate with a demanding race like the Jarada before they gave him the job. Reminding himself that responsibilities always went hand in hand with glory, he projected more confidence into the ritual greetings, hoping the Jarada would read his self-assurance as an emblem of strength and competence.

Finally they reached the last pair of guards, who flanked the stairs leading up to the dais. Zelfreetrollan was seated on a broad black marble bench draped with a hive-standard of deep crimson edged with gold. Looking up at the Jaradan leader, Picard wondered if he had gotten every greeting correct. For him, the walk down the aisle had been almost as long as the spiritual journey the ceremony represented for the Jarada.

He imagined how a Jarada diplomat from another hive would feel, waiting for an acknowledgment from the local potentate to tell him that he had successfully proved he was an intelligent individual and a worthy representative of his own hive. It had to be nerve-racking to be a diplomat among these exacting and temperamental beings.

The task was difficult enough, Picard thought, although he knew he could have Transporter Chief O'Brien beam him and the away team back to the ship if things went too far awry. That, of course, would not complete their mission, nor would it promote better relations with the Jarada, but it would save their

31

necks. After seeing the martial scenes carved into the door to the Council Chambers, Picard wondered how often the Jarada executed one of their own for failing to remember every detail of their complex protocol.

Zelfreetrollan stood and descended the steps, his clawed hands extended to Picard. "We bid you welcome," he said in his multitonal voice. Even though the words were in English, Picard's communicator buzzed as the translator function attempted to cope with what it interpreted as multiple voices speaking at the same time. Behind him Picard heard a grunt of displeasure from Worf and realized the worst of the feedback must be in the lower frequencies, in the range where the Klingon was far more sensitive than most humans. Data was supposed to be monitoring their communications to prevent such difficulties. Picard hoped the android would catch the problem quickly and direct the computer to recognize this peculiarity of Jaradan speech.

At the bottom of the stairs Zelfreetrollan folded his arms across his thorax and gave Picard the ritual crouch. "Your Federation honors us with your presence. May our association be a long and profitable one for both our hives."

Picard bowed, a deep formal bow from the waist. He could not remember being required to be so formal for so long since he had led the Starfleet contingent to the Federation Games held on Yokohama IV thirty years before. Yokohama had been settled in the early years of the Federation by a sect of Japanese traditionalists, and they had insisted on conducting the games according to the exquisite etiquette of sixteenth-century Japan.

Straightening from his bow, Picard extended his empty hands to Zelfreetrollan. "First Among Council, your greeting honors us. We hope this visit may be the beginning of a long and mutually beneficial relation-

IMBALANCE

ship between your people and ours. The Federation is always delighted to welcome new members into our community. The exchange of ideas and cultures makes all of us the richer."

"This is an idea my people are finally coming to accept," Zelfreetrollan bobbed his head in what Picard took to be an approximation of a nod. As he did so, the side facets of his eyes shimmered in the flickering light.

Picard bowed again and then gestured toward the rest of the away team. "First Among Council, may I present the other members of my party. Commander William Riker, a valued advisor. Counselor Deanna Troi, Chief Medical Officer Beverly Crusher, Ship's Botanist Keiko Ishikawa, and Lieutenant Worf, the commander of our honor guard." As they were introduced, each person gave Zelfreetrollan a deep bow. Picard might have imagined it, but he thought he again heard Worf growl in protest, as though the Klingon did not like taking his eyes off the Jarada for a single moment. Picard suppressed a grin. Worf was a good security officer, but he would never make a diplomat; the skills required were mutually exclusive.

"The Prime Council Chamber is this way," Zelfreetrollan said. "Some of my principal advisors will be joining us there." Turning away from Picard, Zelfreetrollan led the way to a door on the side wall, his claws clicking against the mosaic floor.

Picard followed, still trying to figure out whether the negotiations were being conducted by Federation protocol, Jaradan protocol, or some ill-defined combination of both. He was starting to suspect the last and did not find the idea reassuring. Conducting such an important meeting according to rules being made up on the spot by beings known for their strict standards and their intolerance of error put him at a severe disadvantage. It was almost as bad as playing Fizzbin

33

without a chronometer in the caverns of Marel Five, where the locals could tell the time by the smell of the air, and the day and season from the flow of water in the underground springs and rivers.

Two reddish-brown guards stepped out of the shadows. They moved to the center of the door, pressed embossed knobs hidden in the intricate carvings, and stepped forward, pushing the doors open. As Zelfreetrollan passed, the guards crouched deeply. The odor of cinnamon and cloves swirled around the away team as they passed the two guards.

In contrast to the rooms they had seen so far, this one was almost cozy, its walls hung with abstract tapestries worked in a variety of blues and bluishgreens. The floor was tiled with brightly glazed ceramics that reflected the patterns in the wall hangings. A large oval table of gleaming black wood occupied the center of the room. The guards pulled the doors closed behind them, the wooden panels hitting their frame with a solid *thunk* that reverberated like a stroke on a large drum.

Picard inhaled deeply, trying to identify the smell in the room. For a moment he was puzzled, until he realized it was the near *absence* of odors that had caught his attention. Here the overpowering conglomeration of scents that had surrounded them since they arrived on Bel-Minor was muted to a bearable level.

At the sound of the closing door, five Jarada entered the room through openings hidden behind the wall hangings. Picard was reminded of medieval Europe, where friend and foe alike had hidden behind the tapestries in the throne room to eavesdrop on important meetings. The comparison made the Jarada seem less alien, more human, but Picard had to shake a moment's uneasiness. Suspicion and distrust were not the human traits he wanted to discover in the Jarada, and he wished the medieval analogy had not occurred to him.

Zelfreetrollan nodded his head to each of the new arrivals, the flat facets of his eyes shifting colors as his head moved. Turning, he gave Picard a formal nod as well. "Honored Picard-Captain, may I present the Council of Elders for the Hive Zel?" At his words, the five Jarada lined up behind him and each made a deep, formal crouch to the *Enterprise* team.

Zelfreetrollan raised his left true-arm. A large chestnut-colored Jarada wearing a gold and silver sash that was almost hidden beneath badges and medallions stepped forward. The Jarada crouched again, bending its neck to touch its forehead with its true-hands. "This is Zelk'helvtrobreen, head of our hive guardians." Zelk'helvtrobreen rose and stepped back into the line with the other councillors.

Zelfreetrollan introduced the other four. Zelmirtrozarn, the spiritual leader of Jaradan society, was deep brown and of medium height. His sash contained more colors than anyone's except Zelfreetrollan's. Zelbrektrovish, the head of scientific research, was the smallest Jarada in the room, but its strong yellow ochre color and bright purple sash were as distinctive as the commanding presence it projected. Zelnyartroma'ar, the director of medical services, was a pale honey-gold and wore a dark, unadorned sash. She was the youngest member of the council. Zelnyentrozhahk, whose title translated roughly as "minister of education," moved with the stiffness of extreme age. Her exoskeleton was pale orange mottled with darker splotches that looked strangely like age spots to Picard.

With the introductions completed, Zelfreetrollan gestured toward the conference table. "Now we have disposed of the major formalities and can begin working," he said. "We hope you will not mind that we want to discuss matters with you on terms of equality. However, the arrival ceremonies are needful, so that word will spread among the hive that you are indeed intelligent creatures."

"We understand," Picard replied, feeling more confused by the moment. That the Jarada would dispense with their elaborate protocol should be a singularly hopeful sign for the negotiations. However, the idea made Picard extremely uncomfortable, especially when he remembered the history of Federation-Jarada relations. He glanced at Troi, one eyebrow raised. She gave her head a small shake, a movement so tiny he would have missed it if he hadn't been waiting for it. So—whatever the Jarada were up to, Troi still could not read enough of their emotions to interpret their behavior. Zelfreetrollan could be luring them into a trap, or he might be a reformer pushing through something the majority of the Jarada did not want, or this might be normal Jaradan diplomacy. Picard had no way to tell, given the information he had available.

Everyone took their seats, with Picard and Zelfreetrollan facing each other along the long axis of the table. The rest of the group sat in alternating human then Jarada order, with the chairs positioned so that each individual was also facing someone from the other group. As best Picard could tell, the pairings had been done with an eye on function, with Worf opposite Zelk'helvtrobreen, the head of the Jaradan guardians, and Crusher opposite Zelnyartroma'ar, the director of medical services.

Despite his disavowal of protocol, Zelfreetrollan launched into a welcoming speech praising his visitors and hoping for a new era of harmonious relations between the Jarada and the Federation. Unobtrusively, Picard timed the speech, wondering if his opening remarks should be longer or shorter. Longer might be seen as an insult, as though he were trying to upstage his host, while shorter could also be an affront, offering less to the Jarada than they were giving to the Federation. It was a delicate point, and he decided his best course was to come as close to Zelfreetrollan's time as he could manage.

Watching the Jarada's reactions as he finished speaking fifteen minutes later, Picard decided he had chosen correctly. The six Jarada had listened intently, wagging their heads to the side when he touched on the diversity of the Federation and the opportunities for trade and cultural exchange. Picard concluded with an offer to answer any questions the Jarada might have. To his surprise, Zelfreetrollan asked him to explain how the Federation was governed. This led to a lively discussion of the variety of worlds that belonged to the Federation. Then Worf, Keiko, and Troi gave long explanations of how their homeworlds differed from each other and from other Federation worlds. The Jarada seemed fascinated and, before anyone realized it, the afternoon was over.

Zelfreetrollan ordered refreshments to finish the session—sweet nutcakes and fruit nectar served with a pitcher of water so that the *Enterprise's* away team could dilute the syrup to a bearable sweetness. Worf eyed the water suspiciously, since its presence confirmed his deduction that their conversation in the Meditation Chamber had been monitored. However, no one else seemed to notice, so the Klingon filed his doubts to examine later.

"Picard-Captain." Zelfreetrollan dipped his head in an informal bow. "Your happiness to communicate and your generosity in describing the wonders of your Federation honor my people greatly. We regret that we

37

have delayed so long in experiencing this excellent exchange and wish to find ways to make amends for our hesitance. It is our desire to return the honor you have shown us by sharing the spirit of our hive with your council, if you would consent to allow this. Our people would be greatly honored to meet with your most respected advisors and to show them what our world and our people have to offer your great Federation."

"It would be a privilege to meet your people," Picard answered. "It is our greatest wish to learn more about your world and your society so we may understand each other better."

"Then my Councillors will be delighted if your advisors will grant them the pleasure of showing them our city tomorrow while you and I complete arrangements for the exchange of ambassadors. Our medical researchers invite the most excellent Crusher-Doctor to inspect their facilities and the *val'khorret* would be pleased to meet a musician of Riker-Commander's talent." Behind the First Among Council, Zelk'helvtrobreen bobbed its head to the side in time with Zelfreetrollan's words. "Keiko-Botanist is invited to join a learning-outing from the City Academy, so that she may see the plants and trees of our world. And, of course, Worf-Guardian will want to attend an exhibition of our most excellent *val'ghreshneth*."

As Zelfreetrollan began listing the activities planned for each crew member, Picard felt a moment's dismay at being maneuvered into accepting the plan before he saw its full outline. Also, if the Jarada knew of Riker's musical talents, their information about the *Enterprise* and its crew was far better than the *Enterprise*'s information about the Jarada. A frown flickered across Riker's face, his thoughts traveling a course parallel to the captain's. Worf gave a low growl in the back of his throat, like the moan of a rusty hinge. The Jarada would not understand the Klingon's message, but Picard heard it loud and clear—don't split up the away team.

Unfortunately, the offer was so well timed, so carefully placed, that to refuse might undo all the diplomatic progress they had made. After talking about trust and cultural exchange all afternoon, they could not decline the invitations without risking a serious diplomatic incident. "First Among Council, your generosity overwhelms us. If you are certain your Councillors can spare the time, my officers will be delighted to accept your offer."

Zelfreetrollan gave his head two sharp nods, his eyes flickering from greenish to yellowish with the movement. "Then it is settled. We will show you to a chamber where you can spend the night. When you return here in the morning, we will be honored to show you our world. We ask only one thing of you, that you do not display your communications devices where they might disturb our more traditional citizens. We will, instead, give you translation units of our own manufacture, so that all will know how you are able to understand our people."

After a long formal dinner accompanied by interminable speeches and entertainments, the *Enterprise* team was finally escorted to the quarters assigned to them for the duration of their mission. The room was little different from the Meditation Chamber where they had been taken when they first arrived, and the furniture was identical. Three sleeping chambers opened off the room, all with hard, narrow bunks designed to accommodate Jaradan anatomy, and the washroom contained a communal shower.

It was late, but they had one matter to settle before they could sleep. While most of the group found places to sit, Worf prowled the common area of their guest suite, searching for hidden recorders or listening devices.

Picard worked himself into a comfortable position on the low sofa and gestured for the others to join him. The three women found seats, but Worf continued to examine the room and Riker paced the floor to work off his tension. The captain had to struggle to keep from joining them.

Riker spun around at the end of a lap and stopped opposite Picard. "Why? We know almost nothing about these people and yet you've agreed to split up the away team."

"Fair enough." Picard leaned back, tilting his head upward to meet Riker's gaze. After a moment, when Picard gave him nothing to argue against, some of the tension left Riker's posture. The captain nodded. "I agree with you, Will. It's a risk to separate the away team, and you are quite correct to point that out. However, the purpose of any diplomatic mission is to establish trust and understanding between two races that know nothing of each other."

"Put up or shut up?" Riker frowned, trying the idea on for size. "I still think you were maneuvered into accepting the offer, and I want to know why."

"Counselor?"

Troi's face went blank with concentration as she reviewed her impressions of the day's events. Finally, she shrugged. "I sense no hostility, not even as much as might be expected from a reclusive race such as the Jarada. There is something, some disturbance that I cannot identify, but nothing that seems to relate directly to the invitations that First Among Council Zelfreetrollan issued to us."

Crusher ran a hand through her coppery hair. "I for one am very interested to see their medical facilities. The equipment and the sophistication of their research will tell us a great deal about the Jarada and their society." She paused for a deep breath, shrugging apologetically. "Besides, I feel so useless in the negotiations. I'd prefer doing something where I could make a contribution to the mission."

"Ms. Ishikawa?" Picard glanced toward Keiko. "I assume you share Dr. Crusher's sentiments."

Keiko answered with a brief, controlled nod. "I feel I can best contribute to the success of our mission by doing the job I was trained for. And I feel that the Federation will lose face with the Jarada if we do not accept their invitations."

Riker spun away, crossed the room in four quick strides, and returned, again stopping in front of the captain. "That still leaves my original question—why?"

Picard nodded. "If we could answer that question, we wouldn't need to be here. I'm open to suggestions, but at the moment I see no way to gain the information we need without separating the away team. We asked the Jarada to trust us and the Federation, and they responded with an invitation that forces us to do just that. As Ms. Ishikawa said, if we don't accept, the Federation loses 'face.' That is the basic issue we must consider."

After a moment Riker nodded. "However you look at it, it's another test, and we don't even know *what* they're testing this time. Or what the rules are. I don't see a way to avoid going along with it, but I don't have to like it."

One by one the members of the away team nodded. Worf was last, and his deep scowl betrayed how much he disliked the captain's decision. "That's it, then,"

41

Picard said as his security chief stalked away to resume searching for listening devices. "We'll use standard precautionary measures, with Mr. Data monitoring our communicators at all times."

Finally Riker sat, trying to retain his dignity while searching for a comfortable spot on the sofa. "Captain, since Ms. Ishikawa will be outside the settlement areas, I recommend that an additional crewman accompany her."

"I can take care of myself. I don't need extra protection."

Riker flicked his gaze toward Keiko, then returned his attention to the captain. "As I was about to say, Ms. Ishikawa will have a greater opportunity to acquire information than anyone else, except perhaps Dr. Crusher. Another person would be able to record more data for later analysis."

"Make it so, Number One." Picard looked at his officers, pausing long enough to be sure no one had any more questions. "In that case, this meeting's adjourned. I recommend that we all turn in, because tomorrow will be a long day." Although he had deliberately framed the words as a suggestion, the captain knew what would happen. Within minutes everyone had retired to their bunks, leaving Picard to mull over the day's events. Despite his confident words about trusting the Jarada, he could not shake his uneasiness about the mission.

Something about the Jarada disturbed him deeply, but he could not bring the discordant ideas into focus. Picard knew the insectlike alienness of the Jarada would trouble some people, but he didn't think that was what bothered him. As a boy he was fascinated by the mantises and ladybugs he found while playing in the family's vineyard, and as an adult he had learned to value intelligent life in whatever form it appeared.

Still, a subliminal warning tickled at his brain and demanded acknowledgment. What had he missed? What was his subconscious mind trying to tell him? He played with the idea, turning it over and over in hope of finding his answers, until sleep at last claimed him.

Chapter Four

THE AUDIENCE CHAMBER was deserted, lit only by narrow shafts of light from the clerestory windows high overhead. Riker, following their guide through the cavernous room, tried to remember if he had seen those windows yesterday. They must have been screened off, he decided finally. The Beltaxiyan star was slightly bluer than Sol and, even though the planets orbited at a greater distance from their sun than Earth did, the light level was not appreciably less. Today the rays of white light robbed the Chamber of its aura of ancient and barbaric splendor.

Riker shifted his trombone case to his other hand, reassured by the familiar weight but wondering if he should have brought it. Zelfreetrollan's comments about his musical abilities had been unjustified, but Riker knew they were unjustified. He loved music and played well—for an amateur—but he simply did not practice enough. Certain notes, certain passages, required more repetition than he had time to give them, and Riker knew they would always remain beyond his skill.

They reached the Prime Council Chamber, already occupied by Zelfreetrollan and his chief Councillors, and Riker's thoughts were interrupted by the flurry of greetings and the brief confusion of handing out the Jaradan translators. It took Riker a moment to figure out the unfamiliar catch on the strap. Zelmirtrozarn stepped to Riker's side, clicking his claws together in approval when he saw the trombone case. "It is good that you brought your instrument, Riker-Commander. The leaders of the *val'khorret* are most desirous to learn what manner of music so alien a creature can create."

"The leaders?" Riker asked as he fell into step with the Jarada, shortening his stride to accommodate the insectoid's pace. Zelmirtrozarn was of medium size for a Jarada, which meant his head was level with Riker's chest. In spite of the difference in height, he covered ground quickly and Riker got the feeling that the Jarada had reduced his speed to accommodate the human's two-legged locomotion. "I thought you were in charge of this *val'khorret*, Councillor Zelmirtrozarn."

The Jarada clacked his claws in a boisterous rhythm which, after a moment, Riker realized indicated amusement. "In service to my hive, I am 'in charge' of many aspects of our society, Riker-Commander, but only a fool would claim more than titular control of the *val'khorret* unless his spirit ran solely within the rhythms of their days."

They turned a corner and started down a long ramp that led underground, if Riker had guessed their position correctly. The air was cool and damp, with an earthy scent that reminded him of helping his grandfather work in the garden when he was very young. Gramps had been a wizard at growing things, winning first place at the Alaska state fair for the best and the largest vegetables two out of every three years

45

he had competed. It had taken the young Riker a long time to realize that the ability to grow eighty-pound cabbages was a gift, and not one he had inherited from his grandfather along with the genes for his height and his changeable gray-blue eyes.

With a start Riker pulled himself back to the present. "If you are not in charge of the *val'khorret*, Councillor Zelmirtrozarn, then perhaps I misunderstood First Among Council Zelfreetrollan's explanation yesterday. Could I ask you again what your function in the government is?"

Again Zelmirtrozarn clacked his claws together in the Jaradan equivalent of laughter. "To ask that question suggests that you do not understand our naming rules, Riker-Commander. Does your translating computer not tell you how our names are constructed?"

Riker reached for his communicator, clipped inside his sleeve to keep it out of sight, but stopped when he realized the Jaradan unit strapped around his wrist had done no better. Last night Data had said nothing about Jaradan names, although he had supplied them with speculations on most of the information they had gleaned during the day's activities. On a hunch Riker decided that admitting imperfect knowledge might be a good strategic move. So far the Federation's best information suggested that the Jarada were about a century behind the technological mainstream of the Federation. That hundred years had produced dramatic changes for many Federation worlds, improving the quality and style of life almost immeasurably. To the Jarada, the *Enterprise's* technology must seem almost magical, a wondrous and infallible power that they could comprehend dimly and that they could hope to command only in the far distant future.

A little imperfection, Riker reasoned, might lessen the perceived disparity. "No, Councillor. Our computer hasn't given us any translations for your names. So far it's had enough trouble coping with the tonality of your language, without working on such finer points as naming rules. I'd appreciate an explanation, if you don't mind."

They approached a cross-corridor, the first Riker had seen since they reached the bottom of the ramp. From the left came loud noises—the clashing of metal on metal and a loud buzzing, like the sound of the antique chain saw his grandfather's best friend had used to carve totem poles for the Talkeetna Heritage Park. Wondering what was happening, Riker turned toward the noise. Zelmirtrozarn tapped his arm with a clawed true-hand and pointed in the opposite direction. "I had forgotten. The hive guardians are holding a *vrrek'khat* drill in this sector. We had best move quickly, or we shall get caught in their maneuvers."

"*Vrrek'khat?*" Riker stumbled over the word, puzzled. His translator gave him no clue about its meaning. From behind them Riker heard the clatter of a group of Jarada running in unison. When he paused to see what was happening, Zelmirtrozarn grabbed his wrist and jerked him into the side passageway. A dozen large chestnut-colored Jarada charged past them and headed toward the noise without missing a stride. The odor of cinnamon washed over Riker, almost overpowering him with its intensity.

"*Vrrek'khat* are vicious predators native to our homeworld. They attack in swarms, often in the season when the larvae emerge from the eggs. If they breach the Hive's defenses, they will destroy both the queen and the larvae in their chambers. When the guardians are fighting *vrrek'khat*, they will attack anything that is not-Hive."

Something in Zelmirtrozarn's tone told Riker that the Jarada was lying. Why or about what he was not sure, but he decided to test the insectoid. "I would be very interested to watch the drill, Councillor Zelmirtrozam. Would that be possible?"

The large central facets of the Jarada's eyes shimmered from pale orange to greenish-yellow to lemon yellow. Watching the changing interference colors, Riker realized that Zelmirtrozam was scanning the intersection, checking all four corridors without moving his head. The shifting colors meant the lenses in the central elements of his compound eyes could change their orientation, much like the focusing element in a platform scanner. Thinking that fact might be useful, Riker filed the observation along with everything else he'd learned about the Jarada.

The sounds from the opposite hallway grew louder, and Zelmirtrozam started away from them, gesturing for Riker to hurry. "If you wish, we can arrange for you to watch a drill at a later time, Riker-Commander. However, these passageways have no observation galleries and it is unsafe for you to remain unless you have been marked as a member of the Hive. I apologize for the oversight, but it was not brought to our attention that you would wish to observe this aspect of our society."

"Marked?" Riker shook his head, trying to clear it of the reek of cinnamon. How did the Jarada stand being bombarded by such overpowering smells? He could not remember when he had been assaulted by so many concentrated odors.

"Of course, Riker-Commander. Each individual emits a characteristic marker scent determined by one's genetics and role in our society. That way, one always knows the status and relationships of each person one encounters. Under unusual circumstances one may wish to subdue one's scent, but this can create disorientation in the strangers one meets,"

They reached a split in the corridor, and Zelmirtrozam chose the downward fork. Riker suppressed a moment's uneasiness, envisioning a network of tunnels and dungeons beneath the Governance Complex which could swallow him without a trace. To take his mind off that thought, he asked, "How does this relate to what you started to tell me about naming rules?"

Zelmirtrozam clacked his jaws together sharply. "You are very perceptive, Riker-Commander. You have almost the intelligence of a hive-brother. With proper training, perhaps your people may be worthy to be adopted into our hive."

How am I supposed to answer that? Riker wondered. He thought the Jarada intended his remark as a compliment, but his wording was such that Riker could not guess an appropriate response. Fortunately for him, Zelmirtrozam continued talking as though he did not notice Riker's dilemma.

"Our language constructs personal names so that the listener will know the place of each individual in our society. Doesn't your Federation do the same for its citizens?"

With an effort Riker focused his attention on the immediate subject. "There is no one set of rules in use throughout the Federation. Each world has its own customs and traditions."

Zelmirtrozam bobbed his head to the side. "That is odd. It must be very difficult not to know an individual's position in his hive. I cannot conceive of how your people could function with such uncertainty."

The corridor bent to the left and turned sharply downward. Moisture beaded on the walls and pooled in the low spots on the uneven floor. Riker shifted his trombone case to his other hand so he could wipe the cold sweat from his palm. He told himself that he had no cause for alarm, but the signs of disuse were so obvious that it was difficult to convince himself.

He wondered if anyone knew where he and

Zelmirtrozarn were, and he had to struggle to keep from calling Data on the *Enterprise* just to hear a familiar voice. That thought brought him back to the Jarada's question. "When you deal with beings from other worlds and other cultures, you generally must ask what their titles and functions are. We've concentrated on developing rules for dealing with the uncertainties, because there is no way to avoid them when you step outside your own culture."

"This is a concept with an intensely exotic aroma. It will require much contemplation before I can encompass it." The Jarada was silent while the tunnel twisted deeper underground. Finally they passed through a massive undecorated door and into a cylindrical shaft that disappeared into darkness both above and below them. Dim greenish glowstrips dotted the walls at apparently random intervals. Zelmirtrozarn started to climb upward.

"When you decompose the elements of a Jaradan name, the words will tell you the individual's place in our society. The first syllable is always the name of the Hive, for without the association and support of our hive-mates, we are nothing. Everyone on this planet belongs to Hive Zel, because this is a recent settlement. When our population becomes too large, so that the fabric of hive life is severely distorted, the Hive will divide and new units will coalesce from the segments of the old."

"How often does this happen?" For the hives to subdivide when they became too big was a simple thing, and logical, too, but none of their information on the Jarada had suggested such an event might occur.

"It is a variable thing depending on the resources available to the hive and on the quality of offspring produced. In a new world where we have abundant resources, we can expect the fission to occur in perhaps twenty of your years. On the older worlds the queens produce fewer eggs and the hives grow more slowly. However, you asked about our naming rules, and I should not allow myself to become distracted."

Riker shrugged, then realized the Jarada might not understand what the gesture meant. "I'm interested in learning everything I can about your hive. Please continue, Councillor."

"You are most gracious, Riker-Commander. My caste-mates often claim that my calling is for an administrative instructional function rather than an administrative one. At times I fear my explanations do follow as convoluted a path as this diversion we were forced to take."

They had reached a level space on the ramp and Zelmirtrozarn paused, running his claws over the outer wall. Riker noticed the faint outline of a door. A small click sounded, loud in the enclosed shaft, and a moment later a control panel lit beside the door. Zelmirtrozarn fitted his claws into the proper indentations and tapped out a coded pattern. With a grinding protest the panel retreated into the wall. They stepped through, onto the landing of a well-lit shaft similar to the one they were leaving. After closing the door, Zelmirtrozarn started upward again. "We rarely use the old passages anymore, because they collect too much moisture in the damp season. She who designed them for us was from a different hive, and one has to suspect the motives of those who sent her to work for us."

Riker started to ask if interhive rivalries were common, but remembered the battle scenes carved into the Audience Chamber door. Instead, he returned to the earlier topic. "You were explaining about Jaradan naming rules."

Zelmirtrozarn clacked his claws in amusement. "Yes, I do seem to have trouble staying on the subject.

As I was saying, the first syllable of a name indicates our hive affiliation. The second syllable is the name of the caste to which the individual belongs. One's caste is very important, since it is determined by one's genetic inheritance and in turn governs how one serves one's hive. My caste, the Mir, are the keepers of our hive's traditions, rituals, and values. The Nyen raise and train the young, and the Free are the administrators and rulers."

They reached another level stretch of the ramp and the Jarada faced toward the wall, sliding his claws across the surface until they activated the control panel. The invisible controls were a formidable security precaution, and Riker shivered at the thought of what could force a society to so thoroughly hide the locks to their doors. With an effort he shoved the thought away and searched for a less martial topic. "You said that everyone's caste was genetically determined. Do you mean—you're born into your position and can't change it?"

"Of course," As the door opened for them, Zelmirtrozam clacked his claws together in amusement. "You would have to get a Brek—a scientist—to explain the mechanisms to you, but I infer that our genetics have a much greater influence on our abilities than among your people. Of course"—he curled his feeding-arms and true-arms upward to his shoulders, which Riker now recognized as the Jaradan equivalent of a shrug—"we have a larger genome to work with. Our genetic inheritance is a tremendous advantage in building a stable and efficient society."

"I see." They passed through a second door and into a wide corridor. Sunlight poured through a row of skylights overhead. The walls were a pale golden color and the abstract mosaic on the floor was done in various earth tones. Riker blinked, trying to adjust to the brilliance after the subdued artificial light in the tunnels. A short distance away, from behind a closed door, he heard what sounded like someone torturing a small cougar.

"You do not believe me, I think." Zelmirtrozam clacked softly. "Later we will show you that we are right. Now, however, I must finish one lecture before I begin the next. The third syllable in a name indicates one's function—leader, worker, teacher. As you may guess, individuals may wear distinct functions at different times in their lives, and their naming will change to reflect this. Finally, the last syllable is an individual name, which can be used by itself when one is not fulfilling a formal role. It is such a logical system that I cannot believe your society can operate without it."

Riker drew a deep breath, wondering why he had wanted any part of this diplomatic mission. *Is it too late to convince the captain to leave me in charge of the Enterprise?* There were a staggering number of wrong responses to Zelmirtrozam's last statement. If the Jarada had been deliberately setting him up to commit a diplomatic faux pas, if he had been trying to create the justification for an interstellar incident, he could scarcely have laid a better trap. Riker shook himself, trying to dismiss that thought. After a moment he answered in what he hoped was a neutral tone. "Our system isn't quite so formalized, but it functions in a similar manner." The sounds of the dying cat rose to a crescendo and then were lost in the hollow pounding of an army of what sounded like bongo drums. Riker shivered with the awful premonition that the sounds were being produced by the *val'khorret*, the musicians he was supposed to be visiting.

They stopped outside the room where the noises were being made, and Zelmirtrozam reached for another of the hidden control pads. "I hope you will

53

explain your naming rules to me after the *val'khor-ret* makes their presentation for you. I would be fascinated to learn more about your people," Zelmirtrozam said. He entered the combination into the panel and the door slid aside.

The room was bright and airy, with wide, unbarred windows filling the outer wall. They were on the upper story of the tallest building in the city, and Riker was immediately drawn to the view. He crossed to the window, trying to orient himself. A broad river meandered across the foreground, and the misshapen wheel of the Governance Complex sprawled across the opposite bank. Beyond, partly obscured by the thick foliage of various trees, lay the bulbous earth-toned structures that housed the city's population. In the far distance the serrated edge of a mountain range shadowed the horizon.

Behind him Riker heard the subdued clacking of a dozen sets of claws. "We thought you would be impressed with the sight of our city," Zelmirtrozam said. "We're gratified that our judgment was correct."

"Very impressive." Riker turned away from the window. The city's major structures were on his side of the river, he remembered, and he decided to ask to see the corresponding view after the musical session was over. "But forgive me for ignoring you."

"Not at all." Zelmirtrozam dismissed Riker's concern with a wave of his true-hand. That gesture, at least, was common to both humans and Jarada. "Anyone who does not respond to the first time they meet this view has no music inside his cephalon. Consider it an initiation, and welcome to the inner ranks of the *val'khorret*."

Riker studied his surroundings more closely, noticing that the room was large enough to hold a small orchestra. Even spread out, the dozen Jarada facing him seemed lost in the space. Before he could pursue that thought, Zelmirtrozarn began introducing the musicians and letting each demonstrate his instrument for Riker.

All the musicians had mottled carapaces and moved with the stiffness of extreme age. Also in contrast to most of the Jarada he had met, their scents were subdued, faint enough that he was not overwhelmed by a surfeit of aromas. From their names Riker was able to identify individuals from at least eight separate castes and he noticed wide differences in size and color. *Genetics again?* he wondered, making himself a note to ask later.

"And please, call us by our personal names," said the leader of the group, Riis. She was a diminutive female with a primrose-splotched carapace. "When the music starts, we are all equals."

"That is an excellent idea." Zelmirtrozarn extended his arms in apology. "I will take a lesson from my esteemed colleague Riker-Commander. From now on you must call me Zarn."

The instruments were a surprise, although if he had thought about it, Riker would have realized that their rigid mandibles prevented the Jarada from playing wind instruments. Instead, they had a variety of string and percussion instruments—a plucked string instrument similar to a harpsichord, various sizes of drums, bells, xylophone- and glockenspiellike arrays of tuned wooden or metal bars, a harp that required six hands to play, a tabletop instrument that resembled a cross between a guitar and a violin. A large organlike instrument that needed two Jarada to operate it occupied the back wall of the room.

Riis demonstrated the organ briefly but explained that her usual partner had been called away suddenly. She pulled the cover over the keyboard and sat at the harpsichord. "Now, Riker-Commander, would you honor us with a performance of your instrument?"

"Of course." He lifted the trombone case onto a table. "But if we are all equals, you must call me by my personal name, Will."

"It will be our privilege," Riis answered with great dignity. She inclined her head in an abbreviated bow, and Riker noticed again how stiff her movements were, reinforcing his conclusion that the Jarada in the *val'khorret* were quite old.

The trombone was a novelty, its basic principles unknown to the Jarada. He had to demonstrate how the instrument worked—how he formed a tone by blowing air from his lungs through his lips into the mouthpiece of the instrument, how he could vary the tone by modifying the way the air flowed through the mouthpiece, how moving the slide changed the length of the resonating column of air.

Finally Riker played them a brief solo, choosing a piece by the pre-Reformation Vulcan composer, Karbrésh. He had never mastered the micro-tone scales of modern Vulcan music, which the Jaradan music strongly resembled, but the quarter-tone scales of the Karbrésh piece were at least within his reach— as long as no one counted his errors. Fortunately, the Jarada had nothing against which to compare his performance.

"That was most intriguing," Riis said when he finished playing. "But it was so simple, so like a child just finding the first register of its voice."

Simple? Riker struggled to hold back a groan of dismay until he realized what Riis meant. Most of the Jaradan instruments were designed to play chords, echoing the multitonality of Jaradan speech. Therefore, no matter how complex the melody line, to the Jarada it would always sound simple. "Sometimes human music *tries* to emphasize the simplicity of a single melodic line, such as the piece I just played. More often, though, groups of musicians work together to create complex patterns such as your instruments play. For example, several trombones playing together can produce the same chords as your—" He pointed toward the harplike instrument, unable to remember its name.

"*Zheelsray*," Riis said.

Riker nodded. "And the *zheelsray* could produce music the way we humans do, if you plucked one string at a time."

The mottled brown Jarada sitting at the *zheelsray* rubbed the base of his antennae in puzzlement. "But that would be inefficient, requiring several players and instruments to do what I already do."

"True. I was using that only as an example, because many of our instruments produce only single notes. Even on instruments that can play chords, we often emphasize the melody by playing it louder than the chords."

"This is an interesting concept." Riis ran her claws along her keyboard, calling forth a series of chords. "Would you be willing to play with us and demonstrate what you mean?"

For a moment Riker considered refusing. So far these musicians had shown none of the cultural inflexibility the *Enterprise* crew had expected, based on their previous dealings with the Jarada, but he wondered how far he dared push them. Musical traditions were among the most conservative in any society, depending as they did on a strict consensus of acceptable tonality, rhythm, and harmony. On the other hand, the invitation was courteously offered and could not be politely declined.

Diplomacy! Damned if you do and damned if you don't, Riker thought in disgust. However, if he ever left Starfleet, he could put this on his résumé as one of the greatest of all improvisational sessions. Reaching for a smile, Riker nodded his agreement. "But, please, do me a favor—pick something simple so I can keep up."

Riis glanced at the other musicians, her antennae wagging. The harpist suggested a selection. One of the drummers countered with a different title, and then other people offered their favorite pieces. A lively discussion followed as the *val'khorret* debated which piece of music would be most suitable. Finally they reached a consensus and Riis turned back to Riker. "We have chosen a *kazbrey*, which we can repeat as many times as we wish. We will start and you may join us when you understand the essence of the music." She reached for a scriptboard resting on top of her instrument. "I assume that you read musical notation."

Riker glanced at the board and shook his head. "I read music, but I don't know your notation. I'll have to play it by ear."

A rasping sigh went through the room. Riis bobbed her head in approval and left the scriptboard in its place. "It is not often one finds a musician good enough to work with an exotic ensemble without copying their notation slavishly. We approve."

Riis struck a run of chords, signaling the tempo to the other musicians. She paused for the space of two breaths, then nodded. The group began to play. The *karbrey* was a happy, lively piece that reminded Riker of an Alsrayven folk dance. At first he just listened, trying to sort out the different instruments and their roles. The glockenspiel seemed to dominate, its bright tones filling the place in the composition that Riker considered the property of the brass section. The drums carried the complex rhythm in an interwoven patter that echoed the dominant chords in the music, and the stringed instruments, tuned to a scale based on eighth tones, wove complex and shimmering patterns around the glockenspiel.

After the second chorus Riker felt he understood the *karbrey* well enough to try a simple counterpoint. At first he kept it uncomplicated, holding to the standard scale. His notes, sweet and legato, blended into the Jarada composition better than he had expected, and several of the musicians wagged their antennae in approval. On the next chorus Riker picked up his tempo and even attempted a few quarter tones.

He was beginning to relax and enjoy the improvisation when a commotion, much like the sounds that Zarn had told him were a *vrrek'khat* drill, erupted in the corridor outside the room. Immediately the Jarada quit playing and jumped to their feet. Their claws clattered against the floor as they scrambled toward a door on the far side of the room. "Hurry," Zarn said, tugging on Riker's sleeve. "We must get out of here before they breach the lock on the door!"

Chapter Five

DR. BEVERLY CRUSHER fiddled with her medical tricorder as she watched Riker leave the Council Chamber with Zelmirtrozarn. The two made a strange pair—the tall human in his black-and-cranberry uniform and the deep brown Jarada who barely came up to Riker's chest. A smile flickered across the doctor's face, momentarily erasing the slight frown that wrinkled her forehead.

"It's all right, Beverly," Troi whispered. "These are routine diplomatic courtesies."

"I know." Crusher exhaled sharply. "We've done this dozens of times, but for some reason I feel edgy today. Are you sure everything's all right?"

"I sense nothing." Troi's face tensed with concentration as she tried to read the Jarada's emotions. After a moment, with no more success than before, she relaxed and shook her head. "I think you're suffering from stage fright because you aren't familiar with insectoid physiology and are afraid they will laugh at your ignorance."

Crusher chuckled softly. "I hope that's all it is."

Her face went sober as Zelbrektrovish crossed the room and stopped in front of her. The tiny ochre Jarada projected such an aura of command that Crusher found herself starting to curtsy before she realized it. With an effort she turned the movement into the brief nod that they had been told was the appropriate greeting between equals.

"Crusher-Doctor," the Jarada said in a soft, high-pitched, multitonal voice. It returned Crusher's nod and then gestured toward the doorway. "Our research facilities are on the outskirts of the city. If you will accompany me, our transportation is waiting outside."

"Of course." As she followed Zelbrektrovish from the room, Crusher wondered what would happen if she tried to disobey the tiny Jarada. She felt like a first-year medical student, awed by the wisdom and authority of her department chair. With that comparison, Crusher's perspective shifted and she relaxed. Undoubtedly, Zelbrektrovish dealt constantly with the Jaradan equivalent of starry-eyed freshmen and had perfected its command aura for them. Also, given the differences in their height, Crusher realized the Jarada was probably as intimidated as she was. Crusher had not felt so gangling and outsized when she was with another sentient being since Wesley had turned ten.

They left the building by the side entrance, and a small teardrop-shaped groundcar pulled up to the curb. Zelbrektrovish tapped a coded pattern against the window and the vehicle's door slid opened. Crusher climbed into the back and struggled to find a comfortable position on the Jarada-shaped seat. The contoured cushion left awkward gaps where her human anatomy needed support, and several odd-shaped pillows did not completely solve the problem. Zelbrektrovish fastened its acceleration harness

61

and entered their destination into the vehicle's computer, then swiveled around to face Crusher. "The harness fastens like this," it said, demonstrating the unfamiliar catches. "I always find it advisable to wear it, even when I have a priority lane with no cross traffic."

"Thank you." Crusher pushed a stray lock of hair off her forehead. Ground travel had always made her nervous, even when she was younger and living on Earth. High-speed vehicles moving in close formation, and the injuries that occurred when something went wrong, had convinced her that transporters were by far the safest way to get where she wanted to go. She had been in space too long to ever change her mind, but at least the harness gave her a minimum of reassurance. "I'm never completely comfortable with groundcars."

The Jarada clacked its claws together in amusement, and its command aura slipped away, replaced by a focused warmth that was almost as frightening in its intensity. Crusher remembered one or two humans that could pull off the same trick, most notably the High Commissioner from Dalraydy, Sri Janda.

Just after she and Jack had been married, a group of Federation Commissioners had toured the medical research facility where she was working. Crusher had watched Janda work her special magic on the hospital's chief administrator, a man noted for his aversion to outsiders. Janda was a petite woman, barely taller than a half-grown child, but when she concentrated her charm on the administrator, he had been unable to deny her anything, particularly not the in-depth tour she requested.

Janda's twinkling, impish smile and deep, dark eyes were backed by an intellect that would keep a Vulcan on his toes, and most of the researchers she met during that inspection also surrendered to her spell. Finding the same magnetism in a Jarada made the insectoids seem both more *and* less alien.

"If we agree on the subject of groundcars, Crusher-Doctor, then I am certain we will find other things to share. You must call me Vish if you are to be my hive-partner."

"And I'm Beverly." Crusher wondered what the Jarada meant by "hive-partner," but decided to postpone the question. If the computer was having difficulties interpreting the Jaradan world view, it would help to give it more data before asking it to decipher that conceptual cluster again. They had hoped that having the Jaradan translating devices would give them better data on the insectoids' language and culture, but so far she could not see any improvement over the *Enterprise*'s universal translator. Both societies needed more information about the other to obtain good translations.

"Bev-er-ly," Vish said, testing the unfamiliar name. "I hope you don't mind if we do not take the shortest route to the research center. It was thought that you might appreciate a tour of the city to see the landmarks that you would otherwise miss."

When in Rome, Crusher thought. She was not a good tourist, caring little for architectural styles or heroic statuary, but it didn't seem polite to say that to her host. The Jarada were recent settlers on Bel-Minor, and Crusher supposed they had every right to be proud of their accomplishments on their new world. Still, if allowed her choice, she would gladly give Picard her share of the city tours, since he appreciated the artistry that went into designing and constructing beautiful and functional urban zones. However, the gods were not listening to her wishes, so she accepted the invitation with a diplomatic pretense of enthusiasm. "If you're sure we have time, I'd love to see your city. It's not often I get the opportunity to go sight-seeing in the line of duty."

"I'm not sure that 'having the time' is the precise term I would use." Vish ducked its head apologetically. "This is our season for repairing the roads and, unfortunately, the bridge on the direct route is closed while its center span is being refurbished. I fear that you will find I am barely adequate as a tour guide in the city, since I spend most of my time in my laboratory."

"I'm sure I won't notice," Crusher said with a warm smile. "My son makes the same observation about me—all work and no play. Why don't you tell me about your research?"

Vish clacked its claws in laughter. "Gladly. Remind me to point out the main buildings to you, in case someone asks what we saw, but meanwhile we can discuss more interesting matters."

While they talked, the car traveled through a residential area. The earth-toned buildings were circular complexes made of bulbous units similar in style to the Governance Complex. Except for color, each unit was identical to its neighbors, down to the placement of the doors and the spacing of the windows. On any world and in any style of architecture, low-budget housing was always identifiable by its mind-numbing uniformity. For a moment Crusher wondered if the interiors were as absolutely bland and uniform as the exteriors, but she pushed the thought aside. Vish's discussion of its favorite project, research into the link between Jaradan nutrition and genetics, was much more interesting.

"You mean nutrition alone determines whether an individual will be fertile?" Among Earth's insects, fertile female bees developed when the workers fed the larvae a substance called royal jelly. However,

Crusher could not remember reading any studies on intelligent insectoid societies that used a similar process for determining which individuals would perpetuate the species.

"Not completely. The Jarada have a tetraploid genome, and only those individuals with a full, uninhibited complement of chromosomes have the possibility of being fertile. In some cases, even when both the genetic *and* the nutritional factors are present, the individual develops as sterile or as neuter. What my group is trying to determine is the specific nutritional factors that trigger one path of development over another."

"Fascinating. How far are you from producing definitive results?"

"Oh, we've just begun." Vish clacked its claws in amusement, as if Crusher's question had come from a very young child. It pointed out the window, where the housing units had given way to fields of low bushes. The plants were loaded with brightly colored flowers—reds, yellows, blues, and a deep purple that was nearly black. "Actually, this plantation is part of our project. The *breveen* plant is extremely sensitive to the nutritional content of the soil it grows in, which we can monitor by the color of the flowers. By controlling what we feed the plants, we know the composition of the nectar we are supplying to the newly hatched larvae. It's a very fragrant little project and I'm extremely grateful to the young student who designed it. That one will make a worthy successor to lead our studies when I am ready to retire."

Crusher looked at the bushes with more interest, marveling that the wide variety in colors was produced by adding different chemicals to the soil. Did the trace elements produce the colors, she wondered, or did they control the expression of the genes which made the pigments? In a similar vein, how did nutrition control the expression of the Jaradan genome?" "If it's not too delicate a question, Vish, how many genders are there in a normal Jaradan population?"

Vish's central eye-facets shifted from greenish to yellow, and Crusher had the feeling she was being examined like a specimen under a microscope. Before she could answer, however, the Jarada waved a claw to dismiss its own question. "For you, it would be the scientific question. You do not know enough of our society to realize that the other viewpoint exists."

"Then I'd be interested in both answers, so I can understand you better."

"Ah."

Vish fell silent, apparently in no hurry to answer. Rather than pressuring the Jarada, Crusher concentrated on the view outside the window. The road they were following through the *breven* fields had turned back toward the city, and they were approaching it from a more southerly direction. To their right, in the middle distance and near where the buildings began again, Crusher saw the spidery structure of a bridge. To their left, a gray smudge hung over the sector of the city they had bypassed. Smoke? It seemed to be coming from a large area, probably several blocks in diameter. With a puzzled frown Crusher turned toward Vish.

Before the doctor could ask her question, the Jarada anticipated it and brushed Crusher's concern off with a careless flick of a true-hand. "Some types of trees that came with us from the homeworld have become diseased in this climate. That district was scheduled for sterilization this morning."

Crusher looked back out the window, trying to guess how many trees it would take to produce so much smoke. She was no expert on such things, but a small forest would have to burn to create that dense blanket of smoke. She shivered involuntarily, wondering if Vish's explanation was truthful. For the first time she was conscious of how isolated she was, how cut off from the *Enterprise* and all her crewmates.

"You were asking about our gender divisions," Vish said in such a smooth tone that Crusher wondered if the switch back to the original topic was intended as a diversion. "It is a complicated question, because so much of our society is controlled by our caste system, which is directly linked to our genetics. Therefore, if you ask about gender in a philosophical sense, the pure traditionalist will tell you that each caste represents a distinct gender."

Vish paused expectantly, so Crusher asked the obvious question. "How many castes are there?"

"By the latest accounting, there are five hundred forty-three documented trait-packages that are reproducible and distinctive enough to be accepted as formal castes. Of course, some of these groups are very small, since there is little use for their abilities in most situations."

"Five hundred forty-three?" The number was staggering. Any research into the genetics of such a system would require an almost incomprehensible number of controls. That meant some simpler order had to underlie the apparent chaos of the caste system or Vish had no better chance of obtaining answers from its research than the ancient human theologians had of determining how many angels could dance on the head of a pin.

Vish lifted all four arms upward in a "you asked" gesture. "If one works on the genetic level and uses the most basic definitions, the answer reduces to six. The females are tetraploid and the males are diploid, with only a few of each group developing as fertile individuals capable of reproduction. By tradition, the sterile females and males are considered as separate genders from the fertile. Interestingly enough, some of our research supports the traditional view of how deeply the differences run between fertile and sterile individuals. Then there are the neuters, those with inhibited genomes who fail to develop any sexual characteristics even though they have the chromosomal signature for either male or female.

"Finally, within each gender-group are distinctive trait-packages of color, scent, size, and ability that form each caste. We know that certain traits, such as adult height and mass, are controlled by how much the larvae are fed, but certain aptitudes are always linked with size. If the genetic coding for these traits is not present, no amount of food will produce a larger individual." Vish expelled its breath in a buzzing hum. "It's a very complex problem, and the more we study it, the less we seem to understand."

"I've had problems like that." The car swerved into a wide turn and the road climbed a steep embankment to rejoin the main highway as it approached the river. The spidery structure of the bridge, a gleaming web of steel and composite cables, stretched ahead of them. The river was a wide, smooth expanse of dark water, wrinkled here and there by current eddies or ruffled into whitecaps by the wind. Reminded of the raw, unharnessed power of nature on any planet's surface, Crusher shivered. An old Starfleet joke ran through her head, *It's a nice planet to visit, but I wouldn't want to live there.* Suddenly she wished she were back in space, safely enclosed by the hull of the *Enterprise*.

Halfway across the bridge, a metal object clanged off the roof of the car. With an angry squawk Vish swung its seat around and slapped a series of controls. Armor plates dropped over the windows and the windshield. Behind them Crusher heard a muffled explosion and then, like a string of firecrackers, several more in rapid succession. The car lurched, then picked up speed, racing away from their attackers.

"What's happening? What's wrong?" Crusher asked. Vish did not answer. She tried again, but the Jarada still would not respond. Reaching for her communicator, she signaled for emergency beam-up. Silence answered her.

After three more tries Crusher gave up. She was trapped in the speeding groundcar, blind and deaf. Her communicator was not working and, as long as the armor plates remained down, she could not see where they were going. Her only source of information was Vish, and the Jarada was not responding to questions either. *What else can possibly go wrong?* she thought.

Chapter Six

IT SIMPLY WASN'T FAIR, Keiko Ishikawa thought as she stared in angry silence out the window of the school transport. A whole world to explore, fresh and untouched by any human—and the captain had assigned her a partner as though she were a tenderfoot on her first assignment. She was *by far* the most capable botanist on the *Enterprise*, and she didn't see why she should be forced to share credit for her discoveries with anyone.

And, to make matters even worse, her husband had chosen to throw a childish, jealous fit over the matter, as if Reggie Tanaka were *her* choice for a working partner. Reggie was a sweet, likable boy, she guessed, but she *knew* his incessant, cheerful talking would drive her crazy before this assignment was over. Fortunately, for the moment he was quiet, his nose glued to the transport's window as he soaked up his first impressions of Bel-Minor.

Keiko sighed and focused her attention on the scene outside. The seats in the pod-shaped vehicle were designed to face inward, toward the center, but they could be rotated to let the passengers see out the windows. She and Tanaka were traveling through a residential area that contained the most boring assemblage of Jaradan architecture on the face of this—or any other—planet. If she saw another street of gourd-shaped modules plastered together into fairy-rings, Keiko thought she would scream.

This part of the city even lacked vegetation to give it variety. The few places where trees might have grown were now hard brown earth, compacted by Jaradan foot-claws until nothing could survive. The effect was harsh, sterile, and monotonous, characteristics that did little to recommend the people who lived here to Keiko.

"Ms. Ishikawa, is there anything I should know about our assignment before we pick up the bug-kids?"

Bugs? Is that what they're calling them on the ship? From Tanaka's inflection, the name didn't seem derogatory, but with such nicknames, unpleasant connotations could develop rapidly.

She pulled her attention from the window and turned to her partner. They were the only passengers in the vehicle, although as soon as the autopilot delivered them to the City Academy, they would be jammed arm to pincer with three dozen adolescent Jarada. "The first thing you should know about our assignment is that we don't call them bugs. Their name for themselves is the Jarada and we should respect that."

Tanaka gave her an apologetic grin. "You're in charge, Ms. Ishikawa. Whatever you say."

He really is very handsome, she thought. With his dark eyes and smooth olive skin and the slight gap between his front teeth, he looked like her best friend Kiyoshi had fifteen years earlier. If Tanaka really would accept her authority, perhaps this assignment wouldn't be quite so bad after all. "That's what I say. Nicknames are dangerous because you never know what will get tacked onto them. You of all people should remember that."

"I guess I don't study much history, I always preferred looking forward rather than backward."

She closed her eyes briefly, remembering the interminable history lessons of her youth. To maintain the glorious traditions of Japan's past, Japanese history had been drilled into everyone in her prefecture from the time they learned to talk.

In particular, it was difficult to remember that someone who looked so much like her friend had not been surrounded all his life by the knowledge and experiences Keiko took for granted. "You're right about most of the history," she said, letting herself unbend a little. "But perhaps I can recommend a couple of texts for you and the parts that you would find interesting."

"Sure, Ms. Ishikawa. I'm always looking for new reading material." His grin washed ten years off his face, and Keiko wondered how old he really was. Clearly, he was older than he looked or he couldn't have graduated from the Academy, especially not with a scientific specialty. And a fellow scientist, no matter how much she resented his presence, deserved certain courtesies.

"If we're going to be together for the next two days, this formality is going to get tiresome. Why don't you just call me Keiko?" The memory of her husband's face, flushed with anger as he argued against her decision to come to the planet, flashed through Keiko's mind. The picture wavered before blending into last night's quarrel, when O'Brien had all but ordered her to beam back to the ship.

"I'll not be having any wife of mine running around on some strange planet with whatever crewman happens to be handy," he had yelled, so loudly Keiko was sure the rest of the away team must have heard him even though the door to the common room was closed to give her privacy.

"And I will not be humiliated for working with a partner when there is more than enough work for a dozen botanists on this planet!" she had answered in a low, furious voice, stung by his anger into defending Picard's orders. "I'm following the captain's orders, and you have no right to question them. Or me!"

The thought of O'Brien's jealousy stiffened Keiko's resolve to be nice to Tanaka. "And your friends call you Reggie, don't they?"

"That's right. How did you know? I rarely see you on the ship. We always seemed to be assigned to different shifts or different projects."

Keiko shrugged, but his enthusiasm was contagious. The corners of her mouth lifted in a grin. "It's not that big of a ship. We do have a few mutual acquaintances."

The vehicle turned a corner and stopped in front of a large building. The City Academy had apparently been designed by the same architect who had given the rest of the city its monotonous uniformity, and Keiko decided this particular conglomeration of dirt-colored globs was no more interesting than any of the previous ones.

A group of young Jarada was milling around a pile of assorted packs and equipment. The youths came in all sizes and in colors that ranged from brown to red to gold to pale yellow. Two orangy-gold adults, barely taller than some of their charges, were attempting to bring order to the scene. Keiko hid a smile behind her hand, thinking that schoolchildren were the same everywhere in the galaxy. They always wanted to go on field trips and they never wanted to submit to their teachers' control. She doubted that this trip would be any different from the ones she remembered as a child.

Surprisingly, once their transport arrived, the young Jarada settled down. They stowed their luggage in the side compartments and filed aboard, taking their seats quietly. Most paired off with partners of similar height and color, but a few were mismatched for reasons Keiko could not discern. As the vehicle filled, the smells became overpowering. Each Jarada had a characteristic scent—cinnamon, sage, juniper, jasmine, and others Keiko could not identify—and the mixture amalgamated to form a powerful incense. Suddenly Keiko felt everything whirl around her, and her head seemed to float off her shoulders.

The next thing she knew, Tanaka was shoving her face out the window of the moving transport. Light stabbed into her eyes, and she was sure her throbbing head was going to explode, while the blur of the ground flying past then made it difficult for her to keep her breakfast down. Slapping at Tanaka's arms, she struggled to pull herself back inside the vehicle. "What are you doing, you idiot? Trying to kill me?"

Tanaka helped her back into her seat, adjusting the pillows that made the Jaradan-shaped contours more compatible with human anatomy. "You fainted, Ms. Ishikawa," he answered in his most formal tone. "I surmised that you might be experiencing an allergic reaction of some sort."

Keiko rubbed her temples, trying to get the drummer behind them to stop practicing the morning tattoo. At least her stomach was staying put as long as she kept her eyes closed. "That's a fair guess. I suppose our first aid kit is with our luggage."

"I'm afraid so. Do you want me to have them stop so I can get it?"

The thought was tempting and Keiko gave it serious consideration. However, she wasn't sure exactly what medication she needed, and admitting to the Jarada that she was allergic to them could mean an even greater loss of face. She brushed the hair back from her damp forehead, hoping she could manage as long as the window stayed open. The fresh air was reviving her and had reduced the smells inside the vehicle to a bearable concentration. "I'm not even sure they would stop for us, Reggie. The vehicle is on auto-pilot," she said finally. "And I'm sorry I snapped at you."

She heard Tanaka settle back against his own pillows. "That's all right. I knew the harness would hold you. But for that first instant I'll bet you didn't have a clue what was happening."

"That's for sure." Keiko forced herself to relax against the pillows. "I think I'll try to sleep." She had heard once that rest was the best restorative for allergy attacks, and right now a nap sounded like a fabulous idea. The quiet chittering of the Jarada and the smooth humming of the vehicle's tires against the road soon lulled her to sleep.

When she awoke, the vehicle was slowing, its tires bouncing on the uneven surface of a gravel road. Keiko rubbed her gummy eyes, feeling groggy and thoroughly out of sorts. Outside, dense clusters of trees crowded close to the road, reaching toward the windows with gnarled, twisted limbs hidden under plump, waxy leaves. The bus skittered and bounced from side to side, showing more bad moves than a boat on a choppy sea. The rough ride sent lances of pain through her temples and reactivated her nausea.

They couldn't have been on this corduroy road for long, she thought, hoping they were nearing their destination. *Why couldn't we just beam* there? she wondered. The Jarada had transporters but didn't seem to use them much—another example, she supposed, of how thoroughly their society was controlled by outdated traditions. She remembered that kind of thinking from her childhood, remembered questioning and arguing with the elders when their dictates countered her will.

"Are you awake, Keiko?" Tanaka's voice, coming from just behind her, was loud enough to field-test ear protectors. When she flinched at the volume, he continued in a softer tone, "Canjuir—that's the senior teacher—says we're almost there; that there's a clearing up ahead where we'll be making camp. After that the students have some sort of lesson and we're free to explore if we want."

Keiko pushed herself upright, feeling her muscles protest at the movement. The pillows had shifted while she slept, resulting in a configuration that was unfit for either human or Jarada. Groaning, she adjusted the padding until she was sitting level. "How long was I asleep?"

"Almost three hours. I thought about waking you, because you looked terribly uncomfortable, but I figured you might need the sleep, so I didn't."

"It *was* uncomfortable," she agreed, rubbing her neck to loosen a cramped muscle. A lock of her long, dark hair snaked free from its roll and tangled in her fingers. Angrily, she pulled out the pins, shook her hair free, and reknotted it with deft movements. "If the students are getting a lesson after they make camp, can't we listen in?"

Tanaka took his time answering, which told her the answer even before he spoke. "I gathered that we weren't invited to this particular meeting. My impression was that it was more like—well, like a temple chant or something, if these people actually have a religion."

"I'm sure they do. It's almost mandatory for cultures with their sociological index." *Every autocratic society has an equally autocratic religion to reinforce its traditions,* she thought, remembering her childhood again.

"Anyway, they don't seem to want us around, so if you're feeling up to it, I'd love to go exploring. I can't wait to get a closer look at these trees. Aren't they magnificent?"

Keiko risked another look at the dark and twisted growth that hovered over the road. *Magnificent?* The last time she had used that word to describe a tree had been fifteen years before, when she had been granted the honor of contemplating the exquisite perfection of her great-great-grandfather's four-hundred-year-old bonsai. The elegant sweep of the limbs and the graceful, spiraling trunk of the miniature cedar had captured the essence of "tree" perfectly.

Tanaka had to be a secret tree-hugger if he thought the wild, uncontrolled growth outside was beautiful. Still—that meant she could let him cruise the forest, cataloging tree species, while she worked on the grasses and flowering plants in the understory. For the first time Keiko was glad that Captain Picard had ordered her to work with a partner.

The vehicle jolted around a tight curve and into a long, narrow meadow. Bel-Major hung over the forest ahead of them, a bloated, mottled rust-and-tan globe that glared at them like an angry god, its lower edge speared by the misshapen tops of the trees. While she slept, the gas giant had risen, carried above the horizon by Bel-Minor's rotation. Keiko shuddered, thinking the huge planet looked ready to roll from the sky and crush them.

A stream appeared beside the road, dancing over a tumble of boulders and down timber as it left the forest. A short distance farther on, another stream joined the first, doubling its volume. Clumps of bluish grass covered the ground, in some places almost waist-high and in others cropped close to the dirt. A scattering of flowering plants was interspersed with the grass, the details of their structure obscured by the vehicle's movement.

The road curved again, crossing the stream at a wide, sandy ford. Ahead of them, a small lake occupied the center of the meadow. "Beaver-dam pond," Tanaka murmured. "Or, at least, this world's equivalent."

"Perhaps." Keiko looked at the lake more closely, trying to decide if he was right. They were on the upstream end, making it impossible for her to see what blocked the outlet. "If they don't want us around for their lesson, or whatever it is, we can check it out."

"That's a great idea! I can't wait to explore the interrelationships in the ecology. I mean, we're the first humans ever to set foot in these forests, and just think of all the discoveries we'll make. Whole new classes of trees, structures and relationships we've never imagined—" He paused for breath, his eyes bright with excitement.

Keiko twisted toward him, wondering if his eagerness was genuine. "Tell you what—you study the trees and I'll do the rest of the flora."

"Really?" Tanaka's face lit up like a nova. She hadn't thought it was possible for him to radiate more enthusiasm, but apparently she had underestimated his wattage. "You'll let *me* work on the trees? Usually, when I'm on an away team, Lieutenant Deyllar wants me to catalog the lichens or something."

"*I* am not Lieutenant Deyllar." Hearing the sharpness in her tone, Keiko took a deep breath and forced a lighter, almost teasing note. "However, if you do find any lichens growing on the trees, be sure to catalog them. You never know which plants will have unexpected properties."

"You bet!" A broad grin split his face, his square,

uneven teeth flashing against his olive skin. The vehicle made a last turn and stopped on a wide, sandy area next to the lake.

Before Tanaka could say any more, Canjiir called the bus to attention. Holding her true-arms over her head, she clacked her claws together. To Keiko's surprise, she wore a translating unit on her forearm which interpreted her words for the humans. The slender black unit matched the ones that Keiko and Tanaka wore.

"Student-citizens," Canjiir began, "we have reached our destination. As you know, the purpose of this exploration is to learn of our new world and all the life that shares it with us. We are also honored to have with us visitors from another hive, Keiko-Scientist and Reggie-Scientist. They are here to learn from us about our world and about our hive."

Heads bowed to acknowledge the introduction, even though Keiko was sure that the teachers had explained their presence to the class long before the vehicle had arrived at the Academy that morning. Canjiir wagged her antennae to claim the right to continue speaking. "You will have one standard to set up camp, after which we will hold Full Assembly as usual. Our visitors will join us for evening meal at sunset, followed by campfire discussion until sleep-time. At planetset, we will begin tomorrow's activities. Are there any questions?"

Keiko glanced around, noticing how the young Jarada were fidgeting in their seats. Not surprisingly, no one had any questions. Canjiir signaled for the other teacher to open the door and the class marched out. They seemed so quiet and orderly that Keiko wondered if she was missing something. Even the boys she grew up with would have been kidding and jostling each other to work off the excess energy accumulated by sitting for three hours. Frowning, she watched the youths as they retrieved their luggage and headed for the flat area Canjiir had marked as their camp, still strangely subdued.

Their equipment was, of course, in the back of the compartment. When the last Jarada had retrieved its luggage, Tanaka squirmed inside and pushed their packs out the narrow opening. As Keiko struggled into hers and stood, a wave of dizziness swept through her. She caught herself and leaned against the vehicle, waiting for the vertigo to pass.

"Are you all right, Keiko?" Tanaka reached out to help her, a concerned frown on his face.

She brushed his hand away, irritated that he had caught her in a moment of weakness. "I just stood up too fast, that's all." Pushing off from the vehicle, she started down the beach, looking for a campsite away from the Jarada. The two teachers were standing to one side, watching their students and talking in low tones. Again Keiko felt a prickle of worry, a sense of impending trouble. She wished she knew more about the Jarada, to be able to translate her premonition into something more concrete.

A low ridge of boulders separated the sand near the lake from the rest of the meadow. As they passed the area where the Jarada were pitching their shelters, the rock pile bent sharply toward the lake, then retreated to form another curving bay.

"Definitely artificial," Tanaka announced, studying the arrangement. "They must use this place often."

Keiko picked a level spot in the lee of the rocks and shrugged out of her pack. "Why not? It's more efficient than having to locate new places every time you want to run a group outing."

She burrowed into her pack, pulling out her tent. Tabbing the activator switch, she stepped back and let the single-person shelter unfold. The metal poles expanded and burrowed into the ground, anchoring the circular structure, while the double layer of duroflex fabric pulled the upper supports into shape. Keiko clipped the power pack into its socket and programmed the tent's controller for a comfortable internal temperature and for an external camouflage before tucking the unit into its pocket beside the door. Unsealing the flap, she shoved her sleeping bag inside and pulled its tab. It expanded to a mid-weight bag over a firm mattress which compensated for the ground beneath it. Pushing her pack inside, Keiko turned to see how Tanaka was doing.

"Tie!" He grinned, pointing to his own tent. He had programmed it to an orange so bright it was probably visible from the *Enterprise.* From inside came the last hiss of his inflating sleeping bag. "I thought I'd grab some lunch and then go exploring. What do you think?"

At the mention of food, Keiko felt her stomach lurch. She struggled against the nausea, dismayed that she would be catching something at such an inconvenient time. All her shots were current and she had passed her last physical six weeks before. Struggling to hide her reaction from Tanaka, she pulled her tricorder and a couple of ration bars from her pack. "I'm really not hungry yet. I think I'll just walk along the shore a ways. You can catch up when you've finished eating."

"What? And let you be the first to discover that it *is* a beaver dam?" Tanaka's grin took any possible offense from his words. He dived into his tent and pawed through his pack. Finding what he wanted, he dropped his tricorder into its holster and strapped a full pouch of ration bars to his waist. "I'm ready when you are," he said, scrambling to his feet.

They started along the lake shore, leaving a double line of boot prints behind them in the sand. A light breeze gusted off the water, burdened with the scent of mud and water-logged vegetation. Keiko swung her tricorder back and forth, recording a panoramic view of the lake and the meadow for later reference. Detailed scans of individual plants were the core of her work, but without the overview it was impossible to work out a planet's ecology.

Tanaka moved quickly, bounding back and forth like a child just released from class. "I always forget how exhilarating it is to move in lighter gravity."

"It's only point nine. Hardly enough to make a difference." Still, maybe that was what was wrong with her stomach. Keiko tried hard to believe that, tried hard to convince herself that she was imagining her queasiness, but that didn't work either. The next thing she knew, she was kneeling on the sand, vomiting.

Tanaka was there immediately. "Here, rinse out your mouth." Where he had gotten the collapsible cup, she didn't know, but Keiko accepted the water gratefully. The sour taste wouldn't wash away at first, but finally she sat back, feeling light-headed but otherwise much better.

"I'm calling the ship," Tanaka said in a tone that brooked no argument. "If there's a bug down here that doesn't like humans, we need to know about it fast."

He touched his sleeve where his communicator was hidden in deference to Jaradan wishes. Silence answered him. He slapped it harder, but the device still didn't respond. Frowning, Keiko tapped her communicator, but it, too, was dead. She shivered, realizing how much trouble the malfunctions could cause. Without communicators, she and Tanaka had no way of contacting the ship if they ran into serious trouble.

Keiko stood, moving slowly to keep her stomach under control, and brushed the sand off her uniform. "I'm all right now, Reggie. It's probably something I ate."

"I'd still prefer to have the doctor look at you."

She snorted. "I'm not that delicate that I need a doctor for every little problem. You're sounding as bad as my husband."

"I didn't mean to." Tanaka's face flushed. "But I'd feel better if you'd at least take a nap while I run some diagnostics on the communicators."

His suggestion went against the grain when they needed every minute on the planet for collecting information. However, she still felt a little shaky, and without the communicators, regulations dictated that away-team members remain within earshot of each other. That severely limited what she could do. "All right, Reggie. I'll take a nap if you promise the communicators will be fixed when I wake up."

"I'll do my best. Otherwise, we're not going to get much work done, are we?" He gave her a rueful grin, his expression reminding her so much of her childhood friend that a surge of homesickness washed through her. What would Kiyoshi say if he could see her now?

"Certainly not as much as I'd like." Keiko scowled, wondering why both communicators should malfunction at the same time. It was an odd coincidence—if it *was* coincidence. Suddenly she realized they might have more problems than random equipment failure. The communicators were almost indestructible because they had to work under all sorts of conditions. Outside interference was the most likely explanation for two simultaneous breakdowns, but if the Jarada had caused the problem, why had they done so? However she looked at it, Keiko could find no explanation that fit the facts.

Chapter Seven

"CAPTAIN." Worf's deep voice was harsher than normal. That, plus his vigilance in watching every direction of approach, betrayed his continuing distrust of the Jarada. To the Klingon, the layout of the Jaradan Prime Council Chamber, with its tapestries and hidden entrances, suggested a dozen ways to ambush an opponent. "I still believe my duty as your security chief is to remain with you at all times."

Picard turned toward the Klingon with a slight, exasperated shake of his head. "Mr. Worf, your assignment is to go with Zelk'helvtrobreen and discover what Zelfrcetrollan thought you would find so interesting."

"Captain, I must protest. Commander Data's best translation indicates that I will be attending a performance of the local equivalent of the—ballet." He said the last word in a tone usually reserved for some particularly filthy perversion, such as unconditional surrender.

The captain's mouth quivered with the effort to suppress a laugh. "Mr. Worf, we are at the moment guessing at our translations of half the Jaradan words we think we know. I'm sure our hosts are aware of your feelings about ballet, since they seem almost too well informed about us. We need all the information we can gather about the Jarada. Therefore, I'm ordering you to find out why the Jarada believe my Chief of Security would be interested in their *val'greshneth*."

"Yes, Captain." Dissatisfied, Worf turned away from the captain and Troi. Data had spent almost half an hour the previous night puzzling over the word *val'greshneth*. That was a record for the android—to have taken so long to produce so little. *Val* translated to "group" or "troupe," as best Data could determine. *Greshneth* was more of a problem, since it was also a compound word. The first syllable meant "movement" or "progress," while the second syllable was a modifier which, in some contexts, denoted "control."

Unfortunately, Data could not locate a definitive meaning for either of the compound words. He had insisted that "dance troupe" was only an approximation for the literal "group of controlled movement," but that guess had been enough to keep Worf growling for hours. Though Worf's adoptive mother had tried to teach him an appreciation of human cultural values, Worf never understood why she bothered. Such things were frivolous, beneath a warrior's notice, and he had more important things to do than watch a group of Jarada cavort for his benefit.

Worf's mental grumbling was interrupted by the arrival of Zelfreetrollan and his guide. Zelk'helvtrobreen appeared beside him so quietly that Worf's first impression was that the Jarada had beamed in. Seeing the Klingon's reaction, the chestnut-colored Jarada clacked its claws together in amusement. "Appearing as if from thin air is a good trick for a guardian, is it not?"

"I suppose so," Worf replied evenly. For the Jarada,

with their hard claws which clicked against the tiled floors, it should be nearly impossible. Worf felt his curiosity getting the better of his caution. "How do you accomplish it?"

Again the Jarada clacked its claws together. "It is a matter of rhythm and anticipation, mostly. When several people are present, they are always moving, always creating small sounds that can mask a set of random noises. As long as I vary the hesitation between my steps, the sounds will not be noticed. It is the even, rhythmic pattern that alerts one to the coming of a stranger. How do you achieve a silent approach?"

"I use a similar technique. Also, our floors produce less noise." His boot heels made almost as much clatter on the hard floor as the Jarada's claws, Worf thought. With a start he realized that he had seen no carpeting anywhere in the Governance Complex. He filed that fact away for his report on the defensive aspects of Jaradan buildings.

The insectoid gestured for Worf to accompany him through the door. "Today we are no longer sitting in Council, so you should call me Breen. After all, we are fellow guardians of our hives. The full naming title is only for ceremonies and strangers. Are you called only Worf?"

"It is the way of my people to have only one name that is spoken in public." Worf frowned, trying to isolate an impression that nagged at the edges of his awareness. Something about the Jarada Breen was different from the day before, a change in its speech or its gestures that was triggering a warning in Worf. Regrettably, from what little the Federation knew of the Jarada, either behavior pattern might be normal for Breen. There was no way to tell.

They turned the corner and started down a long corridor. Breen bombarded Worf with questions about his work, about what it was like to be in Starfleet, and about minority treatment on a human-dominated starship. In return for Worf's answers, the Jarada supplied anecdotes from its own experience, rarely noticing that Worf's answers were so terse as to be almost uninformative. Even so, after fifteen minutes Worf began to relax marginally in response to Breen's apparent interest. After all, it wasn't often that he could talk shop with someone outside Starfleet.

While they talked, they moved downward along a sloping corridor. When it leveled off, Worf judged they were the equivalent of five decks below ground. A maze of tunnels and side passages branched off from the main corridor, and Worf realized the tunnel system must connect most of the buildings in the city. After ten minutes they reached a spiral ramp that led both up and down.

Breen started upward, still talking about its duties as a hive guardian. Worf found it difficult to concentrate on the Jarada's words; although Breen was talking incessantly, it actually said very little. The chatter was a distraction, Worf suspected, a diversion intended to keep his attention focused on the Jarada rather than on his surroundings.

Worf found the layout of the complex enlightening. The extensive cross-tunnels and the apparent lack of markings or directional devices suggested that defensive considerations had determined the design. Without a detailed map, invaders would soon be hopelessly lost in the underground maze, while the numerous side corridors provided endless opportunities for reinforcements to attack from the flank or rear.

The Klingon suspected that security doors operating on the same principle as a starship's decompression doors were spaced at strategic locations along many of the tunnels. He had not identified any such doors, which aroused his curiosity further. Were they disguised behind a false layer of plaster, or was Breen leading him through the only corridor in the area that was not protected by advanced security devices? The more he thought about it, the more puzzled Worf became. A warrior learned to trust his senses, and Worf's perceptions told him something was not right. He knew he should never have left the captain alone.

When they reached what Worf judged to be ground level, Breen stopped. The outline of a door was sharply drawn on the wall, as clear to Worf as the designs on the floor. Breen scraped its claws across the wall and a control panel appeared. Fitting its claws into the depressions, it entered a code into the panel. Much to Worf's surprise, the relays on the touch points each gave off a slightly different sound. He wondered if the Jarada knew this or if the distinguishing overtones were outside their hearing range. Listening carefully, he memorized the sequence: 1-1-3-2-1-2-3-3-1.

"Our locks are our finest security feature," Breen said as the door retracted into the wall. "If intruders want to open a door, they must first *find* the control panel before they can enter the code. And if they enter the wrong code three times in a row, an alarm alerts the hive guardians that strangers are attempting to enter our home. Of course, no outsider knows where our control panels are, so it is virtually impossible for them to enter in the first place."

"This is a precaution against predators on your homeworld?" Worf could see no way the invisible panels would be effective against other Jarada, unless each hive used a completely unique security system. Given how conservative the Jarada seemed, he was willing to bet that most, if not all, the control panels in every hive were in precisely the same position relative to the doors they controlled. Was it possible the sharp, bright outlines of the doors were not visible in the frequencies detectable by Jaradan eyes?

"There are many dangers on our world." Breen turned its head toward Worf, rainbow interference patterns flickering across the large central facets of his eyes. It started down the corridor, its head turned sideways to watch the Klingon. "We cannot be too careful in the ways of protecting our hive. Is it not the same for you? How do you prevent intruders from entering your hive?"

"That problem is less difficult for us." They turned left into the first hall, a short dead end with heavily carved doors facing each other across the mosaic floor. "A starship is a closed system, with all access systems strictly under our control."

"You must tell me more of this later." Breen pushed open the right-hand door and gestured for Worf to enter first. A thick, heavy smell—of cloves or cinnamon or some other spice he remembered his human mother overusing—swirled out of the room and wrapped itself around them. "Now, however, we have arrived, and I am sure you are eager to witness the presentation."

The room was large, larger even than the Audience Chamber, and the roof was at least three levels above them. Worf was reminded of the *Enterprise*'s shuttle deck, both by the sheer size and by the open space. The floor was wood, its pale surface pitted and scarred, worn by constant use despite its protective coating. The boards flexed under his feet and sprang back, almost alive in their response. Such a surface was made for fighting, and Worf wished he had a partner to help him test it.

Fifty or sixty large reddish-brown Jarada were standing near the far wall, their true-arms crossed over their feeding-arms in a posture that suggested deferential waiting. Near one end, Worf spotted a

89

russet individual with a broken antenna. He had noticed a similar injury on a member of the ceremonial guard the previous day, and he was sure this was the same Jarada.

Examining the rest of the group, Worf recognized other markings—here a discoloration, there a nick on an exoskeleton. He grunted, feeling the first stirrings of interest since Zelfreetrollan had issued the invitation. If these were the guardians entrusted to protect the highest officials on the planet, he *did* want to see what they were planning to show him.

The tallest of the group stepped forward three paces. "Admirably Massive Worf-Guardian, you grace our humble exercises with your presence. When we scented the joyous tidings of your visit, we prepared a special performance for you."

At those words, every Jarada in the room crouched deeply, bending their heads until their antennae brushed the floor. Worf shifted his weight uncomfortably, uncertain whether this excessive obeisance was intended to express their respect for him and the Federation or if they were mocking him. Before he could decide, the leader ordered the group to break ranks. While most of the Jarada scurried around the room, setting up a series of large, strangely shaped objects, two individuals carried a bench with a cut-out seat over to Worf. After they filled the Jarada-shaped indentation with blankets, Breen gestured expansively to Worf and said, "Please accept our hospitality for the duration of our performance."

Reluctantly, Worf sat down, even though his instincts warned him to remain on his feet, ready for action. A few moments later, two more Jarada brought a bench for Breen. As it settled into its place, the other Jarada formed into ranks against the far wall like a troop of soldiers on parade.

"The first performance will commence," the leader announced. Six Jarada, tall and evenly matched for size, stepped out of the group, walked to the center of the room, and bowed to Worf and Breen. Turning to face each other, they paired off and bowed to their partners. On an unspoken signal they began to move, slowly at first, with a carefully synchronized choreography of action and response. Gradually the pace quickened, with each thrust and parry being executed with greater speed and power.

Worf studied their movements, noticing the polished teamwork that bespoke hours of practice. The patterns were stylized and formal, lacking any spontaneity, but one didn't need to be a Betazoid to recognize the essence of this performance. If the *val'greshneth* was a dance company, then Worf was as human as his adoptive parents.

He leaned forward to watch the Jarada more carefully. The extra pair of legs gave the insectoids a decided advantage in unarmed combat, making it much harder to push them off balance. Once down, Worf guessed their anatomy would work against them, with the articulation of their joints making it difficult for them to regain their feet. It was difficult to be sure, since their rehearsed drills stopped short of knocking anyone down. Watching them work out, Worf wondered if they would let him join in the drill. He would learn so much more about their fighting style by trying it rather than by merely watching his hosts.

Before he could ask, the six fighters reached the end of their demonstration. They stopped, turned in unison, and bowed once more to their guests. Another group of Jarada came forward, demonstrating a fighting technique that used long strips of cloth tipped with small weights. Again no one ended on the floor, although Worf suspected that in actual combat the weapon would function like a human bolo or a Vulcan *ahn woon*, tangling an opponent's legs and tripping him.

Several other exhibitions followed, all interesting as much for what they failed to show as for what they did. Something in the demonstrations bothered Worf, something beyond his natural inclination to see deception lurking behind the professional geniality of every diplomat. He wished he had brought a tricorder to record the performances for later analysis. Finally, Breen asked if his people had similar techniques and if he would share them with the *val'greshneth*.

"I would be honored to demonstrate a similar activity." Worf paused to weigh his duty as a Federation representative against his responsibilities as the *Enterprise*'s Chief of Security. Clearly, the latter obligations were paramount. To preserve his advantage should he need to fight the Jarada, he decided not to show them any of the Klingon fighting techniques he normally used. Something human, then; something elementary enough not to compromise anyone who needed the advanced techniques for self-defense.

Worf shook himself to break the mood, to remind himself that this was a *diplomatic* mission. The idea rang false, triggering alarm signals every time he considered it. A warrior was trained to recognize potential enemies before the first blow was struck, and Worf kept sensing danger from the Jarada. However, his orders stated that this was a diplomatic mission and he was strictly to disregard his instincts until the other side made a preemptive strike. He squared his shoulders, accepting that he must give them a reciprocal demonstration unless fighting broke out in the next thirty seconds. "I will show you the human art called karate."

The chitter of balance-legs against the floor told Worf that the name had not translated. "Karate is an ancient human art whose name means 'the way of the empty hand.' I will show you this Earth technique so that you may understand the humans better." It seemed unnecessary to tell them that they would probably never understand humans, that after years of observation Worf was not sure he would ever figure out even the ones he knew best.

He stood, stretching to see how he felt. The long walk from the Governance Complex and the climb up the spiral ramp had been a good warm-up, but he had been sitting for some time.

Surprisingly, he still felt good, ready to take on half a dozen holodeck opponents. To be safe, he started slowly, but as he felt his muscles loosening to peak combat readiness, he could not resist the impulse to demonstrate parts of his personal workout. It was an advanced combination of lunges, feints, and strikes that would have exhausted any other member of the *Enterprise*'s crew. Riker practiced his *katas* against a maximum of four imaginary opponents, but Worf used that number only for warm-ups. However, given his audience, the Klingon limited himself to six imaginary assailants and omitted the kicks from the routine.

When he finished, the room was silent for thirty seconds. Then, as if on a single impulse, every Jarada present began pounding its balance-claws on the floor in approval. "You must teach us that," said the leader of the group. "The power and purity of your movements embody the essence of a guardian's mission."

An insect buzz of agreement rose from the Jarada, swelling louder and louder. The sound swept through Worf, sending shivers through his body. With an effort he fought down the battle cry that rose in his throat. This was neither the time nor the place—but suddenly his warrior blood was singing for a fight.

Slowly, the buzzing quieted and the Jarada calmed.

They were still twitching, still fidgeting with eagerness to acquire his knowledge. Seeing this, sensing how close their desire was to fanaticism, Worf felt his doubts crystallize. There was something wrong here, some force that was out of balance. At that moment he *knew* it would be a grave mistake to teach them anything they could use against his shipmates. The commander of the guardians moved forward, true-arms raised in supplication. "We would take it as the greatest honor if you would teach this karate to us." It crouched until its abdomen touched the floor.

Once again Worf realized how different Jaradan anatomy was. He could use that as excuse to stick with the simplest maneuvers. "I am honored that you wish to learn karate. However, it is not easy, and humans often claim it requires a lifetime to master. I regret that I am not a skilled instructor, but I will show you some beginning movements. If you desire, you may ask Captain Picard for another teacher."

Worf swallowed. His throat felt dry from having to talk so much to the assembled Jarada. He would much rather face a dozen Borg single-handedly than play ambassador to a group of twitchy aliens.

The leader bobbed its head sideways in negation. "We are sure the instruction of so powerful a guardian will be more than adequate."

Worf centered himself, focusing on the essence of the *kata* he wished to demonstrate. Although the ancient warriors who had developed karate could almost have been Klingon, for this demonstration Worf intended to draw attention to the *human* characteristics of the art. To exclude the Klingon elements that had crept into his style and to focus strictly on the most elementary lessons a student could learn increased the challenge for him.

Inhaling deeply, Worf bowed to the watching Jarada. His instincts warned him to keep his eyes on his enemies. He had to struggle to look down as he bowed. One should always show the proper trust and respect to one's opponents. It was a fine point, one he did not expect the Jarada to recognize, but many warrior cultures had similar traditions.

Worf straightened and turned, lunging forward to stop an imaginary attack from his right. His block was perfect, catching the attacker well before his blow could have connected. Spinning around, Worf's right hand swept across his body to knock aside a punch to his midsection. Visualizing how his speed and power would have caught his opponent off guard, Worf followed his block with a counterattack to the midsection. Next he stopped an overhead strike from the side, parrying blows with first his right, then his left, arm. After that the techniques were reversed, the movements executed in mirror image to build strength and flexibility on the opposite side of the body. Worf flowed through the routine, his performance swift and precise. It took him exactly forty seconds to complete the *kata* for his fascinated audience.

Before Worf had straightened from his final bow, the Jarada were forming ranks behind him. They spread out, leaving enough room for movement in all directions. Worf's uneasiness intensified as he realized what the spacing implied. These Jarada were experienced enough with unarmed combat that they recognized what he intended to do before he told them. Part of him rejoiced to meet others with such strong warrior traditions, but he wished the Jarada had identified themselves openly. A true warrior should announce himself to the universe instead of hiding behind ritual and stylized drills. What were the Jarada concealing?

He started at the beginning of the *kata*, taking the movements slowly so the Jarada could copy them.

They caught on quickly, almost too quickly if they were potential opponents. Worf reminded himself that these were the Jaradan equivalent of professional soldiers, but after watching them for a few minutes, he found that thought disquieting. There was something uncontrolled, almost frenetic, in their behavior that made him glad he had decided to teach them only an elementary *kata*.

After an hour Worf bowed to thank them for their attention and announced that he needed to return to the Governance Complex. His pupils returned the bow, but the russet Jarada with the broken antenna charged forward, demanding that Worf continue. The two Jarada closest to it tried to intercept it. Broken-Antenna dodged them, and two more Jarada tried to run interference. Another Jarada started toward Worf, shrieking in three keys for the lesson to continue, and others tried to keep it from tackling the Klingon.

Soon every Jarada in the room was fighting with a savagery that took Worf aback. A Klingon warrior's greatest joy was to get into a good fight, but there was something unhealthy about this melee. He looked around the room, trying to find Breen, but it was somewhere in the confusion, fighting along with everyone else.

The noise was deafening, the shrieks and battle cries of the Jarada blending with the sounds of body blows and the echoing clack and thud of feet and exoskeletons hitting the floor. Several fallen Jarada were trapped in the middle of the free-for-all, unable to regain their footing. The scene reminded Worf of sharks in a feeding frenzy, when the scent of blood sent them attacking anything, even one of their own. Those sharks were no more sane than these Jarada, and Worf knew he must report this to the captain immediately.

He touched his communicator but could not hear

its chirp over the noise. He tapped it again, then maintained the contact so it would transmit the noise to the ship. Even Data should be able to interpret the sounds of a fight and beam him up. All he needed was to get to the ship long enough to give his report and then return to the planet with a phaser to protect the captain.

When the familiar dazzle of the transporter effect did not form around him, Worf began inching toward the door. Outside, where it was quiet, he could call the ship and order them to transport him directly to the captain's location.

One of the Jarada saw Worf starting to leave. It sent up a shriek and suddenly the fighting ceased. A moment later, with a battle cry that sounded as if it came from a nest of deranged hornets, the Jarada charged toward Worf.

Even after their self-inflicted casualties, the Jarada outnumbered him forty to one. With odds like that, only a fool or a berserker would fight if he had any alternatives. Knowing his duty was to warn Picard, Worf took the only sane option available. He snatched the blankets off his bench and tangled them into the legs of the two leading Jarada. They went down and several others piled into them, unable to avoid the obstacle. While the mob was sorting itself out, Worf executed a high-speed evacuation in search of a less exposed position.

Chapter Eight

FOR THE FEW MINUTES after the away team entered the Prime Council Chamber, the room was filled with babble and confusion as those who had been invited to learn about their hosts met with their Jaradan guides. While everyone was sorting themselves out, an aide approached Zelfreetrollan. After a brief consultation the Jarada apologized to Picard for having to delay their meeting a few minutes and left the room. Picard watched as Riker, Crusher, Keiko, and Tanaka left, all plying their Jaradan escorts with questions. Worf had been last, and he was not at all eager to leave his captain. An affectionate grin tugged at Picard's mouth as he watched the door close behind Worf and Zelk'helvtrobreen. The Klingon was determined to take his normal meticulous view of his duties.

"He is not pleased that you ordered him to go," Troi said, echoing the captain's thoughts. She swept a hand through her dark curls, pushing them off her shoulder. "He fears that something will happen while he is not here to protect you."

Letting his grin show, Picard nodded. "It *is* a risk, Counselor. Trust always is."

The clatter of chitin against tile interrupted her reply. They turned together as Zelfreetrollan reentered the room. "Forgive me, Honored Picard-Captain and Honored Troi-Counselor. There was a minor problem that I was required to solve. I hope you have not been left by yourselves for too long."

"Not at all, First Among Council. The last of my people just left."

"I was afraid I would have kept you waiting. I am glad this is not the case." He gestured toward the table, where fruit nectar and nut cakes had been laid out. "Please. Help yourselves. I hope this session can be informal, since my Councillors had very few changes to make to the draft agreement."

"That is excellent news, First Among Council." Picard poured a little nectar into a glass and diluted it with water. Troi did the same and then the three of them took seats near the middle of the table.

Zelfreetrollan laid two piles of buff-colored pebbly-textured paper on the table. One set of documents was covered with the complex symbols they had seen carved into the door of the Audience Chamber. The second copy of the agreement was written in English. In places, the phrasing was stilted, but the meaning was unambiguous. Picard checked the document against his memory of their discussions. The provisions for the exchange of ambassadors and the conditions for widening communications between the Federation and the Jarada were as he remembered.

"The Council has given its approval for these agreements," Zelfreetrollan said when Picard finished reading. "It remains only for your Federation to accept our work."

Picard slipped the documents into a case. "When I

return to the *Enterprise*, I will transmit these documents to the Department of External Affairs for them to relay to the Federation Council. Since the Council is expecting my message, ratification should take only a matter of hours. The longest delay will be the transmission time between here and there."

"Our people are honored that you should give us so much of your consideration, Picard-Captain. It is with the greatest anticipation that we look forward to exchanging ambassadors with your Federation."

They talked a little longer, discussing how the agreement would benefit both their cultures. To Picard, it was amazing that the negotiations with the Jarada should have gone so easily, after the long years of tension and mistrust. *Picard's luck*, some of his friends at Starfleet Command would call it, ignoring the massive amounts of hard work he usually needed to make luck go his way. That was the thought he took with him as he and Troi beamed back to the *Enterprise* with the Federation's copies of the agreement—that they hadn't yet put enough effort into the negotiations and that somewhere a nasty surprise was waiting to undo the promising start he held in his hand.

"Captain, we have made the most amazing discoveries about this system." Data stood, vacating the captain's chair as Picard strode onto the bridge. "We have cataloged forty-seven previously undiscovered moonlets in orbit around Bel-Major and have already confirmed the orbits of fifteen of them. In addition, we have greatly improved our descriptions of the orbital parameters of four objects that are in complex orbits around both Bel-Major and Bel-Minor."

Picard suppressed a groan. Data had accomplished a phenomenal amount of work in the last twenty-four hours, and he wanted to give his captain all the details immediately. "Thank you, Mr. Data. However, if you could postpone your report, I'd appreciate it if you could examine these documents before we transmit them to the Federation Council." He held out both versions of the agreement.

"Certainly, Captain." Data took the sheaf of paper, fingering the rough surface. "We know relatively little of the Jaradan language, either spoken or written. I assume you wish me to extract everything I can from these documents?"

"Yes, Mr. Data." As he lowered himself into his chair, Picard took a deep breath, cataloging the smells and appreciating their unobtrusiveness. There was the bright electric scent of the bridge's consoles, the whiff of stray lubricant that Geordi could never quite banish, Lieutenant Mendosa's soft floral perfume. It was a relief not to be assaulted by industrial-strength odors at every turn. "If it's going to take too long, we'll have to send them off before you finish. Commissioner T'Zen has convinced the Council that any delays might cause a war."

"I believe the commissioner is overreacting, sir. I estimate the probability is—"

Shaking his head, Picard waved Data to silence. "I agree, but Commissioner T'Zen fears that we are not civilized enough to avoid fighting unless we have a signed agreement to prevent it." At times it was hard to say who had a weaker grasp of emotional behavior —his ever-curious android officer, who had none of the biological prerequisites, or the ultraconservative Vulcan, Commissioner T'Zen, who denied her own physiological drives while overestimating those of other races.

No matter how much control people exercised over themselves, the underlying biology *did* influence their actions. That was Picard's strongest reason for believing they had not yet determined what controlled Jaradan behavior. He would have to discuss the matter with Troi before they transmitted the agreement. Perhaps after a few hours away from the planet, she would be able to organize her chaotic impressions of their insectoid hosts. "Mr. Data, I would be happier if we had some solid information before we generated any more projections of how things are going."

"In that case, Captain, I shall give these documents my utmost attention." Data shuffled the papers together and turned away, anticipating Picard's next order.

"Make it so, Commander." Picard watched the android stride effortlessly up the ramp to the turbolift, his movements so different from the four-legged walk of the Jarada. With a start Picard realized that he had gotten used to the insectoids' odd, rolling gait. He had seen so many of them in the last day that they were starting to seem like the norm. Giving himself a mental shake, he turned his attention to the ship. "Status report, Lieutenant Chang," he ordered.

Chang's report was crisp and concise and very normal. With a feeling of pleasure mixed with relief that matters would be simple for a few hours, Picard settled back in his chair to command his ship.

The buzzer to Troi's cabin door sounded as she was dressing after her shower. She gave her bright blue skirt a tug to settle it into place and reached for a band to hold back her hair. "Who's there?"

"It's Miles O'Brien. May I talk with you for a few minutes, Counselor?" The transporter chief's voice sounded unusually tense.

"Of course." Troi signaled for the door to admit him and ordered the computer to adjust the light level in her sitting area to its professional setting. She had known this discussion was inevitable since his fight with Keiko last night, although she had not expected it to happen so soon.

O'Brien entered and crossed to the sofa, his movements stiff and awkward. Troi didn't need her Betazoid perceptions to realize that he was fighting a battle with himself even to come here. He perched on the edge of the sofa, his back as straight as a ramrod, and fidgeted with his hands rather than looking at her.

Troi let the silence stretch, waiting until she judged the time was right. "Is there something you wish to talk about?"

"Yes. No." He twisted his fingers together, clenching them so tightly that his knuckles showed white against his fair skin. Finally, the words exploded from him. "It's Keiko. Sometimes I don't understand her. Like now, when she's run off to that planet. It's dangerous down there. She might get hurt!"

Troi closed her eyes, briefly probing O'Brien's mental state. Beyond his anger and frustration, she sensed a deep puzzlement over his wife's actions. Marriage had yet to improve O'Brien's insight into the woman he loved, any more than it had increased Keiko's comprehension of non-Japanese ways. "It upsets you, then, that your wife is doing her job on the away team?"

"She can do her job on the ship! If anybody gets in trouble on that planet, it should be a regular Starfleet officer who signed on for that type of duty."

"If you're so sure that there will be trouble, why are you here instead of in the transporter room, waiting to rescue her?" Troi's voice was soft, deliberately pitched to make him work to understand her. Until he released his anger, there was little chance he would listen to anything she said. "Or are you afraid she will be angry over that too?"

O'Brien's cheeks flushed with anger. "She always wants to do things her own way! She never listens to my opinion on anything!" O'Brien's jaw set into a hard line. "I'm her husband! She should listen to me!"

The problem unfolded itself for Troi, complete with its misunderstandings and cross-cultural confusions. "Like your mother always listened to your father?" she asked in a gentle tone. O'Brien's records showed that his mother had been a quiet woman who enjoyed family life and loved children, even to fostering troubled children after her own offspring had left home. Keiko could hardly be more different from O'Brien's mother if he had set out to find his mother's opposite.

His head snapped up, surprise written across his features. "Of course. Isn't that what marriage is about?"

"That depends." She paused, letting him wonder what her next words would be. "Have you ever asked Keiko about the marriage customs she grew up with?"

"No. Why?" He frowned, confused by Troi's question.

A gentle smile played around the corners of Troi's mouth. The idea that Japan's traditions might still influence Keiko had never crossed O'Brien's mind. "Have you ever considered how much of Japan she brings with her wherever she goes?"

"I don't see what that has to do with our marriage." O'Brien shook his head emphatically. "She rejected all that when she married me."

Troi sighed, thinking that both O'Brien and Keiko came from backgrounds best known for trying to remold the universe to their own specifications. *And* that she would have to repeat this lecture on tolerance to Keiko, once the away team beamed back from Bel-Minor. "It is not surprising that you and Keiko are not understanding each other, Miles, when you know so little of Japanese culture. For example, did you know that in certain regions of Japan the husband is expected to take his wife's name if her family is of higher rank than his?"

"No, I didn't." His anger returning, O'Brien glared at Troi as if, through sheer indignation, he could alter her words. "It's a stupid rule, anyway. A man's name is his heritage, his roots. It's what he is."

Troi nodded and smiled, as if he had agreed with her. "Precisely. In Japan, heritage and family are *everything*. It's a high honor to become a member of an influential family. Sometimes, when a man shows promise of great achievement, he will be adopted into one of the senior families. In that case, he is proud to assume the name of his new family."

"What kind of fool would *want* to change his name?" O'Brien's mouth compressed into a hard line. He stared defiantly at Troi, but she waited, letting his irritation force him into making the next move.

"What does that have to do with me? I don't know anything about Keiko's family. For all she's told me, they could be the lowliest peasants."

"I assure you they are not. And even if they were—by Japanese standards, a non-Japanese is lower than the lowliest peasant. In the more traditional districts, a man of Japanese descent from another country or from off Earth would be expected to adopt his wife's family name." Troi cocked her head to the side, studying his face as the words soaked in. Anger, disbelief, and outrage warred for control of his mind.

"That's absurd. What right do they have to make me deny who I am? I'm just as good as any of them, and better than most!"

"I think Keiko's inclined to agree with that, since it was you she decided to marry. But would you do me a favor, Miles?" She paused, waiting until he gave her a grudging nod. She could tell that he suspected a trap somewhere but didn't know quite how she'd set it.

"I'll flag some references for you in the computer and I'd like you to read them. I think they'll help you understand Keiko better."

"I suppose."

His agreement was none too willing, Troi sensed, but it was a start. Until O'Brien quit expecting Keiko to act like the tradition-bound Irish girls he had grown up with, and until Keiko quit assuming O'Brien lived in a world governed by the same rules as the latter-day samurai she was used to, their marriage was in trouble. "I will have the material ready for you when you come off duty this evening, Miles. Is there anything else you wish to discuss?" She knew there was from his agitation and the tension that remained in his posture. The question was—did he really want to talk about it?

O'Brien stared at his hands, again refusing to meet Troi's eyes. It was a familiar pose, one she had seen more times than she could remember. Stronger even than the conflicting emotions he was broadcasting, the taut lines of his body screamed denial to her—denial both that he had a problem and that anything she said could help him. Troi gave him enough time to answer, but he said nothing.

Today, at least, Troi knew his pride was winning and he could not bring himself to admit to her that he was jealous of Reggie Tanaka or even that he had heard the rumors of the crush Tanaka had had on Keiko when he had first come aboard the *Enterprise*. Somehow, Troi thought that Tanaka's inability to follow through on his infatuation would not carry much weight with O'Brien just now.

"Everything will be all right, Miles. You'll see." She gave him a reassuring smile when he finally looked up at her. "And if you need to talk some more later, I'm always available."

Seeing her words as permission to escape, O'Brien

scrambled to his feet. "Thank you, Counselor," he mumbled, and then bolted from the room.

Troi heaved a deep sigh and reached for her computer to flag the references on Japanese traditions. It was at times like this, when people tried so hard to justify their difficulties instead of overcoming them, that she wondered why she hadn't gone into a simpler field—like theoretical n-space warp dynamics. At least those problems didn't change at the precise moment you thought you'd gotten a grasp on them.

She logged off the computer and decided to visit Ten-Forward. After talking to O'Brien, she owed herself a break before the captain needed her to help unravel the Jaradan agreement.

Geordi discovered O'Brien in the far corner of Ten-Forward, shoving his sandwich around the plate. Through his VISOR, O'Brien's hands showed cooler and darker against the warm colors of his body, a sure sign of stress. He got his lunch and crossed over to O'Brien's table. "Mind if I join you?"

"Sure." O'Brien's tone said differently. Ignoring Geordi, he continued to toy with his food.

"That bad, huh?" Geordi slid into his chair and bit into his own sandwich while he studied O'Brien's face. The wash of light from the table, coming from below and from such a short distance, distorted Geordi's perceptions and made it difficult to read the nuances of O'Brien's expression. Equally, O'Brien was not showing any great eagerness to help him out. "Want to talk about it?" he asked finally.

"What's to talk about?" O'Brien muttered in a resentful tone. "My wife is down on that planet and everyone seems to think talking will help."

"Oh." Geordi took another bite of his sandwich. If he waited, he was sure O'Brien would spell out his problem in excruciating detail.

"Is that all you've got to say?'" O'Brien's face flamed brighter as Geordi's VISOR sensed the angry heat in his cheeks.

"What do you want me to say?" Geordi kept his tone deliberately casual. In O'Brien's present mood he was having trouble telling whether the transporter chief wanted reassurance or if he was trying to pick a fight. "That I don't understand why you're angry?"

"I told her not to go! She should be *here* helping me plan our six-month anniversary! How would you feel if your anniversary was coming up and it was *your* wife down there?"

How, indeed? Geordi thought, resisting the impulse to let his exasperation show. As much as he liked O'Brien and respected his abilities, there were times when his attitudes were too much. If he had wanted a full-time wife, why had he married a working scientist? And why did he keep expecting her marriage vows would convert Keiko into a traditional Irish woman raised in the Old Country? Geordi let the silence stretch while he considered his reply. "How I would feel is—my wife has a job and the captain expects her to do it. Sometimes personal holidays have to take second place to that."

"But why is she teamed up with Reggie Tanaka? Why couldn't she work with Leila Koryev?"

Geordi suppressed a shudder at the thought of working with Koryev on an away team. It wasn't that she was incompetent, exactly; but disaster had a nearly miraculous way of finding her, the way iron filings materialized around a powerful electromagnet. "If it's all the same to you, Miles, Keiko's much safer with Reggie. Leila'd manage to pull down a lightning strike from a clear sky, or run them off a cliff, or something. Besides, I think the captain chose her partner, not Keiko."

O'Brien scowled, not at all mollified by Geordi's logic. "I still don't trust him alone with her. I've seen the way he looks when someone mentions her name."

Geordi decided to try another tack. "You work with Jennie Li all the time. How's this any different?" As soon as he said the words, Geordi realized he should have picked another example. Keiko had made more than a few unfavorable comments about the easy partnership between O'Brien and Li.

"Jennie and I are just friends, that's how." Abruptly, O'Brien shoved his plate away and stood. "And just because you're my superior officer doesn't give you the right to pry into my personal affairs!"

"Cool off, mister!" Although Geordi kept his voice low, the order stopped O'Brien where he stood. "Being your commanding officer *does* give me the authority to order you to correct any problems that affect your job performance. And this definitely falls into that category. You've been impossible to get along with and your work has been substandard for the last day and a half. So I'm ordering you to talk to Counselor Troi or to your wife—or both—before you return to duty. Is that clear?"

"Yes, sir." O'Brien's glared at Geordi, his grudging tone saying how much he resented the order.

Geordi stared back, wishing his VISOR were better for such confrontations. O'Brien needed to acknowledge his jealousy, needed to come to grips with his doubts about himself that provoked his unreasonable reactions—and needed to understand his wife better to prevent such problems from continuing.

For a brief moment Geordi wished he could knock O'Brien's head against the bulkhead until some sense penetrated it. Of course, someone would have to do the same to Keiko, who was showing no better judgment than her husband. Both were projecting all their personal insecurities onto their partner. *If this is what love is about, I don't want anything to do with it!* It was a depressing thought that two people so strongly attracted to each other should have so much trouble seeing the other's viewpoint.

"Dismissed." He watched O'Brien leave, shaking his head. He had hoped that talking to someone would help O'Brien, but Geordi didn't think he had done much good. The transporter chief seemed unwilling to listen to anyone.

Most of the lunch crowd had left Ten-Forward by the time Troi got there—after concluding an impromptu session with Ensign Handler in the corridor. Troi ordered a triple chocolate sundae and took it to the far corner of the room. The first half disappeared quickly, but then she started playing with it, morosely dabbing her spoon in the melting ice cream. Usually, chocolate helped pull her out of the doldrums, but today it didn't seem to be helping much. Dealing with Chief O'Brien's jealousy and his yo-yo moods was taking more out of her than she liked to admit, even to herself. When she finished the sundae, she stared at the empty dish, wondering if she should get it refilled. Maybe more chocolate would improve her mood.

"I recognize that look." Guinan plopped another dish—chocolate-chocolate chip ice cream on a fudge-frosted brownie, topped with fudge sauce and more chocolate chips—in front of Troi before she took the chair opposite the counselor. She had a small dish of peach ice cream for herself. "Do you want to talk about it?"

Troi shrugged and took a mouthful of the ice cream. Her eyes widened in surprise at the rich, sweet-bitter contrast of the flavors.

Guinan gave a knowing smile. "Selvairian swirl. It's four different flavors of chocolate ice cream mixed together like rainbow ripple. The food synthesizers hate that particular program."

"I'll bet." Troi took a smaller bite so she could appreciate the individual flavors.

"That's better." Guinan's white teeth flashed against her dark skin. "Now, do you want to tell me why you're in here in a chocolate funk?"

"It's Chief O'Brien. I just had another long talk with him. Nothing I say seems to do any good." She scooped up some of the fudge sauce, wondering what Guinan had programmed for it. Nothing exotic, she realized as her taste buds reveled in the flavor, just a piece of chocolate lover's heaven. Guinan had ordered up the best, richest, *plain* fudge sauce made from the galaxy's premium chocolate.

"Have you considered that he may not want your help? Some people want to be right more than they want to solve their problems." Guinan tasted her own ice cream while she studied Troi's troubled face. *Who counsels the counselor?* was not a subject that the Starfleet medical division considered often, and sometimes Guinan wondered if the top brass didn't believe their recruiting literature a little too much. Sure, Starfleet officers were the finest individuals in the Federation, but that didn't mean they were perfect. All living beings had a certain amount of innate recalcitrance, which tended to surface at the most inopportune times. Chief O'Brien was certainly trying to prove the adage in a spectacular way.

Troi sighed, frustration written large in the frown that crossed her face. "I *have* considered it. I have also considered that it is my job to see that everyone else's problems *are* solved. *And* I have considered the problems his attitude causes for everyone around him." She stabbed at her sundae, taking out her anger on the brownie. On the third try she got an oversize bite to her mouth.

"And you concluded that the only cure for it was a chocolate binge," Guinan grinned, a twinkle in her eye. "Such a waste of good chocolate, to spoil it with so dreadful a mood."

"You're right," Troi's voice was flat, lacking enthusiasm. "But I didn't have any better ideas."

The twinkle in Guinan's eye grew brighter, more mischievous. "You could go program yourself a nice holodeck simulation, I suppose. One where you crack everyone's head against the wall and they instantly see the light."

In spite of herself, Troi began giggling. Once started, she couldn't stop until tears ran down her cheeks. Guinan watched her with one eyebrow raised, a quizzical smile on her face. "Personally, I didn't think it was *that* funny," she said when Troi had quieted.

Troi rubbed her knuckles across her cheeks. "I was imagining myself doing that to Chief O'Brien and wondering if it would have any effect on that thick Irish head of his. You know, I'm not sure it would make any greater impression than talking, but the idea made me feel better." She tackled the ice cream with greater cheer and decided that Guinan was right. The chocolate *did* taste better now that her mood had improved.

Guinan gave her a knowing grin. "I thought that might be the case. And maybe he'll start listening, if enough people quit telling him he's right."

Troi smiled at Guinan over another large bite of her brownie. "You know, this sundae is one of your better prescriptions, 'Doctor' Guinan."

"Yes, I have been told that recipe was rather good." Guinan's expression was smug, like a cat licking out the cream pitcher. "That's why I keep it in reserve for emergencies."

By the time she finished the sundae, Troi was

almost purring with contentment. She was still enjoying the feeling when her communicator beeped and the captain summoned her to the bridge. Glancing at her chronometer, she realized it was almost time to transmit the Jarada agreement to the Federation. She wondered what Data had discovered from analyzing the documents.

By the time Troi reached the captain's ready room, Picard and Data were seated at the table. The android was fidgeting through the draft agreements the Jarada had given them, looking impatient to give his report. The humanness of the action amused Troi, and she wondered where he had found his model for that particular habit. If she asked, he would no doubt tell her—in detail. Troi promised herself she would *not* ask.

"Counselor, have a seat." Picard's tone carried more than a little relief. Clearly, he was fighting his own battle to ignore Data's latest experiment. "Mr. Data, would you tell us what you found?"

"Certainly, sir." The android aligned both stacks of paper, as if to refer to them, even though they were recorded in his memory down to the stroke weights of the pen used to make the Jaradan characters and the crossouts in the English translation. Another mannerism he was testing, Troi was sure.

Data straightened his shoulders and cleared his throat. "My first observation is that the Jaradan written language is ideographic, like the ancient High Vulcan texts or the traditional Japanese forms of Earth. However, many of the symbols seem to be contextually determined, so that in one place an ideograph will mean one thing, while in another place the meaning is completely unrelated."

Troi slid her elbows forward, cupping her chin in

113

her hands. "Are you sure, Data? In most languages where the symbols change meaning, there are modifiers to indicate the differences. Particularly in legal documents, where neither side wishes to have any ambiguity in the wording of their agreement."

"I have checked the Jaradan ideographs against all forty-seven known styles of modulating the significance of a written communication. I found no correspondence between those methods and the Jaradan version of the document. Given the wide tonal values of each word in their language, I had expected some such system for indicating those values in the written language."

"Yet you did not?" A slight frown creased Picard's forehead as he tried to remember the more esoteric studies of linguistics he had read over the years. Verbal systems as complex as the Jaradan often had a simpler written language and, in the most extreme instances, the written symbols were little more than mnemonics for the spoken word. In that case, however, he would have expected the Jaradan version of the agreement to be significantly shorter than the English translation, which it was not. Something was not right. Before Data could answer, the message light in front of him lit. Picard touched his communicator to acknowledge the signal.

"Captain, we just received a message from Commissioner T'Zen requesting to know if you have relayed the agreement with the Jarada yet," Lieutenant Chang's voice said.

Picard suppressed a groan. With a twenty-seven-hour transmission lag between here and Earth, T'Zen had sent that message while the *Enterprise* was still approaching the Beltaxiyan system. "Relay my compliments to the commissioner," he told Chang, fighting to keep his annoyance out of his voice. "And tell her the draft agreement will follow shortly. Picard, out."

"Why is Commissioner T'Zen so anxious to receive this agreement?" Data tilted his head to the side and twisted his face into a caricature of a puzzled frown. "She could not have known how our negotiations would proceed when she sent that message. Therefore her request for transmission of the draft agreement is illogical."

Troi ducked her head, her mouth twitching in amusement. That left Picard to field the android's question. "The logic of avoiding a war, Mr. Data, outweighs such minor inconsistencies. Commissioner T'Zen wished to hurry us in the negotiations if we were not getting results as fast as she would like."

"That, too, is illogical, if I understand what I have been told about diplomatic proceedings. Am I not correct in saying that negotiations 'take as much time as they take'?"

Picard hid a momentary grin, wondering where Data had found that particular quote. "Yes, Mr. Data. You are correct, but the commissioner has concluded that we must negotiate this treaty quickly or our irrational natures will lead us into fighting with the Jarada. However, back to the agreement. Can you tell us if the English version is an accurate translation of the Jaradan document?"

Data squirmed in his chair, reminding Picard of a schoolboy who had just been caught passing messages to a friend. As a visual demonstration of the concept of "guilt," Data's act was effective, but—guilt about what? As usual, the android had chosen an inappropriate model.

Fortunately for the captain's patience, Data dropped his affectation as he began speaking. "No, Captain, I cannot draw any definite conclusion about the accuracy of the translation. In spite of the progress we have made on the Jaradan language, thanks to the recordings transmitted by the away team, our knowledge is too fragmentary for me to determine what the document actually says. I had hoped that it would provide a Rosetta stone and that I would see correlations between both versions which would add considerably to our Jaradan vocabulary. This has not been the case."

"Data, what *can* you tell us about the documents?" Troi's voice held a note of urgency, as if she were on the verge of solving the mystery. "How many explanations have you considered for the problems you're having?"

"I have examined three major hypotheses. If we assume that the documents are an exact translation, then the Jaradan language is written using a completely unknown system of grammar and syntax. A system, I should add, which is in no way a reflection of their spoken language. A second possibility is to assume that the translation is imprecise, with the words chosen to convey similar meanings without necessarily using identical ideographs each time a specific concept-cluster is discussed. This would be closer to what the document appears to be, but there are still difficulties with this interpretation. Working from the second hypothesis, I am still unable to determine a consistent grammar for the written Jaradan language."

"And all languages must have structure," Troi murmured, thinking aloud. "How a society perceives its surroundings is reflected in their language, and the grammar and vocabulary of the language in turn influence what an individual will notice in his environment."

Picard looked from Troi to Data, not liking the direction his own thoughts were taking. The problem was that none of their explanations made any sense.

"Mr. Data, you said you had a third hypothesis."

"Yes, Captain." The android refused to look directly at Picard, again inviting comparison to a guilty schoolboy. If that were the case, the captain decided, he would have to speak to Data about this particular experiment in human behavior. But he would do it later, when they had less pressing matters on the agenda.

"My other hypothesis is that the Jaradan document is a random collection of words with no apparent meaning. This would explain why I have been unable to discover a reasonable correspondence between the two documents, since there is none. However, this would raise fundamental questions about the underlying reasons for this mission."

"Indeed." Picard drew a deep breath to give himself time to think. If the Jaradan document was meaningless, why was the *Enterprise* here at all? "Counselor?"

"There are several explanations, of course." She ran her hand through her hair, fanning the dark curls across her shoulder. "The first is that we do not have sufficient information to analyze the written Jaradan language and that the fault is in our translation. It's also possible that for similar reasons they were unable to translate the agreement into their language. However, this seems highly unlikely, since they are able to communicate verbally with us and they have provided our away team with translators that seem to function adequately."

"And your perceptions of them, Counselor? Are they dealing honestly with us?"

Troi twisted her fingers through a lock of her hair. The reflection of Data's pale face, his brow wrinkled in another exaggerated frown, stared at her from the polished surface of the table. "I have sensed no deception from them, certainly nothing deep enough to cover a spurious agreement. However, I must admit that I have not sensed any clear feelings or reactions from them. It's almost as if something is blurring their emotions, spreading them out so far that I am unable to read them."

"In that case, could they be hiding something from you, Counselor? Putting up some kind of screen to keep you from sensing their emotions?"

After a moment Troi nodded. "It's possible. At the moment I cannot tell you how likely it is, but we should give the idea further consideration."

"And, Mr. Data, how long would you estimate that it would take you to establish an accurate translation of the Jaradan version of our agreement?"

"I am unable to determine that, Captain. With the information I currently have available, I consider it unlikely that I can improve upon the work I have already done. However, we should anticipate that the crew members on the planet's surface will provide additional information when they return."

"While Commissioner T'Zen sends us hourly requests to transmit the draft agreement." There was no one Picard found more difficult to reason with than a Vulcan who "knew" she was about to prevent a war, however shaky the logic she had used to reach that conclusion. Reluctantly, he concluded there was only one thing he could do. "Computer, summarize the preceding discussion and append it to *both* versions of the Jaradan agreement. Transmit the documents to the Federation Council along with my recommendation to study everything carefully before agreeing to the terms."

"Working," the computer answered, then paused briefly before concluding, "Transmission sent to Federation Council, Stardate 44840.8."

"Anything to add?" Picard asked, looking at Data

and Troi. Both shook their heads. "Then the meeting's adjourned." He stood, feeling a weight lift from his shoulders as he realized the next step in the diplomatic process was *not* his responsibility.

He had just settled into his command chair, looking forward to a few hours of uneventful duty, when O'Brien called the bridge. The transporter chief sounded upset. "Captain, I was trying to talk to Keiko and she won't answer her communicator. The computer keeps telling me she's not on the planet's surface. I can't seem to reach anyone else either."

Deciding to ignore the fact that O'Brien's personal call would have interrupted the botanists' work, Picard glanced upward to tell the computer to relay his answer. "We'll look into it. Picard, out.

"Computer, contact Ensign Tanaka and Keiko Ishikawa immediately."

"Unable to comply. Neither Ensign Tanaka's nor Keiko Ishikawa's communicator registers on the ship's sensors."

A surge of anger, quickly replaced by apprehension, swept through Picard. "Then get me Commander Riker."

"Commander Riker's communicator does not register on ship's sensors."

"What about Dr. Crusher and Lieutenant Worf?"

"Their communicators also do not register on the ship's sensors."

Picard shot the computer an angry glare, realizing that O'Brien must have also been through this sequence and had obtained the same results. He turned to the crewman at Ops. "Mr. Chang, why weren't those communicators being monitored constantly as I ordered?"

Chang touched a control to replay the communications log. "Ship's log reports locations were recorded for all away-team members until Chief O'Brien attempted to initiate contact with Ms. Ishikawa. I would surmise the signals we received were spurious."

Picard scowled at the report. If the signals had been falsified, then the Jarada were definitely up to something. "Open a channel to the Jaradan Council of Elders. I want to speak to Zelfreetrollan at once."

After a few moments Mendosa reported, "The Jarada are not acknowledging our transmissions. I can't get a positive fix on their receiver, but I think their equipment's been taken off line."

Picard glanced at Troi, who rose and headed for the turbolift to tell O'Brien what had happened. Five malfunctioning communicators and the jamming, *plus* the Jaradan refusal to answer their message, were not a coincidence, and O'Brien would not take the news calmly. For a moment the captain wished *he* could throw a temper tantrum because their worst suspicions had just been confirmed, but he knew it wouldn't get his away team back. "Data," he ordered, "begin a full-scale sensor sweep of the Jaradan city and the surrounding countryside. I want our people located and beamed up immediately."

"Yes, sir."

Picard settled himself into his chair, trying to look calm and in control. He felt neither, but the illusion would increase morale considerably. For him, it was going to be a *very* long search, while his mind replayed the events that led up to it and he tried to see what he could have done differently.

"Damned bugs!" Chang muttered, his tone just loud enough to be overheard. "Can't trust an insect as far as you can throw its chitin-armored hide!"

He should lecture Chang on tolerance, Picard thought, but the volume of the remark had been carefully gauged to let him pretend he hadn't heard it. Chang wanted his opinion known, but had chosen a method that avoided confrontation. Besides, Picard was feeling less charitable toward their hosts than he should. The Jarada had maneuvered him into separating the away team, a danger he had discussed with the others after Zelfreetrollan had proposed the guided tours. Still, given their orders to learn more about the Jarada, accepting the invitation had been a calculated risk that should have paid off handsomely.

The malfunctioning—no, sabotaged, he corrected himself—communicators were the factor that changed the equation. *Why?* That was the key question. If they knew *why* the Jarada had set this up, they would understand everything that had puzzled them about the situation from the beginning. Unfortunately, Picard realized, the answers to his questions lay with his missing crew members.

Chapter Nine

RIKER FOLLOWED the Jarada musicians through the narrow door and onto another of the spiraling ramps. This one led only downward, in tight curves that disappeared into darkness below them. The walls were damp and the floor slippery with what Riker guessed was the local equivalent of slime mold or perhaps a form of algae capable of growing in dim light. The enclosed shaft smelled damp and musty, as if it were rarely used.

Despite the poor illumination from the irregularly spaced glowstrips, Riker saw narrow ridges running across the ramp, wide enough to act as steps for Jaradan claws but too small to do him much good. Grimacing in distaste, Riker started after his hosts. Most of the Jarada were scrambling downward at top speed and were drawing ahead of him despite the obvious stiffness of their movements. Zarn lagged back, slowing his pace to match Riker's.

"Do you want to tell me this is another *week'that drill*?" Riker asked, his tone colored with more than a little irony. In spite of the chill and the dampness, sweat trickled down his back.

"Yes, I would tell you that," Zarn answered in a perfectly level tone, "if it would get you to move faster."

"I see." From the clattering of their claws, the Jarada musicians were at least two levels below them. *And* they're *the "senior citizens,"* Riker thought in disgust, realizing just how efficient Jaradan locomotion was. Above them, loud bangs echoed down the shaft, as though someone were taking a battering ram to the door where they had entered. Perhaps Zarn had good reason for his concern. Riker grunted and tried to move faster down the slick, uneven, sloping surface. "However, if you don't mind, I'd like to ask you again when I have more time to hear the answer."

"While it is not my intention to insult a distinguished visitor from another hive, if you do not travel faster than a youngling in its first shell, we will not have the luxury of discussing anything later." Zarn quickened his pace, moving a quarter turn ahead of Riker.

A loud thud, followed by a splintering sound, reverberated down the shaft. Without looking to see if Riker was keeping up, Zarn broke into a trot and disappeared around the curve of the ramp. Another loud crash and the screech of tortured wood chased the fleeing Jarada downward.

From the sound, Riker thought the door might withstand another dozen blows, but he knew he didn't want to meet whoever was trying so hard to get on his side of the barrier. He lengthened his stride, keeping to the middle of the ramp and putting his feet where the musicians had scraped away the slippery organic carpet with their claws. It was risky to hurry too much, but from the silence below him, Riker guessed that an exit lay only a few turns farther down. If he could reach that door soon enough, he would be safe.

Riker kept his footing for the first turn, although his feet and hands were sweating from the nervous tension. The second turn seemed easier, with less slime on the ramp. He guessed there was an entrance somewhere along the wall, letting drier air seep into the shaft, but he didn't see any markings to show him where it was. From several levels farther down, he heard the clatter of Zarn's claws against the stone. Above him the tortured wood of the door shrieked in protest as the attackers struck it again. Riker realized it was going to last only another minute or so.

Distracted by trying to interpret the sounds he was hearing, Riker did not see the thick mat of algae that crossed the ramp below the dry zone. His boot heel hit the slime and kept going. Landing on his seat, Riker shot down the slippery, wet ramp. His head cracked on the concrete, stunning him for a moment, and he continued to slide downward, picking up speed. Although the narrow ridges made the ramp's surface uneven, the coating of algae was like grease, giving him no purchase.

Riker pulled in his arms and legs to minimize his body profile and concentrated on controlling his descent. He tried to imagine that his body was a toboggan and the ramp was his track. Even so, he bounced between the outer wall and the center column, collecting more bruises with each ricochet. He rounded the last bend and crashed into the end wall, all the breath knocked from his body. Just then the upper door gave way with a wrenching groan that echoed and reechoed in the enclosed space. A multitonal shriek of triumph from a horde of Jarada roared down the shaft.

A clawed hand gestured from the darkness beside

him. "Quick. This way," Zarn whispered, his voice a single note instead of the usual chord.

Riker, stunned and battered by his precipitous descent and its equally sudden ending, struggled to get to his feet. His lungs gasped for air and his abused muscles refused to cooperate.

"Hurry," Zarn ordered, scurrying out to help Riker. "We must get the door closed before they discover where we went."

Realizing Zarn lacked the strength to pull him to his feet, Riker waved the insectoid away. The yells of their pursuers were growing louder by the second. He still felt too shaky to stand, so he struggled to his hands and knees and crawled after the Jarada. It was undignified, but it worked. He had barely cleared the opening when he heard Zarn tap in the command to close and lock the door. It slid into its frame, shutting out the cries from the Jarada charging after them.

The tunnel was dark and poorly lit, its tiled surfaces as damp and slimy as the ramp they had just left. Riker collapsed on the floor, desperately trying to regain his breath and his equilibrium before they resumed their flight. The stone beneath his body was cold and damp, and the chill worked its way quickly through his uniform.

"Come. We must hurry," Zarn whispered, still with only a single note in his voice. "It won't take them long to figure out which door we used."

Riker shivered and pushed himself to a sitting position, his muscles shaking both from the temperature and the tension. His right shoulder protested, and he probed gently, finding a large tender spot that was already starting to swell. From the pull on his muscles he judged he had similar bruises on his hips and buttocks. "What's the hurry?" he asked, as much for the information as to delay climbing to his feet.

"They are extremists. Xenophobes who don't want relations with your Federation. Do you not have this problem among your people?" Zarn started along the corridor, his claws tapping impatiently against the floor.

"We do." Riker pushed himself up on one knee, pausing when his head started spinning. Something in Zarn's manner told him the insectoid was lying, but Riker was not sure what rang false. The dank, moldy air clogged his lungs, making it hard to breathe and harder to concentrate. He clenched his fists, fighting the urge to bolt for the *Enterprise* without getting to the bottom of this mystery. "Why didn't you mention this to us before?"

"It is not right that they should oppose the will of the Hive. However, at the moment, they have us outnumbered. We must hurry before they find us."

Riker struggled to his feet, ignoring the protests of his bruised muscles. "I think Captain Picard will be very interested to hear this. We'll beam up to the ship and you can explain it to him." Through the door, Riker heard the high-pitched yells of their pursuers.

Zarn's claws tapped out an impatient jig. "We don't have time for that now. We must hurry."

Riker flipped over his sleeve and tapped his communicator. To his surprise, nothing happened. He hit it again, harder. The dampness in the tunnels shouldn't have affected it, and he didn't remember striking it against anything in his wild descent. However, the device wasn't working and, judging from the sounds on the other side of the door, his options were fast slipping away. He started after Zarn, surprised at how unsteady he felt.

Zarn set a mean pace, his four legs covering the ground with surprising ease. After a few minutes Riker was breathing hard and sweating from the exertion, despite the chilly air. The insectoid followed a twisting, circuitous path that soon had Riker completely disoriented. He was not sure whether the Jarada intended to confuse him or if the complicated route was needed to throw off their pursuers. Riker thought they were headed farther underground, but by the eighth or ninth odd-angled transition from one curving, sloping corridor to another, he was no longer sure where they were or in which direction they were traveling.

Finally, Zarn stopped beside a narrow door, the first Riker had seen since they left the ramp. The Jarada coded the door open and gestured for Riker to enter. "We can hide here for a while. No one would ever think to look in this place."

The room was long and narrow, almost a corridor, with the only light coming from a single feeble glowstrip in the far corner. Piles of trash were heaped along one of the long walls and the dank, mildewy smell was overpowering. Reluctantly, Riker limped inside and looked for a place to sit.

Zarn followed him in and keyed the door closed. "Forgive the poor accommodations, Riker-Commander. This place is never used now, and no one ever comes here."

Easing himself to the floor in the cleanest spot he could find, Riker studied his surroundings carefully. Glowstrips were spaced along the wall behind him, their surfaces dull and inert. Even the one remaining strip was mottled and unsteady, as if the photoactive bacteria in it were dying too. Badly eroded lines etched the wall opposite him, intersecting here and there at blobs of decaying materials. After several minutes Riker realized the lines described a hexagonal pattern like the cells in a honeycomb. The moldering refuse on the floor was probably the remnants of material that had been attached to the wall. "What was this room used for?"

"It was one of the original hatching chambers." Zarn moved to Riker's side and folded his legs under him, the closest the insectoid could come to sitting. "When we first built on this planet, it was a very dry year. We have since come to discover that the ground in many places is damper than we thought and we have been forced to abandon most of our original tunnels. This is one of the worst areas, where we were unable to exclude the moisture from our living and working spaces."

Riker ran his finger over the rough tiles, feeling the film of dampness that clung to them. The floor here lacked the brilliant glazes and elaborate mosaics that characterized the other Jaradan floors he had seen. "If your people wish, the Federation has many techniques for dealing with this type of problem. We would be more than willing to assist you in reclaiming these tunnels."

"That is an interesting proposal, and I am sure the Council of Elders will be happy to discuss it."

The tone of Zarn's voice caught Riker's attention. The words themselves seemed encouraging, but Riker sensed the Jarada was withholding something. He shivered with an unwelcome premonition that more things were wrong on Bel-Minor than he already knew. Forcing that thought away, Riker reached for his communicator and again tried to call the *Enterprise*.

"I do not think your communications device will work here," Zarn said as he watched Riker try for the third time. "There is something in the rocks in this area that blocks out the signals."

Riker scowled, thinking the excuse was a little too convenient. Still, the communicator was not working and he lacked the means to test it. Zarn's explanation was barely plausible, and certainly no more unlikely than the idea that he had managed to break the nearly indestructible device on his rapid slide down the ramp. Whatever the explanation, he now lacked any way of contacting the ship. He would have to rely on Zarn to guide him back to the Governance Complex, where he could rendezvous with the rest of the away team when they returned from their excursions.

"I believe we must stay here for some time." Although Zarn kept his voice low, he had returned to his usual multitonal mode. "I did not hear the alarms to signal the guardians, so we must wait until we are sure all our attackers have been captured. In these tunnels, I fear that will not be accomplished soon."

Again Riker had the feeling that Zarn was not telling him everything, but he did not know how to get the full story from the Jarada. If diplomacy was the creative art of telling only what you wanted known, then Zarn was possibly the greatest diplomat Riker had ever met. Somehow the Jarada had told him so little that Riker did not even know what questions to ask in order to uncover Zarn's duplicity or his omissions.

The effort of trying to outguess his companion, combined with the bad air in the room and his reaction to the day's events, hit Riker all at once. He felt as though he had just run a marathon, and his body was so wrung out that he could not keep his eyes open. Locking his arms around his legs, he lowered his head to his knees, hoping that Zarn would think he was just resting. For some reason, it was important not to let the Jarada know how tired he was. Even so, he was soon fast asleep.

A light, repeated tapping on his shoulder finally wakened Riker. He stirred, trying to remember where he was. The surface beneath him was cold and hard, and dampness had soaked into his uniform. Finally the smell, dank and moldy, registered and memory returned.

He had slipped from his sitting position while he slept and was now lying on his side, curled up against the cold. A shiver ran through his body, and then another, as awareness of the temperature returned along with wakefulness. Riker tried to lever himself upright, but the bruised muscles in his shoulder had stiffened while he slept. Waves of pain washed through him and the arm collapsed. For a moment he just lay there, willing his body to respond to his orders.

"It is time to go now, Riker-Commander. I am sure the bad ones are no longer here." Zarn's claws chittered against the rough tiles as the Jarada started toward the door.

How does he know that? Riker thought. He pushed himself off the floor again, moving more slowly this time and gauging the effect of each movement on his battered muscles. The chill and the inactivity had taken its toll, making him feel as though he were a hundred years old. In truth, he supposed, the cold had probably reduced the swelling of his bruises, but that did not make it easier for him to start moving again.

It was a struggle, but finally he made it, sweating from the exertion despite the icy leadenness of his limbs. The cold and stiffness, at least, would go away when they began walking. Zarn was doing an impatient tap dance by the door, but Riker ignored the Jarada while he stretched some of the kinks from his muscles. If they had to move fast, he wanted to be ready. Besides, although Zarn was calling the shots here, Riker was reluctant to let him know how completely he was at the insectoid's mercy.

"Will you please hurry?" With a visible effort Zarn slowed his jigging and looked toward Riker. In the weak light his eyes glowed a pale green. "There's no one in the nearby corridors, and I can get you to safety before there is any more trouble."

Riker moved toward the door, testing his legs as he went. Aches and twinges greeted every motion, and he certainly would not want to go into hand-to-hand combat against a Klingon or a Vulcan—but he decided he could manage. In any case, he would be glad to see the last of this smelly, damp room. "How do you know that no one's around?" he asked as he reached the door.

"I don't sense anyone. They're not there." Zarn tapped the code into the door and it swished open. He walked out into the corridor without even looking to see if it was occupied.

"Sense? How?" Riker glanced both ways before he followed Zarn out of the room, even though he knew that anyone waiting in ambush would already be alerted to their presence.

"We of the Hive are always aware of each other, to a greater or lesser extent. Don't you always know what is happening with the others of your hive?" Without waiting for an answer, Zarn started down the corridor at a rapid pace.

At first Riker had to struggle to keep up with his guide. His battered body protested at the speed, and he wondered at Zarn's hurry. After fifteen minutes of twists and turns, of ducking around corners and down short ramps, he felt better. The exercise was working out the soreness, loosening up his muscles, and dispelling the chill that had penetrated to his bones.

He began to take more notice of his surroundings, trying to orient himself and to figure out where they were heading. The walls and floors lost their dampness, suggesting they were moving into the drier, inhabited parts of the complex. This impression was reinforced by the glowstrips, which were brighter and more closely spaced. However, they saw no one and

Riker concluded that Zarn was going out of his way to avoid any encounters.

They had been moving for almost half an hour, with Zarn setting a pace that left Riker with no breath for asking questions. He wondered if it wasn't deliberate, since the number of riddles that demanded his attention multiplied with each step. Was Zarn's explanation for the attack, that the assailants were xenophobes, correct—or was there some other reason for the event? Why was Zarn trying so hard to avoid meeting anyone? Was it truly to avoid danger, or was his guide kidnapping him? If the circuitous route they were traveling was deliberately planned to take him away from the area where the *Enterprise* could find him, was Zarn acting with or against government orders? And, finally, how was Riker to determine the true answers to his questions, when he had no accurate way of deciding when the Jarada was lying to him?

They turned onto a ramp that spiraled upward at a steep angle. An intense floral odor assaulted Riker, as concentrated as though someone had crammed a hundred square kilometers of jungle blossoms into the volume of a turbolift car. The suffocating fragrance made his head spin and he paused to catch his breath. A turn and a half above him, he heard Zarn stop too. Hoping they had reached the end of their tunnel odyssey, Riker started up the ramp. Zarn's claws hit the controls harder, and Riker realized that he had not heard a door open in response to the command.

He rounded the curve in time to see Zarn drop his hand from the control pad. *Vrel'keth brefleew!* the Jarada muttered, his voice thick with a nasty buzz. From the tone, Riker did not need a translation. Swearing sounded remarkably similar in every language in the galaxy.

Zarn started up the ramp again, his movements stiff and jerky from anger. Two turns higher, they came to another door and Zarn tried to open it. This time the barrier slid aside on command, sending a suffocating wave of floral perfume down the shaft. Beckoning to Riker, Zarn moved into the corridor beyond.

Riker stepped through the door and slammed into an oppressive wall of heat and humidity. The temperature was at least twenty-five degrees Celsius warmer than the tunnels through which they had been dodging, and the humidity now approached a hundred percent. Combined with the overwhelming floral reek, Riker felt as though someone had dumped a ton of Tribbles on him. Sweat sprang out on his forehead and poured down his back. He struggled to breathe, to drag the thick air into his lungs and extract oxygen from it. His head felt as though it had been detached from his shoulders and was floating away, making for the *Enterprise* by itself.

"Come. Hurry," Zarn whispered, gesturing impatiently. "I shouldn't have brought you here."

With a supreme effort Riker forced his legs to move. The heat sapped his energy and sent thoughts of sleep tumbling through his head. Zarn's form swam in and out of focus—one moment hard and sharp, as dangerous as his current predicament, the next moment fuzzy and dreamlike, a phantasmagorical monster from a children's story. Fighting his disorientation, Riker kept moving, following his Jarada guide even though he was no longer sure of where he was or if he even dared trust the insectoid. In his curiously detached state, nothing seemed to matter, and it was easiest to follow Zarn because that was what the insectoid had told him to do.

Part of Riker's mind observed his actions, cataloging his surroundings and his peculiar reactions to the heavy odors. Unlike the parts of the complex he had seen before, broad archways opened off this corridor, giving him a clear view of the rooms beyond. Through one opening he glimpsed the yin and yang of two Jarada locked together in rut. As they passed, the white female sank her teeth into the ebony male's throat.

The male's final shriek was cut off by the crunching sounds of the female's teeth shearing through his exoskeleton, but even after death his body continued to convulse beneath hers. Farther along, a female with an obscenely distended abdomen was sprawled beside a wall covered with hexagonal cells. Pale gold attendants stroked her thorax, encouraging the contractions that rippled her softened and leathery exoskeleton. Slowly, with each pulse accompanied by a high-pitched whistle of pain, she expelled the eggs from her ovipositor.

The attendants lifted them into the waiting cells and sealed them inside, their movements taut and jerky. Seeing the attendants' tension, Riker knew that the queen was dying, that this agonizing labor was as unnatural for the Jarada as it was normal for humans.

"Hurry!" Zarn spat out. "We haven't much time before the guardians discover us."

The urgency in Zarn's voice made Riker realize that the lack of a challenge had been bothering him. Even in his strangely drugged state, he knew that the Jarada would not wish anyone to see what happened in these chambers. What the penalty for his intrusion was, he did not wish to find out. Sobered enough by that thought to be worried for the first time, Riker broke into a jog. Zarn increased his pace, maintaining his lead.

As they turned a corner, a loud, high-pitched chord roared from the walls. From three directions came the sound of massed foot-claws chattering against the tiled flooring. Riker tried to estimate how many guardians were approaching, but without actually counting them he could not begin to guess their number. With a deep certainty he knew he did not want to see these Jarada, did not want to discover what his punishment would be for witnessing the deepest secrets of their race.

"*Vrel'keth brefteev!*" Zarn growled viciously. He dashed to the end of the corridor and pounded a code into the door's control panel. The mechanism was slow to respond, starting and then cycling back shut. Zarn had to repeat the sequence before it registered properly on the lock. By the time Riker had caught up with him, the door was sliding open.

Zarn gestured for Riker to enter first. The shaft was dark and its walls gleamed suspiciously in the band of light from the corridor. A gust of stale, mold-scented air washed over him. Riker took a hesitant step forward, uncertain of what lay ahead but reluctant to be caught by the approaching guardians. The next thing he knew, Zarn kicked him in the pressure points on both calves. Predictably, his legs buckled and he landed on his seat. Before he could react, Zarn shoved him. Riker shot forward, gaining speed on the algae-slick surface of the disused ramp. Once more he was tobogganing into the darkness, unguided and out of control.

Chapter Ten

THE GROUNDCAR DUCKED AND WEAVED, tossing Crusher back and forth against the safety harness. The pillows that filled out the Jaradan contours to roughly human shape were not anchored to the seat, and they shifted with each violent lurch. Grimly, the doctor braced herself against the side of the car, hoping the restraints would keep her from serious injury. They had been designed for the lighter Jarada and she wasn't sure how much extra stress they could withstand.

Wesley could have calculated it instantly, could have told her how many sharp turns and violent lurches the fastenings could withstand before they parted from their anchors and let her go flying against the far wall. She was glad Wesley was *not* around to tell her that, glad he was away at Starfleet Academy, where he would hear nothing of this adventure until she was safely back aboard the *Enterprise*. Then she could tell him the story with the proper humor and self-deprecation to let him know she had not *really* been in danger, that it had been an exciting but completely harmless little adventure to liven an otherwise dull week.

She tried to rehearse the letter to her son, tried to focus her mind on describing the events in the proper light, but somehow the exercise didn't work. Her palms were sweaty with fear, and if she let up on her control for one second, she knew that hysteria would overwhelm her. This was the classic example of a situation where you called your ship to be beamed back aboard, leaving the work of unsnarling everything to the captain—and her communicator wasn't working.

Get a hold on yourself, Beverly. Maybe it was just the car's armor; maybe the plates were too thick for the signal to penetrate them. She knew that wasn't likely, but it was at least possible and it gave her a small grain of hope. When they escaped their attackers and Vish raised the armor, everything would be all right. Things would be *just* fine then and she would be able to contact the ship.

She kept repeating that thought to herself, over and over, in the long minutes that the car twisted and dodged through what sounded like the mine fields she had seen in ancient flat-screen entertainments. This situation—being blind and isolated and alone with an alien who suddenly wasn't talking to her—was not something she had imagined in her worst nightmares. Ship's doctors were virtually *never* cut off from the rest of their crewmates.

Finally, the car left their attackers behind. Vish was still hunched over the control panel, its ochre body screening the status boards from Crusher's view. She wasn't sure she could make any sense of the panels, but it would give her a feeling of security to think she knew where they were going, like the virtual reality of the star fields on the ship's viewscreens. "What's happening?" she asked, hoping Vish would answer.

The Jarada did not move, did not acknowledge Crusher's question with so much as a twitch of its antennae. Clenching her fists to fight off the panic of its being unable to affect—much less control—her surroundings, Crusher forced herself to take several deep breaths. When she felt calmer, she adjusted the cushions and settled herself in her seat, braced for a ride of indeterminate length.

After half an hour the car slowed from its breakneck speed and turned sharply to the left. To judge by the jolting and bouncing when they picked up speed, they were on an unpaved road seamed with ruts and pitted with potholes. Crusher hoped that Vish would lower the shields so she could see where they were, but the Jarada still was not responding to her questions.

She felt more and more as though she were being kidnapped, but could see no reason for the abduction. Nothing Crusher had seen so far on Bel-Major pointed to problems that anyone would use terrorism to solve. Except for whoever had dropped the bombs on the groundcar, Jarada society seemed peaceful, orderly, and lacking the stresses that normally caused such disruptions. Nothing made much sense.

Crusher chased the problem around in her head, not reaching any conclusions except that she was missing several major pieces of the puzzle. Something in their information about the Jarada, or at least these particular Jarada, was so totally wrong as to make nonsense of everything else they knew. Captain Picard had thought the negotiations were going too easily, and the events of the last hour were proving his instincts correct.

She remembered discussing her own uneasiness with Troi earlier and wondered what had triggered her doubts. Something subtle, certainly, or Troi would have perceived it with her empathic abilities. The more she thought about it, the more Crusher remembered the clues that revealed how nervous all the humans had been, the little gestures and phrases that said how unsettling they found the Jarada even though Troi had not detected anything from their hosts in the way she normally sensed duplicity in strangers.

In most situations Crusher would have dismissed the away team's uneasiness as premission jitters or latent xenophobia, which affected everybody once in a while, no matter how hard they fought it. Still, reviewing their discussion last night, she spotted what they had all overlooked at the time—when as experienced a group as theirs *all* were on edge, something was wrong. Subliminally, they had recognized a problem, but no one had been able to articulate their perceptions as more than vague uneasiness. Given their mission, Picard would need much stronger evidence before he took any action that might destroy the trust he was trying to build.

I guess you've got that evidence now, Jean-Luc, she thought, forcing herself to relax against the seat. She wasn't sure how long it would take for the *Enterprise* to discover her predicament, but she knew it would mean the end of their mission. Meanwhile, she might as well use her time to collect whatever information she could. Anything she learned would help them sort out the situation later. She hadn't heard any explosions for some time, which probably meant she wasn't in any immediate danger. Certainly, if Vish had wanted to hurt her, the Jarada could have turned her over to the attackers. That meant Vish wanted her alive, at least for a while, and that gave her time to observe and to plan.

The groundcar slowed again and began climbing a steep incline, its engines laboring from the strain. After a short distance it slewed around a sharp hairpin turn and continued to climb. Five switchbacks later, Crusher was glad the armor plates still covered the windows. She was no judge of how far they had traveled, but from the tightness of the bends and the straining of the car's engine, she knew they were fairly high up a steep mountain. Again she wished for the safety of the *Enterprise*, for the security of the thick bulkheads and the multiple layers of force shields that protected the ship. Planets were inherently dangerous, and traveling mountain roads in underpowered vehicles ranked just below refereeing Klingon war games on Crusher's list of activities she expected to shorten her life expectancy to zero.

To pass the time, Crusher tried to remember the briefing on Bel-Minor's geography. There had been something about a mountain range—to the south and east of the city, she thought—but she couldn't bring up any details. Given her ignorance of the speeds and directions they had traveled, she could be almost anywhere on the planet.

After four more switchbacks, two of which they negotiated by backing and taking a second run at the turn, the road leveled off. Crusher hoped they had reached the top, but that left her wondering what would happen next. She thought about asking Vish, but decided she would rather let the Jarada pilot the car, if that was what it was doing. Since the armor still covered the windows, they could be traveling along the edge of a cliff, for all she knew. Under the circumstances, distracting the driver did not seem prudent.

They traveled for fifteen more minutes, but encountered no more sharp curves or steep inclines. Despite her previous resolutions, Crusher was almost ready to demand an explanation from Vish when, unexpectedly, the surface beneath their tires went smooth. A *paved road? On the top of a mountain?* The doctor's first thought was that she had taken leave of her senses, that the whole trip was an elaborate simulator hoax and that her wild imaginings were all paranoid fantasies.

The groundcar rolled to a stop. From behind them Crusher heard a loud thump, like the sound of the shuttlebay doors seating themselves against their seals. Vish tapped a pad on the control panel and leaned back in its seat, giving a low hum that reminded the doctor of nothing so much as a sigh of relief. The shields slid away from the windows, giving Crusher her first view of their surroundings. They were in a large, poorly lit cavern that extended deep into the mountain. Several other groundcars of various sizes were parked near them, but most of the area was empty.

Vish removed two small buttons from the base of its antennae and turned to face Crusher. "Please forgive the manner of our bringing you here. As you saw, there are those who do not believe in the wisdom of deciding that your people should be allowed into this place."

"You mean, this was where we were coming all along?" Crusher inhaled sharply, fighting to keep from screaming at the Jarada for putting her through the hair-raising ride when they could have transported so much more easily. "Why didn't we just use the transporter to get here? I could have survived without the tour of the city."

Straightening itself to its full height, Vish gave Crusher a stare that she guessed would have paralyzed a graduate student or made a junior researcher quiver in its exoskeleton. "We do not permit transporters to operate within a seventy *belevi* radius of this complex. That translates to"—the Jarada cocked its head to one side, its antennae bobbing, as it did the calculation—"about fifty of your kilometers. Our work is too sensitive for us to risk giving marauders easy access to our facilities."

"Marauders? Do you expect attackers even near your scientific facilities?" Crusher shivered at this new aspect of Jaradan life. They knew so little of these people—and most of their information was clearly wrong. Nothing in any report had suggested that violence directed against scientists, or against any other segment of their society, was a problem for Bel-Minor's Jaradan population.

Vish released its safety harness and leaned over to unfasten Crusher's. "So many questions. Come inside and we will answer them all." The Jarada opened the car door and stepped out, waiting for Crusher. Reluctantly, although she was not sure why, she climbed out of the vehicle and followed the insectoid.

They crossed the cavern to the near wall and Vish tapped a coded pattern into the door panel. The door opened and Crusher noticed that it looked thick enough to withstand a direct phaser hit from the *Enterprise's* main batteries. She shivered, wondering what sort of assault force they feared would attack the facility.

From her Earth history, she would have expected to find such a door on a secret weapons research facility, dating from the Eugenics Wars. Here, though, the occurrence was disturbing. Zelfreetrollan had invited her to visit a medical research facility, not a manufacturing plant for biological weapons. Either she had been given deliberate misinformation about the work done here, or the role of scientific researchers in Jaradan society had been grossly misrepresented. *Or something even worse is going on.* She shivered, not liking any of the possibilities.

Inside, the complex consisted of broad, well-lit corridors and large, well-equipped laboratory spaces. Vish led Crusher around, introducing her to the researchers and explaining the various projects. At first Crusher tried to keep the different individuals straight, but soon she lost track. Everyone she met was small, though most of them were taller than Vish, and all had large heads. All were various shades of ochre and tan, but the shadings were so subtle that Crusher knew it would take her weeks to keep the differences straight. Each gave off the faint scent of sage or oregano or some other cooking spice Crusher could never remember even when she was reading the label for it. And, Heaven help her, most of the names began with "Zel-brek-k'vel," and despite the invitation to address them informally, she had trouble sorting the individual names from the first three, which she knew meant "worker of the scientific caste of the hive Zel."

Many of the projects she was shown centered around Vish's favorite topic, the role of nutrition on Jaradan development. Other groups were working on plant biology, on genetically engineering imported plant species to survive Bel-Minor's radiation, and on exploring the effects of that radiation on the Jarada. The researchers were all friendly, eager to show her their work and excited when she made comments on what they were doing.

As the afternoon wore on, Crusher became more and more puzzled. Nothing she saw justified the secrecy with which she had been brought to the facility nor the elaborate security precautions that guarded the researchers. She began watching the Jarada around her, looking for anything abnormal, trying to spot any differences that separated these people from each other or from any other Jarada she had met.

The first clue presented itself as she was listening to a young researcher discuss its studies into the link between *breveen* genetics and nutrition. It was showing her a series of glass tanks, each containing plants with different colored flowers. "We've isolated the genes that control every blossom color except one.

The most common color for *breveen* on our homeworld is a pale lavender, which we have been unable to produce in any of our tests."

The Jarada paused, its eyes shifting color as it focused on various parts of the room. After a moment it gave its head a couple of sharp jerks and returned to its explanation. "Reproducing the pale lavender flower, which is the most common shade on our homeworld, has proved impossible in all our tests. Since all the colors are determined by the genetics, with the expression of the genes being controlled by the effect of certain trace elements on enzyme function, and since even the first-generation plants display this problem . . ."

When the young researcher paused again, its head twitching violently, every Jarada in the room began running toward it. Even so, they were not fast enough. With a falsetto shriek it launched itself at Crusher, its claws slashing toward her eyes. She threw her arm across her face and retreated until a lab bench hit her legs. The Jarada raked its claws against her arm, ripping her uniform and gouging deeply into her flesh. Crusher jerked backward and overbalanced, landing across the bench in a crash of breaking glassware and smashed experiments.

The other Jarada overwhelmed the young researcher and hauled it away. It continued to twitch and to shriek, its behavior reminding Crusher of her brief stint as a young intern on the mental wards after the Kadreelan plague killed swiftly and horribly, but a few people survived with their mental faculties ravaged. Crusher shuddered at the memory of what it had been like when the sudden and unexpected influx of incurably insane, triple what anyone had dealt with in over a century, had stretched the Federation's resources beyond their capacity.

Slowly, Crusher pushed herself upright, trying to avoid cutting herself further on the broken glass. The claw gouges on her forearm were bleeding freely and her back felt as though slivers of glass had cut through her uniform in several places. She ought to be furious, she thought, but couldn't summon the emotion. The attack had been too sudden. Her hosts had recognized the symptoms, had known what was going to happen, but even for them, things had happened too quickly.

Vish waited for her to get to her feet. As she separated herself from the broken glassware, Crusher realized that the Jarada's posture was far more deferential than she had ever seen it. "Forgive the attack, Honored Crusher-Doctor. If we had known that one was so unstable, we would not have brought you to see its most important project."

"Does this sort of thing happen very often?" Her temper was finally starting to waken, and Crusher made no attempt to rein it in. It was about time the Jarada gave her some answers.

"We will show you to a place where you may cover your injuries, and afterward we will answer any questions." Vish started for the door, as if to pull Crusher along by its movement.

The tactic might have worked if the throbbing in her arm hadn't compounded Crusher's irritation. She planted her boots on the floor and refused to budge. "I want some answers and I want them now. Does this happen very often?"

Vish turned to study Crusher with eyes that flickered from amber to green to red. Finally, it lifted all four hands to its shoulders in the Jaradan equivalent of a shrug. "As you wish, although this is not the place I would choose for such discussions. Since we have come to this planet, it has been happening with increasing frequency. None of our researchers know why this should happen, and as each one becomes crazy, the ripples of its madness pass through the rest of our group.

"We are now so diminished that only the strongest are still able to continue our work. Soon all of us will lack the support of our hive-mates and will become as lost and insane as the youngling that attacked you. Since you are a solitary being and can function without the support of your hive-mind, we brought you here to help us. You will find the cause of this insanity before it destroys our entire hive."

Crusher stared at the Jarada, wondering what she had missed. Of course she would help them; she was a doctor and never refused help to anyone who needed it. However, the implied threat in Vish's words made her uneasy. What was it they wanted of her? "I'd be glad to help you. Let me beam the relevant materials back to the *Enterprise* and I'll put all my research facilities to work solving the problem."

"No. You don't understand." Vish's voice was flat with certainty. "We cannot let word of this affliction go beyond this place. You will work here, without contacting anyone, until you have solved the problem."

Chapter Eleven

LONG SHADOWS lay across the campsite when Keiko finally crawled out of her tent. She looked around and groaned, thinking of the entire afternoon lost. Tanaka was sitting beside his tent, fussing with his tricorder and with something on a cloth in front of him. "Why didn't you wake me up sooner?" she asked. "You know we have work to do."

Tanaka looked up, noticing that she was outside her tent. He glanced around, taking in the shadows and the low angle of the sun as if he hadn't been aware of them either. "I didn't realize what time it was." He pointed to the ground in front of him.

Keiko looked at the scattering of miniature electronic components, miscellaneous bits and pieces of metal, and assorted tools. At first she couldn't fit things together into anything she recognized. Her second thought was that, just like Kiyoshi, Tanaka had managed to cram more tools and gadgets into his pack than was humanly possible. Finally, with a sense of dawning horror, she recognized the scattered components. "Our communicators? What have you done

147

to them?" She hadn't thought anyone could disassemble them without access to a complete diagnostics and repair unit.

If her attack insulted him, Tanaka gave no sign of it. Instead, he examined his handiwork with a rueful grimace. "The damage was done long before I touched them." He picked up one of the components and handed it to her on the flat of his palm. "This is the frequency modulator. Without it, we don't send anything anywhere."

Gingerly, she took the tiny object and examined it. When it came to electronics, her entire knowledge could have been inscribed in readable letters on the part she held, with room left over for the complete works of Shakespeare. However, the modulator looked strange, almost as if it had been heated with a plasma torch. "It looks melted," she said with a frown.

"That's a good description, for a nonspecialist." He took the modulator back, examined it critically, and replaced it on the cloth. "Someone wanted to cut us off from the *Enterprise* pretty badly. I'd guess they zapped us with a high-gain subspace transmitter at very close range. Whatever it was, it put out far more power than these circuits were designed to absorb. It also seems to have overloaded the data links in the tricorders, although everything else works."

She knelt beside the cloth and looked closer at the other parts. Now that she knew what to look for, she could see that most of the components showed signs of damage. "Could it have been an accident? I mean, could we have driven past something that did it?"

"Oh, we drove past something, all right." He gave the scattered bits of circuitry a final scowl and then began putting them into a specimen bag. "But it wasn't any accident. Otherwise, the tricorders and my diagnostic equipment wouldn't work either. Whatever it was, they picked the precise frequency that would burn out the communications relays without damaging anything else."

"That means we could be in a lot of trouble." Keiko sat back on her heels, thinking. Before she could deal with their next step, though, there was something she needed to know. "How come you've got all that repair equipment in your pack? It's not standard policy to bring an electronics kit with you."

Tanaka's expression went grim. "I've been on away teams with Lieutenant Deyllar. Have you ever seen what that man can do to a tricorder?"

Keiko groaned in sympathy, remembering the time Deyllar had managed to get sulfuric acid from a particularly unpleasant carnivorous plant *inside* the casing of his tricorder. To this day she had no idea how he had gotten the acid into the sealed device while *not* getting any on himself. The tricorder, however, had been a dead loss and the captain had ordered Deyllar to return to the ship until the doctor had checked him over for acid burns. Several other members of the away team had received multiple burns before they finished the survey, but Deyllar had emerged unscathed, except for his tricorder.

Tanaka continued. "Since he ranks me, when we're on a survey together, he always takes my tricorder after he ruins his own. If I want to get any work done—even if it is on lichens—I have to repair his junk before I can do anything."

"Why don't you just call the ship for a replacement? Wouldn't that be easier?"

"I tried that—once. Deyllar put me on report for damaging Starfleet property."

"Because he ranks you." Keiko shook her head at her own foolishness. Deyllar was the botany section's albatross, completely incompetent but with connections somewhere that kept him from being booted out

149

of Starfleet for his offenses. She shuddered, wondering why they were wasting time on unsolvable problems. "Enough. We should be planning our next move."

Thumbing the lock tab to activate it, Tanaka sealed the bag with the damaged pieces of their communicators. "I'm open to suggestions, but right now I'm a little short on ideas." He glanced over his shoulder in the direction of the Jarada camp. "Since our hosts sabotaged our communicators, you could say that I'm feeling somewhat reluctant to trust them."

Keiko leaned forward, resting her chin on her hands while she considered their situation. As per standard policy for such excursions, they had enough ration bars and water purification tablets to last them several days, so they wouldn't starve or die of dehydration. They were scheduled to be gone two nights, but the captain would probably start looking for them sooner.

She was sure Miles would insist when she failed to call him and when neither of their communicators showed up on the ship's scans. On the down side, she had no idea where they were and she doubted that anyone on the *Enterprise* knew which direction away from the city their vehicle had gone. Separating the sensor traces of two humans from a busload of Jarada shouldn't be too difficult once the sensors were pointing in the right place, but she had no idea how long it would take for the ship to focus its search in their area. After a long silence she spoke. "The problem as I see it is that we don't have any transportation. And we could be upward of three hundred kilometers from the city in almost any direction."

"Northwest." Tanaka stared out over the lake, a glum expression on his face. "But the only way the ship would know that is if they were tracking our communicators while we were riding out here."

She studied his face, thinking how transparent he was. Reading his moods was like reading a book, with everything spelled out in terms only a fool or a blind man could miss. "You're positive that the communicators were damaged before we left the city?"

He shrugged, his expression still bleak. "That would be easiest. Besides, wouldn't the point be to separate us from the rest of our people? If they waited until the ship got a bearing on us, it wouldn't work. The bus would have to change directions and double back onto another heading, or why bother?"

"What's the point? What do they want with us?"

The whole situation was ludicrous. Kidnapping them would only antagonize Picard and, through him, the Federation. There was nothing she or Tanaka could do for the Jarada that they could not better achieve by completing their negotiations with the Federation.

"Maybe they want hostages. Maybe they want to hold us for ransom or something." All the animation left him suddenly, and he reminded Keiko of a lifelike wooden doll. She wondered what had caused the sudden change, but this didn't seem like the time to pursue the matter. They had other problems to settle first.

She pushed herself to her feet, determined to force some answers from their hosts. A wave of dizziness swept through her as her body struggled to cope with the sudden movement. Tanaka reached for her, steadied her until her head cleared. "Thanks, Reggie," Keiko murmured, unsettled by her reaction.

She had done that hundreds of times without being dizzy, so why should she have problems now, when she needed all her faculties at peak efficiency? Squaring her shoulders and straightening her back, she mentally ordered her body to stay under control for the rest of the mission. Crossing to her tent, she pulled out her jacket and shrugged into it. "As I recall, the Jarada are expecting us for dinner. I for one would like some answers. Are you coming?"

Tanaka climbed slowly to his feet, still in the grip of the strange mood that had hit him along with the idea that the Jarada wanted them as hostages. "I can't let you go alone." His words came slowly, in a flat, dead voice. "But I don't think I'd trust them very far if I were you."

"About as far as I can throw them." She gave him a sharp look, wondering what had come over him. "You don't have to come if you really don't want to."

He shook his head, a little life returning to his face. "Regulations. We've got to stick together now that our communicators don't work."

"In that case, let's go hunt some explanations." She started off, wishing she had a phaser to back up her brave words. She started to ask Tanaka if he had one somewhere in his collection of nonregulation field equipment, but decided he would have volunteered it if he did. Besides, she wasn't sure she would trust him with a weapon in his present mood. "I don't suppose you have a phaser hidden somewhere in your pack, Reggie?"

"No." He sighed, his expression still oddly remote.

"I never thought about needing one."

It was probably just as well, Keiko thought. She wasn't sure she could trust herself. The more she thought of Miles, worrying about her because she hadn't talked to him in six hours, the angrier she got at the Jarada. It was one thing to insist on away-team duty, even though it separated them for a few days, and quite another to be deprived of all means of communications for the duration. The longer she thought about it, the more furious it made her. By the time they reached the outskirts of the Jaradan camp, Keiko had decided she was going to demand an explanation from the teachers and insist that she and Tanaka be returned to the city immediately.

The Jaradan camp was laid out in clusters of domed

tents half buried in the sand. The tents ranged in color from pale gold to almost black, much like the Jarada themselves. No two tents were the same color, although within each cluster the colors were similar. Looking at the sand piled around the base of each dome, Keiko realized Tanaka had been correct about the artificial beach. From her brief survey of the meadow's ecosystem, she knew the soil in the area was mostly clay. Such large amounts of sand were not natural in that environment.

The second thing she noticed was the camp's silence. She looked around, trying to find anyone at all. This close to the announced dinner hour, she expected to see part of the group fixing the meal while the others relaxed or worked on their lessons. Instead, the camp appeared deserted. The only sounds were the rustle of the wind through the grass and the distant call of a bird or bird-analog.

"This is damned odd!" Tanaka muttered, twisting his head around as if trying to watch every angle at once. "Where did they all go?"

"I suppose they're still at their assembly." She looked around, trying to convince herself Canjiir had said that the evening meal would be at sunset, and already Beltaxiya had dropped below the treetops. Unless the Jarada had a unique interpretation of the word "sunset," the food should be served within minutes. Keiko shivered with a cold premonition, wondering if she and Tanaka had been deliberately abandoned here or if there was some other explanation for the complete absence of their hosts.

"I don't know. The Jarada don't strike me as the sort of beings that ever change a schedule once it's announced." He looked around the encampment, as if searching for a way to force it to reveal its secrets. Instead, he ended up staring at the empty level area at the end of the road. "They've taken the transport."

Keiko, turning to see where he was looking, felt her hope shrinking fast. The Jarada had probably sent the vehicle back to the city and it would return only when the students were ready to leave. That complicated their situation, though, because it deprived them of any means of getting back to the *Enterprise* until the Jarada were through with the field trip. She heaved a sigh of frustration. "I don't think they took it, Reggie. I think they sent it back to the city until they need it again."

"Still . . ." Tanaka looked at the empty parking space and shivered. His eyes had a flat, empty look that frightened and angered Keiko more than the Jarada's apparent treachery. What was wrong with him anyway?

"Let's see if we can find where they went." She started through the camp, keeping her eyes on the ground to see what story she could piece together from the tracks. As she expected, the sand near the tents was too churned up to tell her anything. She cast wider, hurrying now to find any clues before it became too dark. Even with flashlights and the buttery glow reflected off the three-quarters-lit gas giant, she did not want to go charging through an unexplored forest on an unsurveyed planet after dark, pursuing some-one who didn't want to see her. Still, for her own sanity, she could not stand around waiting for the answers to find her, and she desperately needed to shatter Tanaka's passivity.

Finally, when she had almost given up finding anything in the churned sand, she spotted a line of indentations running in a straight line toward the trees. She gestured for Tanaka to join her and pointed to the tracks. They followed them across the beach, away from their own tents and to the edge of the meadow. Where the trail left the sand, the stems of the grass were bent over or broken. Keiko crouched down, examining the soil until she found the sharp imprint of a clawed Jaradan foot. "They definitely went this way," she said, pointing toward the trees. "Let's see what they're up to."

"Do you think that's wise?" Tanaka's hesitant tone was what she would have expected from a green cadet, not an experienced officer.

"It beats sitting around waiting for them to do something to us! What's your problem anyway?" *The last thing I need right now is a partner who goes to pieces at the smallest sign of trouble!* Keiko thought. Since the captain insisted on assigning her a partner, at the very least he could have given her someone who could handle the pressure. She started for the trees without waiting for his answer.

After a few moments Tanaka's footsteps followed her. "I'm sorry. I didn't mean to tick you off, but it's getting dark and we don't know anything about the local predators. Wouldn't it be wiser to wait till morning?"

Keiko heaved an exasperated sigh and picked up her pace a little. "Use your head, Reggie. On this planet sunrise is almost thirty-six hours away. I for one have no desire to wait that long to find out what's happening."

"I just meant, without the communicators, we don't have any access to the ship's sensor scans of this planet. It really isn't safe to go exploring after dark without getting as much information as we can."

They entered the trees, ducking under the dense branches that formed a screen along the edge of the meadow. Overhead, the trees tangled together, forming an interlocking web of limbs and foliage. Vines twisted around the trunks and looped over the branches, adding to the massed greenery above them. Despite that, it was light beneath the trees, a curious half-light that diffused downward from the canopy.

Tanaka moved up beside Keiko and thumbed his flashlight to its minimum setting, although they barely needed it to follow the line of tracks. The scuffs and gouges in the litter of dead leaves and twigs that covered the forest floor could mean only that a large group had passed that way recently. When she inhaled deeply, Keiko caught a whiff of the mixed, spicy scents of the Jarada, even though the smell of damp soil almost overwhelmed any other odor.

Glancing around, Keiko decided that Tanaka's nervousness was probably justified. There was something eerie about the forest, something ominous that reminded her of the forests in the old Japanese stories her grandfather had read to her as a child. Nothing good had ever happened in those stories, and to be caught in a place that evoked the same feeling of menace was decidedly unsetting. "Tell you what, Reggie." Keiko hoped her voice did not betray her own jitters. "If we don't find anything in the next twenty minutes, we'll head back. As much as I'd like some answers, I don't think we should leave our camp undefended for too long."

Tanaka touched his tricorder case to assure himself that the device was still there. "I've got a full pack of ration bars if we need them. But the rest of our stuff is in our tents, and we both know how secure those are."

"Yeah. They're good for about thirty seconds in a buffalo stampede or against a determined thief. Neither of which are we supposed to meet in the line of duty." Keiko paused, her head cocked to one side. From somewhere ahead came muffled pounding, like someone playing a large drum. She glanced at Tanaka to see if he heard it too. "Do you think that's them?"

He shrugged. "If so, they're not being quiet about whatever they're doing. And if not—I'm not sure I really want to know who else in this forest can play the bongos."

She frowned, considering his words. The sounds she heard were too rhythmic, too purposeful, to be caused by an animal—or even a child—banging on a hollow log. If the unknown drummers were not the Jarada they had come with, then they needed to find out fast who else was here. Zelfreetrollan had told Keiko that their group would be the only people for many kilometers around the study site. Gesturing to Tanaka for silence, she moved forward as quietly as she could. He dropped behind a step, watching her back, although that meant someone could take him from the rear if he was not sufficiently alert.

After ten minutes they reached a dense wall of bushes that extended as far as they could see in both directions. The claw-tracks led through the only break in the foliage. Flickering orange light suggested a fire in the open space beyond the trees. As they approached, the drumming became louder, until the heavy, monotonous throbbing filled the air with its insistent beat. Shrill, ululating cries punctuated the rhythmic pounding. The mixed scents of the Jarada clogged the air and overwhelmed the commonplace odors of soil and trees and night-blooming flowers.

Keiko and Tanaka exchanged glances. The sounds were unsettling, like the battle cries of a horde of primitives psyching themselves up to attack their neighbors, and their translators did nothing to interpret the sounds. They looked at each other and simultaneously thumbed the devices off. Keiko nodded to their left and Tanaka shrugged, indicating he had no preference. He turned off the flashlight to avoid attracting attention and slid it into the pocket of his jacket. Moving as quietly as they could, although Keiko doubted that anyone could hear them over the drums, they left the trail and crept along the curving line of bushes.

Finally, Keiko spotted a gap, small and close to the

ground. Dropping to her stomach, she wiggled forward to see what was happening beyond the barrier. After a moment Tanaka followed her example, squeezing beside her to share the tiny hole.

A broad meadow, much larger than the one where they were camped, opened beyond the bushes that hid them. Keiko tried to guess how far the open space extended, but the twilight distorted the perspective and blurred the more distant trees with shadow until she was unable to estimate the distance. The mottled orange and beige ball of Bel-Major hung over them, the cloud patterns on its sunlit side glaring in brilliant contrast to the darkening sky.

Keiko shook herself and tore her attention away from the giant planet. She and Tanaka were concealed by a narrow tongue of bushes. Except for one small break, the undergrowth formed a dense, leafy wall between the main meadow and a satellite clearing. In the smaller meadow the Jarada were dancing around a bonfire. Except for the teachers, who were pounding the large, wooden drums with all four hands, everyone was running and leaping in unison, as though they were a dance troupe performing a choreographed number.

At first Keiko thought their timing was perfect, with each Jarada repeating the set patterns flawlessly. However, the longer she watched, the more discrepancies she saw. One tan-colored youth kept jerking its head in an erratic rhythm, while a red-brown individual and another tan Jarada twitched their upper limbs in spasmodic gestures that sent shivers up her spine.

"You see it too?" They were lying so close that Tanaka's lips brushed her ear.

"Like they're just a little crazy?" She, too, felt the need to whisper her answer, although she doubted that anyone could have filtered their voices from the noise the Jarada were making.

Suddenly a large black Jarada broke from the circle, screeching furiously. The two nearest youths raced after him. The black swung on his pursuers, knocking the smaller one off its feet and slashing his claws across the eye of the other. Several more youths charged toward the black, overwhelming him with sheer numbers. Canjiir dropped her drum and dashed over, crouching to reach the black's exposed neck. Even over the drumming Keiko heard the crunch of Canjiir's teeth shearing through the shell that covered the black's throat. She crammed her hand into her mouth to keep her stomach from emptying itself.

The black's dying shriek descended into gurgles that were covered by the sound of the remaining drum. He twitched and jerked spasmodically, fighting to hold on to life. Finally, he went still and, one by one, the other Jarada got to their feet.

Canjiir returned to her drum, pounding it with furious intensity. Slowly the youths rejoined the circle, resuming their dancing as though nothing had happened. However, as she watched them, Keiko realized that more of the young Jarada showed erratic behavior—twitches and jerks and breaks in the rhythm that seemed to upset the others in the group.

"More than a little crazy," Tanaka murmured, starting to wiggle backward. "Let's get out of here."

Keiko nodded and waited for him to squirm free. She had just started her own retreat when more loud screeches interrupted the chanting of the dancers. Glancing toward the meadow, she saw three Jarada attacking their classmates. A fourth, the largest student in the group, was streaking for their hiding place. By sheer bad luck he would trip over them no matter what they did.

"Run!" she ordered Tanaka. Twisting around, she tried to force her way out of the bushes. The branches were tough and springy, and they pushed back.

Tanaka grabbed her wrist and pulled, jerking her clear of the slapping, scratching foliage. As soon as she was free, they ran, racing to put as much distance between themselves and the insane Jarada as they could.

Behind them the large Jarada hit the bushes and crashed through, seemingly oblivious of the grabbing, tearing limbs. His shriek, when he saw the fleeing humans, was echoed by more distant yells and then by other crashing noises. Keiko risked a quick glance over her shoulder and saw that several more Jarada were struggling through the barrier in pursuit. The large Jarada was gaining on them fast, even though Keiko was sure she had beaten her personal best time for the two hundred meter dash. Her lungs screamed for oxygen and she knew she wouldn't be able to hold her speed much longer. Even though he had gotten a head start, Tanaka couldn't be in much better shape, since his preferred sport was swimming.

She glanced in his direction and saw that he was slowing, angling toward a sturdy tree slightly off their course. He extended his arm and swung around it, using the change in direction to stop himself. "Up!" he said, pointing toward the treetops to emphasize the message. Keiko veered toward him, feeling her speed lessen in spite of herself, but she was still moving too fast to stop when she reached him. Tanaka grabbed her arm and swung her around the tree in a repeat of the maneuver he had used to kill his own momentum. Before she could catch her breath for the climb, he knelt and offered her a boost. She set her foot into his cupped hands and let him shove her upward.

For a moment she felt as though she were flying, and then her right hand hit the lowest branch of the tree. She wrapped her fingers around it, struggling to keep her hold, and threw her other arm and her legs around the trunk, pressing as much of her body as possible against the bark. After several tense seconds she halted her downward slide. Taking a deep breath and pulling on the branch, she dragged herself up to the next limb and freed the first one for Tanaka.

The next branch was closer and the one after that, even closer. Above that the limbs separated from the trunk in groups, with the branches and the trunk at each split all having nearly the same diameter. The tree shuddered as Tanaka leapt for the first handhold. Keiko continued working her way upward until she found a secure spot in the crotch between the trunk and a sturdy limb.

Leaning against the tree to catch her breath, she risked a glance downward to see how Tanaka was doing. A wave of vertigo swept through her, but she forced it away. Tanaka was two meters away from the tree, bracing for a running start at a second jump, and the pursuing Jarada had almost closed the distance. Launching himself at top speed, Tanaka raced for the tree and leapt, catching the branch with his outstretched hands. For a moment he just hung there, swinging, before he started pulling himself upward.

With a shriek the Jarada flung itself at Tanaka, jaws open and claws outstretched. Tanaka almost made it to safety, but he wasn't quite fast enough. The Jarada's claws caught his leg, slashing through his uniform and deeply into his flesh. Tanaka continued to climb upward, as if unaware of the injury, although Keiko could see the blood welling through his ripped pants. *Adrenaline*, she thought, realizing that the need to escape had probably blocked his awareness of the wounded leg.

Below them, more Jarada had arrived. In a hysterical frenzy they threw themselves at the tree, attacking again and again. The tree shuddered under the blows and Keiko wondered how long before the Jarada tried something more active and more effective. And whether she and Tanaka could survive without water or medical supplies until the *Enterprise* found them. For the first time ever, she wished she had listened to her husband. Then she wouldn't be in this situation—trapped with an injured partner twenty meters off the ground at the start of a thirty-six-hour night on an unsurveyed planet, with no water or communicators, and surrounded by hostile aliens. It was enough to make her wish she had never left Japan. Unable to help herself, Keiko laid her head against the tree and cried.

Chapter Twelve

WORF RACED DOWN THE CORRIDOR and turned right, with the Jarada guardians hot on his heels. Having so many enemies so close behind gave him no chance to test his theories about the door locks. Even if he were correct, his pursuers would be on him before he could finish entering the nine digit code to open the door. What he needed was a hiding place where he could observe his enemy and study the terrain while he planned his next move. Given his observations of Jarada architecture, he had about the same chance of finding what he needed as he had of getting rescued by Romulans.

On the off chance that Data might be listening, he tapped his communicator again. This time he could hear the dull click of the pressure switch, but that sound was not followed by the chirp that indicated the device was active. Somehow, the Jarada had managed to deactivate the communicator, isolating him both from the captain and from the *Enterprise*. A low growl escaped Worf's throat. If these insectoids wanted to test the prowess of a real warrior, then he was ready to oblige them.

He had seen no windows since he and Breen left the Council Chambers, which meant he had only a rough idea of where he was. His first priority, he decided, was to find a spot where he could see the city and the position of the Beltaxiyan sun. He would have liked to have a map as well, but he doubted that the Jarada would give him the key to their defenses. Remembering the layout of the Governance Complex, Worf took the first upward-sloping corridor that he encountered. After that, each time he had a choice he continued to move upward. Surprisingly, his pursuers lost ground, their shrieking and the clatter of their claws diminishing as he put more distance between himself and the workout room.

Finally, Worf slowed his pace to a jog, both to conserve his energy and to concentrate on the sounds behind him. After a brief lull, the shrieks rose to a crescendo punctuated by dull thuds. Apparently his pursuers had begun fighting each other again. If that was the case, it was time for him to get out of the corridor before he encountered someone else eager to take up the fight where the Jarada behind him had abandoned it. With the warriors of this society acting like lunatics, who knew what the ordinary Jarada might do? He had to get back to the captain!

Dropping to a walk, Worf began scanning carefully. Although the corridor was well lit, the light exaggerated the rough texture of the plaster walls. It was an effective camouflage, and Worf was beginning to worry that it might delay him too long, when he finally spotted the telltale dark line of a door. He studied the surface carefully, locating the exact outline of the opening before he made his next move. He scraped his thumb, forefinger, and little finger across the wall at waist height. After a moment, as if the computer that controlled the mechanism had to repeat the analysis of his stroke before giving him access, the control panel lit up. Worf fitted his fingers into the touch points and entered the code Breen had used: 1-1-3-2-1-2-3-3-1. Again there was a delay while the computer processed the code, but then the door slid into the wall.

Worf stepped into the shaft, listening for the sound of someone moving inside it. Silence, broken only by the hum of the air circulators, greeted him. Quickly, he moved farther inside to let the door close behind him. If Breen's boasts about the Jarada's faith in their security locks reflected a general attitude, then he had shaken his pursuers and needed to worry only about chance encounters delaying him. What he could not guess was how to find the quickest route back to the Jarada Governance Complex. He wondered if the Jarada memorized the entire maze of tunnels beneath their city or if the major passages were marked in some way the *Enterprise's* away team had not discerned. Neither method was going to do him much good. He had to get outside, where he could see enough landmarks to orient himself.

He started downward, testing the ribbed surface of the ramp. It was well suited for the Jarada, with narrow shelves to catch their claws, but the ridges were badly spaced for a Klingon, particularly one as large as Worf. A growl rose in his throat, born of his frustration at running from a fight *and* from being in the wrong place at the wrong time. With an effort he suppressed the outburst, knowing it would attract attention that he didn't need.

Three turns down the ramp, near the level where he thought he had lost his pursuers, he heard shrieking and pounding in the corridor outside the shaft. Apparently the melee was still in progress, with the Jarada tearing into one another with reckless abandon. Worf would have loved to watch the fight and to observe how the guardians handled actual combat, but he knew he would become the target as soon as they saw him. While he couldn't fault their zeal in defending their hive, he had no intention of letting it interfere with his duty to return to the captain.

Four turns farther down, Worf judged he was nearing the ground floor. As he started to search for a door, he heard the sounds of several Jarada entering the shaft a level above him. Quickly, he deactivated the Jaradan translator before its sounds could betray him. Hoping they were not going far, he started downward again, moving as fast as he dared. One level, two levels, three—still they descended, the chittering of their footsteps unhurried and the singing interplay of their conversation betraying no hint that they suspected his presence. Worf noticed that a heavy, spicy smell floated down the shaft ahead of them.

The acoustics in the enclosed space multiplied the noises, making it hard to separate out source and distance. From below, Worf thought he heard echoes of the Jarada behind him, which meant they were approaching the bottom. However, as he listened, he realized the sounds were growing louder. He rounded another turn and almost collided with three russet-colored guardians.

At the sight of the Klingon on the ramp above them, the three Jarada shrieked a battle cry and charged. The Jarada behind him echoed the shriek and the clattering of their foot-claws speeded up. Worf roared an eager response and dropped into a defensive crouch, letting the Jarada bring the attack to him. On this sloping ramp the disadvantage lay with the attackers, and as a true warrior, he knew how to exploit his enemies' weaknesses.

The first Jarada reached him, and Worf lashed out

with his leg, landing a perfect kick to the Jarada's thorax. The Jarada was unbalanced from running up the ramp, and Worf's kick threw it off its feet. It landed on its back, limbs flailing in all directions, and skidded into one of its companions. The second Jarada fell too, its limbs tangling with those of the first insectoid. Both slid downward, their exoskeletons bumping and scraping against the rough surface of the ramp.

The shrieks of the group above Worf reached deafening proportions and five more Jarada clattered into view. The leader launched itself at the Klingon, its claws extended like daggers. Worf braced himself and grabbed for the Jarada's arms. Closing his hands around the bases of the lethal claws, he pulled the insectoid forward and flung it into the last of the Jarada below him. That Jarada went down under the impact and two more insectoids started the downward slide on their backs.

The approaching Jarada slowed when they saw how Worf disposed of their leader. Taking advantage of their momentary hesitation, Worf gave a loud roar and charged them. Caught off guard, they were slow to respond, and he got past them before they could take advantage of the close quarters. One swiped at him and caught his arm, slicing his uniform and drawing blood with its sharp claws. Then he was above them, where his height and greater reach would serve to best advantage.

Turning, Worf kicked the nearest Jarada, landing a well-placed blow on its thorax. As it fell, its body slammed into the legs of the fighter next to it. While the second guardian struggled to keep its balance, Worf closed in and grabbed its arms. For someone who followed the Klingon's daily exercise regimen, the Jarada was not a major challenge. He jerked the insectoid from its feet and swung it into the two remaining fighters. All three smashed into the wall with a satisfying crunch.

With all his opponents temporarily disabled, Worf headed back up the shaft, searching for the first available exit. He found it around the first turn on the opposite side of the shaft from the other doors. Still, he had to get away before anyone raised the alarm or reprogrammed the locks, so he located the control pad and tapped in the combination.

The door started to open, hesitated partway, and began sliding shut again. Afraid that his access would be cut off, Worf jammed his shoulder into the opening. The mechanism grumbled and protested as he forced his way through. At the last minute the panel snapped shut on his wrist. From beyond the door he heard the shrieks of a horde of guardians swarming into the shaft.

Growling under his breath, Worf braced his foot against the doorjamb. Curling the fingers of his free hand around the door, he pulled on it. At first nothing happened. He threw his entire weight into the effort, and finally the panel moved barely enough for him to work his hand loose. He released the door and jumped clear, just as a dozen guardians clattered past.

Worf looked about, checking his surroundings. He was in another shaft, this one damp and poorly lit. Streaks of black mold and greenish slime covered the walls and most of the floor. The air stank from the dampness, from mold and mildew, and from other things he was reluctant to name. He was on a landing at the top of the shaft, which descended an indeterminate distance. Briefly, he studied with longing the door he had just come through. A warrior should die in battle, even if dishonorable opponents resorted to overwhelming odds to defeat him. He should not be expected to fight cold, and slime, and unnameable biological horrors.

Growling under his breath, Worf started downward. His duty was to get to his captain any way he could. If that meant wading through ankle-deep slime or swimming frigid rivers, then that was what he must do. With any luck the Jarada would find this shaft as distasteful as he did. Looking at the carpet of grayish-green and black stuff that covered the ramp, he could well believe that he was the only living creature to have blundered into this shaft in decades. Even the bioluminescent glowstrips were fading, their internal nutrients all but exhausted and the bacteria inside them dying.

It was slow going, keeping his footing on the tricky descent. At each door he paused, listening to the sounds in the adjoining shaft. The shrieks and the massed clatter of Jarada claws made it obvious that an entire army of guardians was searching for him. If they ever thought to check this shaft, he was in serious trouble. However, at least for the moment, their oversight let him put more distance between himself and the location of the attack.

The shaft grew damper as he descended, until the water flowed in runnels along the walls. He approached one door where the noise on the other side was so loud that he was sure he had been discovered and the Jarada were about to pour into the shaft. As he crept closer, he saw that the bright crack that marked the opening was uneven, the door warped too much to form a tight seal against the jamb. A dozen Jarada were milling around on the other side of the door, their chittering claws and discordant voices reverberating inside the shaft.

Worf continued downward, descending the equivalent of five more decks before he found another door.

Its outline was dim, barely brighter than the surrounding walls, and he almost missed it. However, a rivulet of water leaking through a crack between the warped door and its frame caught his attention. Holding his breath, Worf listened for several minutes, but nothing moved in the corridor beyond the door. It was either a clever ambush, worthy of a Klingon, or he had reached an unoccupied portion of the complex. The only way he would find out was by leaving the shaft.

It didn't take him long to decide. Vertical movement would not bring him back to the Governance Complex and, when the Jarada finally realized where he had gone, this shaft was the ultimate trap. Also, while the ramp continued downward, the last thing he wanted was to take the predictable exit on the lowest level.

His decision made, he raked his fingers along the wall, shuddering as he touched the algae- and mold-covered stone. Nothing happened, but three light-colored streaks marred the organic coating on the wall. Worf growled under his breath, realizing there was no way to escape this slime hole without leaving road signs to mark his passage. He tried again with no better luck. The control panel, if indeed there was one for this door, appeared to be dead.

He was about to start downward again, when he remembered his fight with the door at the top of the shaft. Maybe this one would succumb to the same treatment. Worf checked the edges and found that the door was warped enough for him to force his fingers into the crack. Bracing his feet against the jamb, he pulled with all his strength. A low, tortured groan came from somewhere inside the wall. He kept up the pressure and felt the mechanism yield marginally. Encouraged, he summoned another all-out effort and was rewarded with the shriek of metal dragging against metal. Slowly, he forced the door back into its frame. From the sounds, he thought the door was operated by a spring and piston device. With luck it would hold the door against his pursuers, if he could get it closed again.

When the opening was large enough, Worf squeezed through the door and released it. It rebounded partway and stuck, a beacon to anyone that he had forced his way through. He examined the door, surprised to find its surface incised with carvings. Much of the wood veneer was rotten and crumbling, but he found enough purchase for his hands. Grunting with the effort, he pushed the door toward its closed position. The squeals and moans were almost as loud as when he had opened the door, giving him hope that the Jarada would have as much trouble with it as he had had.

Worf couldn't seat the door completely into its frame, but the final gap was only a finger's width. He doubted that the Jaradan exoskeleton provided enough leverage to open the door by brute force, and he hoped his pursuers would not realize the full potential of his superior Klingon anatomy.

With his back protected as best he could, Worf examined his surroundings. A tunnel, in no better shape than the shaft he had just left, stretched before him. The flickering glowstrips, the mold-streaked walls, and the damp floor told him that this area had long been abandoned. He concentrated on his location for a moment, trying to decide where he was in relation to the Governance Complex.

Breen had headed generally east when they left the Council Chambers, and he thought the tunnel ahead of him was pointing south, which meant that he would have to go to his right when he got the chance. To the right and *up*, he promised himself, looking at the wet and moldy passageway with distaste. If someone had tried to design a Klingon's worst nightmare, this would be a championship contender. The only thing left to complete the horror was a swarm of Tribbles. Suppressing a shudder, Worf started down the corridor, his boots squelching in the damp slime.

Chapter Thirteen

THEY WERE ENTERING the third hour of the search and still Data had found no sign of the missing crew members. He had concentrated his scans around the city, where most of the away team should have been located, but so far he had had no success. Once or twice he had registered a trace that might have been Riker, but when he tried to focus in for a transporter lock, he lost the scan. Either Riker had been moving very fast or someone was deliberately screening his sensors. At the moment either hypothesis was equally likely, although the android suspected his human colleagues would favor the sabotage theory.

Data adjusted the settings on the scanners for the tenth time in as many minutes, trying to improve their resolution. As he watched the results scroll across his screen, a part of his brain kept returning to the idea of how one might disrupt a sensor scan without making it immediately obvious. It would take some subtle programming and a complex algorithm to simulate random noise, but the more he considered it, the more the idea seemed plausible.

The only way the *Enterprise*'s sensors could have missed the entire away team for so long was if all of them had been removed from the city. Keiko and Tanaka were probably outside the range of his scans, since he had no idea what direction they had gone when they left the city. He should have found the others, however, since their destinations were supposed to be inside the city limits.

While part of his brain monitored the sensor readings, Data started working on plausible mechanisms for disrupting the scans. Given how little the Federation knew about the Jarada or the precise levels of their technology, he had no hard evidence for rejecting any known jamming technique. For that matter, they had no firm idea of how much the Jarada knew about the Federation. What he had was two very large systems of unknowns—which he had to solve to locate the missing away team.

While he was working on that problem, two unrelated facts swam to the surface of his brain. First was how much the Jarada had seemed to know *specifically* about the *Enterprise* and its crew from the beginning of this assignment. They had requested the *Enterprise* and its captain by name, they had known the first officer was a competent amateur musician, and—despite their adherence to strict protocol in previous encounters with the Federation—they had presented a friendly and genial façade to their visitors, almost as if they had known the exact approach that would win Picard over with the least amount of effort.

The second fact was the scan that the Jarada had run on the *Enterprise* when the ship had met them for the first time at Torona IV. After briefly disrupting key elements of the ship's computer and control systems, the Jarada sensors had apparently done no further damage to the *Enterprise*. But what if the disruption had been a side effect, the result of a high-speed data grab from the ship's main computer? The computers were heavily shielded to prevent such thefts, but the protection could never be absolute in a dynamic system. As long as the computer's users needed to get information into or out of its memory, vulnerable access paths into the computer existed which could be exploited by a determined enemy. In the relief of successfully completing their mission at Torona IV, they had not questioned what the Jaradan scan had been looking for, but now Data wondered.

He called up the ship's logs and sorted through them to find the unreduced scan records he needed. It took several minutes to find the information, since much of it had already been archived to provide working space for current projects. Even when he located the records, they were too complex and too ambiguous to give him an immediate answer. After ordering the computer to run simulations on the readings and to show him the most likely scenarios of what had happened to the computer's memory banks when they were scanned, Data turned his attention back to the current sensor readings.

A warning light caught his attention, indicating an anomaly in the orbital scans. He switched to those inputs, checking for the signals that had triggered the alarm. The number of objects in their immediate area—in orbits around Bel-Major, Bel-Minor, or both—was staggering. In the last day he had seen more collision warnings than he had ever encountered outside a simulator, but a brief look at his screens told him that a stray moonlet was not what had triggered the computer.

Radiation trails of the kind normally associated with old-style nuclear propulsion systems fanned out from the planet like the lines in a children's hypertext on gravity potential. The readings were faint, difficult to separate from the high background radiation in the area. Data ordered the computer to repeat the scans and to refine its calculations to minimize the uncertainty. It still reported the same results. To the limits of the analysis, between ten and twenty one- or two-person nuclear-powered spacecraft had taken off from Bel-Minor within the last six hours and were in all probability hiding among the moonlets that littered the area. Data was about to report his findings to the captain when the proximity detectors sounded yet another collision warning.

The three small fighter craft swooped from behind a large asteroid so quickly that they were on top of the *Enterprise* almost before they had registered on the sensors. Picard signaled for red alert and the emergency lights began flashing. "Collision alert," Data announced for broadcast throughout the ship. "Brace for impact. This is not a drill."

"Mr. Data, report! Conn, warn them off!" Picard snapped, his words overlapping the warning from the proximity detectors. Chang's voice, telling the approaching ships to change course, wove a muted counterpoint to the android's report.

"The ships are single-man fighter craft, Captain. They apparently lifted off from Bel-Minor when our orbit carried us to the far side of the planet," Data said. "I had just finished analyzing our sensor data, which is extremely ambiguous due to the high radiation levels around Bel-Major, and was about to report the probable presence of up to twenty of this class of vessel in orbit with us. From the sensor readings I am getting now, I surmise the pilots are Jarada, but the information is extremely peculiar. It does not correspond to anything else we have on the Jarada."

"Twenty—" Picard glanced at the screen, saw the smaller ships still headed straight for the *Enterprise*, and interrupted himself. "Chang, warn them off!"

"I'm trying, sir. They are not responding to our signals."

Data answered Picard's next question before he even asked it. "The shields will hold against a direct impact, Captain. Some people may be affected by radiation on the decks nearest the collision point, but the *Enterprise* should sustain no permanent damage. However, the approaching vessels will be completely destroyed."

"Chang, get a tractor beam on them and try to keep them from hitting us."

"Aye, sir." Chang punched in the coordinates of the leading vessel and activated the tractor beam. However, the small ship was under heavy acceleration and the tractor beam could not lock onto the ship's hull. The fighter plunged straight for the *Enterprise* and disintegrated against its shields. The viewscreen flared white and the ship rocked briefly before the inertial dampers compensated.

"Do the same thing on the next one, Mr. Chang," Data ordered. "I will work Tractor Beams Two and Three to shift it away from us."

"Yes, sir."

While Chang tried to hold the next fighter with his tractor beam, Data programmed two additional beams to help force the Jarada ship away from the *Enterprise.* Despite the android's speed and his ability to work each hand independently, Data and Chang managed to get only a partial grip on the attacking ship. It tumbled away from them and crashed into the *Enterprise*'s shields, exploding in a blaze of hard radiation.

"Get the pilot first," Picard ordered as Chang and Data tried for the next ship. "Security to Transporter Room Four."

Data relayed the coordinates for the pilot of the third vessel to the transporter room. While they waited for the report, the sensors picked up three more fighters approaching under extreme acceleration.

"Mr. Data." Picard's voice held a note of frustration. "What are our chances of stopping these vessels?"

For a long moment the only sounds on the bridge were the mechanical chirps of various status indicators and the brush of Data's fingers on the touchpads of his console. After what seemed an eternity to the waiting bridge crew, Data answered. "The probabilities are that we will do no better getting a tractor beam on any of these ships than we did on the others. Our shields are holding, with two small radiation leaks reported on the lower decks. All projections indicate that there will be no significant damage to the *Enterprise* even if all three of the approaching vessels collide with us. The radiation levels from the explosions will make transporting the pilots risky, but the chances for the pilots surviving are significantly greater than if they crash their ships against our shields."

"Make it so, Commander."

Just then the report came in from the transporter room. "We couldn't keep the signal lock on him, Captain. The radiation levels were too high."

After a moment's hesitation Data relayed the coordinates for the three approaching ships. "Pull these in as fast as you can, Mr. O'Brien," he added. "Their ships are rapidly approaching the danger zone."

"Aye, sir."

With an outward show of calmness Picard waited for word from the transporter room. Watching the fourth ship burst into a spray of blinding light against the shields, he considered destroying the fighters before they hit the *Enterprise's* shields. However, if he fired the phasers too soon, O'Brien would not be able to rescue the pilots. And to protect himself from any more attacks, Picard wanted those pilots. If there was any reason behind these suicide runs, any explanation for his missing crew members down on the planet, Picard's instincts told him he would get it from the Jarada in those ships.

"Data, try contacting the Jarada Council of Elders again. I wish to speak with Zelfreetrollan." Picard felt the deck shudder beneath him as the fifth ship destroyed itself against the *Enterprise*'s shields.

"Aye, sir." There was a brief pause while the android tried to open a channel to the planet. "They still are not responding, Captain."

"Captain," came O'Brien's voice from the transporter room. "We've managed to rescue two of the pilots from those ships, but they're in pretty bad shape. Security had to stun one of them and the other is under restraints. Raving like a lunatic, he is."

Picard suppressed a groan. It figured that the Jarada pilots would be incapable of answering his questions. "Have security take them to sickbay for observation, O'Brien, and keep them under restraints at all times." He glanced up at the ceiling, signaling a new call. "Sickbay. Dr. Selar."

After a moment the Vulcan doctor answered the page, her voice calm and unruffled even though Picard could imagine the sudden influx of patients she was having due to the collisions. Somehow, despite the warnings and the drills, people always managed to get hurt. "Selar, here."

"Doctor, security is bringing you two prisoners. I need a full medical workup on them as soon as possible. Also, notify me the minute they are able to answer questions."

"Yes, Captain. Do you need anything else?"

Was that a hint of irony in her voice? Picard wondered. If it had been Crusher, the sarcasm would have bordered on insubordination. All doctors, it seemed, learned that skill as part of their medical training. "Thank you, Doctor. That will be all."

He shifted position, wondering why his chair should suddenly feel so uncomfortable. After a moment he remembered something Data had said earlier. "Data, how many of those ships did you say were out there?"

"Between ten and twenty, Captain. The radiation levels in this system create too much background noise for me to get any more precise readings than that."

"Thank you, Mr. Data." Picard settled back in his chair, trying to look calm and in control. It was going to be a very long night, waiting to see what would happen next. Too many lives were at stake for him to move before he had enough information. At the same time—what could he do to speed up the process? Somewhere in the last day and a half the away team must have discovered something he could use to reach the Jarada. The attacks on the ship, the disappearance of the away team, even the apparent ease of the negotiations—all had to be part of the same pattern.

The question still was—why? If he knew the *why* of the Jarada's puzzling behavior, he should be able to anticipate their next move. And for the safety of his ship, he *had* to anticipate it. The Jarada's next attack might be with something more lethal than antiquated one-man ships. Picard shuddered, feeling desperation finally kick his brain into overdrive.

"Why?" O'Brien demanded angrily, pounding his fist against the engineering console. "Why does the captain insist that I rescue the damned bugs who kidnapped my wife? We ought to just blast the lot of them to oblivion!"

"Calm down, Chief, and keep your mind on business! The captain wants those Jarada for questioning." Geordi's voice contained a steely edge. While he understood O'Brien's anger, it was getting in the way of the transporter chief's work. However, Geordi had to admit that despite his bluster, O'Brien had performed brilliantly getting the Jarada pilots out of their craft.

Geordi skimmed through the results of Data's latest simulation, which postulated one way that the Jarada might be jamming the *Enterprise*'s sensors, and then dumped the numbers to O'Brien's console. "We need a plan for holding the transporter lock against this kind of interference."

"This is all hypothetical," O'Brien snarled. "Why don't we just take a landing party down there and rescue them? Before the Jarada kill them?"

Geordi heaved an exasperated sigh. "If you have any suggestions on how to find them, I'm sure the captain will be eager to hear them. Otherwise, the best thing you can do is make sure we can keep a transporter lock on them when we find them, regardless of what the Jarada throw at us. Is that clear?"

"Yes, sir," O'Brien replied in a tone that contradicted his agreement. However, his hands moved across his panel, calling for information and cuing in the tests he needed to decided the best way to transport people through the Jaradan interference.

"Good." Geordi sent another set of reports to O'Brien's console. "Let's get cracking, so we've got the answers when they're needed."

Chapter Fourteen

RIKER SLAMMED INTO the bottom of the shaft, and the wind whooshed from his body. Dazed and battered, he slumped to the wet floor, gasping for breath. Every bone, every muscle, every *nerve* in his body screamed from the beating he had taken as he plummeted down the ramp. He had lost track of the number of times he had banged his shoulder or his knee as he descended, struggling to keep some control of his course but not daring to stop himself for fear that the guardians would pour down the ramp before he reached the bottom.

He tried to move, testing his body to see how badly he was injured. By now he knew his bruises had bruises, each puffy swelling embellished with its own satellite injuries. His left knee was swelling rapidly and soon, he feared, he would not be able to bend it. Moving slowly, he rolled on his side and started to get up.

A loud scraping hum, accented by random clatterings and knockings, poured down the shaft.

Before Riker could wonder who or what was descending so rapidly, Zarn shot around the corner. The Jarada was on his back, using his exoskeleton like a toboggan. He crashed into Riker, again knocking the human to the floor.

The impact flipped Zarn over and he scrambled to his feet. "That was most exhilarating. I see why you find so much enjoyment in descending in that manner." The insectoid moved to the outer wall and raked his claws over the mold-covered wall, activating the control panel.

Riker groaned and tried to stand. Somehow it was harder the second time. To make matters worse, when Zarn had hit him, the Jarada's claws had nicked him in several places and the cuts were smarting from the contact with his wet uniform. He shuddered at the thought of what could happen if he didn't get proper treatment soon.

"Hurry!" Zarn ordered, his voice hitting three shrill, discordant notes. "I overrode the standard setting on the door where we entered, but that won't keep them away for long. They'll be after us as soon as a squad reaches the door on the next level."

"Oh, great! That's all I needed to hear." Riker forced himself to his feet and cautiously put his weight onto his left leg. The knee was very tender and too swollen for him to bend it more than a few degrees, but it held his weight. Heaving a sigh of relief that the injury was not worse, he hobbled over to the door. "If we're in such a hurry, what are we waiting for?"

Zarn pounded on the control panel, which flashed a message at him in lavender characters. "Security breach? *Vrel'keth brefteev!* I'll give you 'security breach?'" His claws twitching against the control pads, he entered a long string of commands. A message in royal purple answered him, and Zarn tapped in another long sequence of coded symbols. Finally the door began to open.

Zarn dashed through, beckoning for Riker to follow. "Hurry up! Someone is trying to lock us in the shaft. I overrode their program with my Council authority, but that won't last for long. When it occurs to them, they'll block all the overrides for this part of the complex."

Limping heavily, Riker stumbled through the door. He had barely cleared the frame when it began closing. He paused, listening for sounds of pursuit, but the shaft behind them was silent. "They're not on our trail yet. If you have any good ideas for throwing them off, this would be an excellent time for them."

Zarn started down the tunnel, moving ahead of Riker before he realized the human was not keeping up. The Jarada slowed, swiveling his head around to see what the problem was. His four-legged stride covered the ground with an easy lope that Riker envied, but at the moment he would have gladly settled for two sound limbs. "You must hurry if you don't want them to catch up with us," Zarn said.

"I'm doing the best I can," Riker grumbled, more than a little annoyed at his own weakness. The worst of it was that he didn't know how much he dared admit to Zarn about his injuries. He thought the Jarada was on his side, but he was beginning to wonder. His inability to contact the *Enterprise* and the repeated attacks were making him less and less inclined to trust Zarn. If he could have gotten himself out of this interminable dungeon on his own, he would have declined any further help from his host.

The Jarada watched him, studying Riker's limp for so long that he began to feel self-conscious. Finally Zarn pivoted his head forward and slowed his pace. "Truly, if your people are so fragile, how do you manage to survive? And why do you indulge in such activities as the sliding if you are not capable of absorbing the damage?"

"It wasn't by choice," Riker muttered, envisioning Zarn with a bruised joint. The swelling against the Jarada's exoskeleton would indubitably be even more painful than the pressure in Riker's knee.

"I don't understand your answer."

Without waiting for Riker to explain, Zarn dashed into a side corridor. The floor was coated with mud, and a trickle of water meandered along one wall. Several passageways split from the tunnel, each looking more dark and unhealthy than the last. Zarn chose one, apparently at random, then selected another tunnel that branched from it. With each turning the floor became muddier and the number of surviving glowstrips fewer. *Where are we going?* Riker wondered, but decided it wasn't something he wanted the Jarada to tell him. His instincts warned him that the answer would be unpleasant at best and, at the worst, he would find the story completely unbelievable.

After three or four turns Zarn entered a tunnel whose end was blocked by a huge pile of mud and dirt. His antennae sprung outward, giving his face a decidedly smug expression. For a moment Riker had to fight against an irrational impulse to wipe the look off Zarn's face. When the Jarada spoke, Riker was almost sorry he had resisted. "We will climb through there," Zarn said, pointing at the mound of dirt. "There is a short stretch of tunnel between two cave-ins. No one will look for us there."

Riker eyed the blocked tunnel dubiously. He was not sure he could fit through a Jarada-size opening, and he was certain he didn't want to try. However, he didn't think he could retrace their path and find a way out of these deserted tunnels, so he had to stick with Zarn. Reluctantly, he followed the insectoid up the pile of dirt, discovering that there was a large gap at the top where the ceiling of the tunnel once had been. He squeezed through and slithered down the other side.

"We will wait here," Zarn announced. "They will search these tunnels for five standards if they use the customary procedures. After that we will be free to go."

Riker heaved a sigh of frustration. The last thing he wanted to do was sit around in cold, wet mud for several hours. However, he had little choice. He lowered his head to his knees and, in spite of himself, was soon fast asleep.

He awoke slowly, unable to place where he was. It was cold, so cold and wet he thought at first he was still dreaming. Mud was everywhere, supporting him, surrounding him, and oozing into every pore of his uniform. Surely, he thought, so miserable a place could not exist outside a nightmare.

The sluggish plop of water into a puddle, as monotonous and maddening as the proverbial Chinese water torture, finally convinced Riker he was awake. Carefully, he pried one eyelid open to confirm his worst fears. He was alone in the blocked-off section of passageway, with no sign of where Zarn had gone or if he intended to return.

Riker shoved against the ground, trying to push himself upright. He got nowhere, his muscles too stiff and battered to respond. With a groan he flopped on his back, and the cold mud found new places to penetrate. As it seeped into his hair, Riker decided that whoever said hell was hot had never been there; eternity in a frigid mud hole like this seemed an infinitely worse punishment. Suddenly, his stomach growled, reminding him that he hadn't eaten in many hours. He gritted his teeth, knowing there was no food available, and willed himself to ignore the hunger pangs. His first priority was to get himself out of here.

Concentrating on his hands first, he began moving his fingers. Slowly, carefully, he worked the stiffness from his wrists and arms, flexing and warming each muscle until he regained use of it. Moving to his toes, he repeated the exercises for his legs, gently stretching and bending them until he could stand. He was pleased to find that the cold had taken down some of the swelling in his left knee. The joint was still painfully enlarged, but the fabric of his uniform no longer stretched taut across the injury.

He levered himself to his feet, his movements slow and awkward as he tried to keep his balance on the greasy mud. The middle of the tunnel seemed firmer, the floor less muddy. Riker squelched the five steps over to the driest area, thinking how mud had lost its attractiveness after he reached the age of ten. Before that he remembered the fights he had had every summer with his cousins in Oklahoma, when his aunt had sent them off to play in the creek that ran through the back forty. The four of them, with Riker the youngest by two years, had always returned covered from head to toe with the clayey red muck with which they had pelted each other.

With a shake Riker brought himself back to the present. The mud was much more like the gummy sediment along the rivers of his native Alaska, icy rock powder as cold as the glacial waters that poured off the serrated white mountains. Testing the footing to be sure he had guessed right, Riker started a series of stretches and lunges. At first he worked slowly, just to get his blood circulating, but gradually he picked up the pace until he felt able to take on almost anything. Beads of sweat dotted his hairline and, for the first time in hours, he felt deliciously warm.

As he paused for breath, he heard a rock bounce down the far side of the mound of dirt where he and Zarn had entered. Was it Zarn returning, or had a hostile Jarada discovered his hiding place? Quickly, Riker clambered up the slope and crouched in the darkness beside the entrance. A strong scent of pine preceded the Jarada through the opening. The deep brown chitin-armored legs that appeared in the opening were the right color to be Zarn, but Riker was taking no chances. His arm swept forward, chopping against the Jarada's strong-legs. The blow upset the insectoid's balance and he fell, skidding to the bottom of the slope. He ended on his back, and with all eight limbs waving in the air, revolving slowing on the small patch of semidry floor.

Riker straightened slowly and took his time to descend, watching the Jarada. His face twitched as he fought to control the amused grin that tugged at his mouth. Zarn *did* look rather silly in that position and, after the pain and misery and uncertainty of the last few hours, it felt good to see the Jarada at a disadvantage. Riker knew it was a petty thought, but he acknowledged the source—after everything that had happened, he was no longer sure if he could trust Zarn. To see the tables turned on the Jarada reassured him that he was not entirely helpless, no matter how much he needed the insectoid to lead him out of this maze.

"Why did you do that?" Zarn's voice sounded flat, the triple notes of his speech oddly compressed. "Fighting is only for those of the warrior castes, and you could have been seriously injured if you tried that maneuver on one of them."

Riker stared down at the Jarada, trying to decide if his statement was the truth. If it was hard to read Zarn under normal circumstances, deciphering his expression was almost impossible while the Jarada drifted in a leisurely circle with his limbs flailing in the air. Flipping a mental coin, Riker decided Zarn had not exactly lied to him, but that he had, in all probability, omitted enough of the truth to make the remainder of questionable usefulness. However, the insectoid was still his best chance for escaping from this slimy mud hole, so he needed to keep their relationship on as cordial a footing as possible. "I didn't know who was coming," he said finally. "Since you didn't tell me where you were going or when you would be back, I thought it might be an enemy. And I was afraid if I waited too long, I wouldn't have a second chance to protect myself."

"I told you they'd quit searching after five standards. No one else knows you're here," Zarn said in a disgusted tone. "Now, quit dithering around and help me up off this floor."

Riker extended his foot, shoving it against Zarn's side to stop his spin. For his size, the Jarada *was* heavy, and Riker grunted with the effort. All the insectoid's mass was in his torso, a fact that might be helpful if Riker ever met a Jarada in hand-to-hand combat. Leaning over, Riker braced himself and offered Zarn his hand.

The Jarada locked his claws around Riker's wrist and pulled himself over on his side. From that position he completed his flip and scrambled to his feet. He started up the mound toward the exit, gesturing to Riker to follow him. "Come. Hurry. We must leave here before someone discovers the transportation I found for us."

"What? Transportation to where?" Escaping from the tunnels sounded like a good idea, but Riker wasn't sure how far he wanted to commit himself until he knew what Zarn had in mind. By now he was long overdue to check in, and the *Enterprise* was surely searching for him. He didn't want to get too far away from where they would be looking, especially since his communicator seemed to be malfunctioning. Although he wasn't sure exactly where he was, he knew he was still within walking distance of the Governance Complex. If the search was being run according to standard procedure, the scans would have started from his last confirmed position and moved outward in concentric circles. Unless the ship was having other difficulties, they should find him, literally, any minute.

"I will take you to a safe place where there are no crazy ones. It isn't too far from here, but if they see you before we get there, the insane ones will try to attack you as they did before." Zarn paused at the top of the mound, swiveling his head to look back at Riker. "Now, will you hurry before someone else requisitions our transportation?"

Riker started to climb, thinking that Zarn seemed a little too eager. Still, he had seen more than enough of these muddy, moldy tunnels to last him a lifetime. Perhaps when they got closer to the surface, it would be easier for the *Enterprise* to locate him. Normally, the ship's scanners should have found him long before this. The radiation levels in the Beltaxiyan system weren't high enough to disrupt the sensors, although some compensation would be necessary to process the data. Since he hadn't yet been found, something in the tunnels must be interfering as well.

They met no one, although Riker saw streaks and scrapes in the dirt and scum on the floor that told him other Jarada had passed that way recently. In a few places the scent of cinnamon or cloves still lingered, striking an almost pleasant contrast to the dominant odors of mud and mold.

After ten minutes they began moving upward a level at a time. In most places they found open ramps that led in the direction Zarn had chosen, but twice they were forced to use the enclosed spiraling ramps. Each time Zarn muttered about the dangers of coding the entry sequence into the locks, but nothing happened either time. Riker wondered if the Jarada expected the computer that controlled the locks to identify them, or if the complaints were to keep him on edge. Given how long it took Zarn to work the locks, Riker didn't need more reasons to be nervous. It was far too easy to imagine someone accidentally stumbling across them in the restricted confines of the shaft.

Finally they reached the surface, ducking out of the building through a narrow door located near the end of a long corridor. It was dark outside, and a dense row of bushes screened them from view. Zarn scuttled along the building, crouching to avoid the branches that arched against the wall. Riker had to bend almost double to keep from being slapped in the face by leaves and thorny twigs.

They turned the corner and crept halfway down the next wall before Zarn found a gap in the bushes. Spreading the branches apart, he gestured for Riker to go through. He stepped out onto a walkway beside a major thoroughfare, lit only by the reddish glow from the gas giant overhead. Fortunately for them, the street was deserted except for a small teardrop-shaped groundcar parked in front of them.

"Hurry!" Zarn whispered, stepping clear of the bushes. He trotted over to the car and tapped its window. The door slid open and the Jarada climbed inside. "Hurry!" he repeated, his voice strident with anxiety.

Riker started forward, still debating whether to get in the car. His instincts told him that he probably wouldn't find a better chance to strike out on his own, but he wasn't sure how far he could get. The empty street offered few possibilities for cover and fewer distractions to keep Zarn from finding him. All he had to do, he told himself, was stay in the clear until the *Enterprise*'s scanners located him. He ran the calculations again and still disliked his chances. Showing Zarn he distrusted him didn't seem like a good bet.

He stepped clear of the overhanging bushes. Above him, Bel-Major hung like a huge rust-striped balloon. Riker stopped, caught by the wonder of the sight. Bands and whirlpools and festoons of white and orange and ochre swirled across the surface of the planet, a glorious reminder of how varied and marvelous the universe was. Riker had flown past Jupiter many times, but he could not remember being on a habitable planet this close to a gas giant.

A distant rhythmic clatter broke into his awareness. Before Riker could identify the sound, Zarn shouted, "Hurry! The guardians are coming!"

At the thought of facing an entire phalanx of large, aggressive Jarada, Riker made up his mind. Now was *not* the time to separate from Zarn. He dove into the car and the door swished shut behind him. Pulling himself around on the rear bench, he found some loose blankets to stuff into the Jarada-shaped indentation on the seat. While he wrestled with the padding and the safety harness, Zarn programmed their destination into the control panel. Riker had just tightened the last strap, when the car shot into the street, accelerating heavily. At the same time, armor plates slammed down over the windows, completely blocking his view of everything. Blind and helpless, Riker could do nothing as the car raced into the night.

Chapter Fifteen

"LET ME GET THIS STRAIGHT." Crusher glared at the five Jarada facing her around the polished black table. They were, as best she could remember, the four senior researchers at the Complex and Vish, acting in the dual role of researcher and chief administrator. Right now, however, her annoyance at their tactics was making it difficult for her to care which small tan insectoid was which. "You want me to stay in this complex without contacting my ship to let them know where I am or what has happened to me, and while I am here you want me to solve a problem that has defeated your best minds. *And* you want me to do this without any of the equipment, or databases, or assistants that I normally have at my disposal to do such work. Am I leaving anything out?"

Vish had the grace to shift uncomfortably in its seat. The rough plaster wall behind the Jarada was a brown ochre, several shades darker than the insectoids facing Crusher. "You must understand, Honored Bev-er-ly, that this problem is so uncomfort-

able to us that we do not even like to admit to it
among ourselves. It would be exceedingly disturbing
to us if others of your hive were to know of our
problem. Since it is known that your race is not
composed of hive creatures, you have no need of the
support of your hive-mind to accomplish your work."

Crusher groaned, wondering where the Jarada had
conjured that conclusion. And how, she wondered,
did their hive-mind function that was so different
from the give-and-take of a well-balanced team of
human researchers? She shifted uncomfortably, trying to find a position where the Jaradan contours of
the chair did not gouge her all-too-human anatomy.
The throbbing cuts on her arm added to her discomfort, jabbing her with sharp pains every time she
moved. With the exception of her tricorder, every
piece of equipment in her medical kit was as nonfunc-
tional as her communicator, although Vish claimed
ignorance of the malfunctions. Crusher had been
forced to treat her injuries by primitive methods,
daubing the cuts with an odd-smelling herbal ointment and covering them with gauze. The jury was still
out on the effectiveness of the treatment, particularly
since the medicine was intended for Jaradan physiology.

Glaring at the Jarada, she heaved an exasperated
sigh. Let's get a couple of things straight. I don't know
how your group mind works, but my people are not
isolated units with each person capable of doing
everything entirely by himself or herself. We're spe-
cialists, with each member of the team contributing
their unique skills and knowledge to the group effort."

"That is not relevant." Vish planted its claws
against the surface of the table in a gesture of finality.
Around the table, the other Jarada bobbed their heads
in agreement. "You do not sense the other workers in
your group. Your mind does not lose its rationality

when it touches the madness of one of your fellows. You will solve our problem for us."

"Let's get *that* straight, as well." Crusher took a deep breath to rein in her anger. She needed to keep her thoughts clear to argue with the Jarada, although she would gladly have let loose with a full-scale tantrum, if she thought it would accomplish anything. Among humans, who expected her temper to match her fiery hair, it was a weapon she kept in reserve for use when logic failed.

The Jarada, however, seemed blind to her annoyance. "You still haven't given me a single reason *why* I should work on your problem. You kidnapped me, you're holding me prisoner and won't let me talk to my ship—and you think I should be willing to help you. *Why* should I want to do anything at all for you?"

Vish straightened to its full height. "Because you do not know how to get back to your hive-mates without our help. Because, if the madness takes us, you will be trapped here with no escape. Because we five in this room are the oldest and the most stable workers in this complex, and I swear to you we will do nothing to return you to your hive until you have solved our problem."

Crusher started to protest, searched the group around the table for the most susceptible individual at which to aim her arguments, and snapped her mouth shut. She had never seen five beings who looked so uniformly adamant about anything. Their triangular heads with the hooked jaws and the faceted, shimmering eyes which reflected her face over and over could have been stamped out of the same mold, for all the differences she could identify.

If she tried to argue them into releasing her, she would be here until sometime in the next decade, with the Jarada ignoring her reasoning until insanity claimed everyone in the room. A random thought wandered through her head: some races conducted their intraspecies business by exchanging hostages for information or favorable treaties, similar to the system used by the ancient Romans. Were the Jarada planning to trade the Federation her research for her freedom? she wondered. From the information she had, she could not determine the rules they were using. With a sigh of frustration, Crusher yielded. "I will need all your records, both from before and after you arrived here on Bel-Minor. I need access to your computer and all your databases. I need the best analytical equipment you have in the complex."

To Crusher's dismay, Vish promptly agreed, as if all her requests had been anticipated. "Our main laboratory has been prepared for your use. You will find everything there that you desire."

"Not so fast." She waved her hand to forestall the Jarada's next words, which she knew would be a politely phrased order for her to begin work at once. "I also need assistants to operate the computers and the equipment."

The large facets in Vish's eyes flickered from green to reddish to amber. "I do not believe that would be advisable."

With a start Crusher recognized the uncertainty in the Jarada's manner. The situation must be far more serious than she had been told, if the thought of lending her a couple of technicians to operate their equipment caused so much concern. But how, without their help, was she to manage? She couldn't speak the Jaradan language, much less read it, so the instruction manuals and the analytical reports would be useless without an interpreter.

"I will require assistance," she said in a tone that brooked no argument. "In the first place, the more help I have, the faster I can solve your problem. And in the second place, I cannot speak or read your language. Since you refuse to allow me any contact with the *Enterprise*, I will have to use the equipment and databases you provide. However, without someone to translate, everything will be useless. It's your choice—I can work on your problem or I can spend the next six months learning your language well enough to conduct scientific research." Crusher allowed herself a moment's regret that her Jaradan translating device worked only on spoken sounds.

Vish's antennae vibrated uneasily. "We do not have six months to wait, Honored Crusher-Doctor. However, we also do not have workers we can trust to assist you. What happened with Mren is but a foretaste of the unpleasantness that will occur if you do not find the solution quickly."

Crusher folded her arms across her chest and leaned back in her chair. The glare she turned on Vish was very familiar to her son, but the Jarada was unaffected. "It seems to me, given the urgency of your situation, that you would want me to use the best tools available. However, since you refuse to allow me access to my laboratory aboard the *Enterprise*, you must provide me with a minimum of help if you want results."

The five Jarada exchanged glances, their eyes flickering through the spectrum as they refocused on different members of the group. Finally, Vish curled its true-arms to its shoulders. "We will comply with your request, although it is against our better judgment. You must understand that we cannot be responsible if the madness should strike all of your assistants at the same time."

"How likely is that?" Crusher suppressed a shiver, not liking the ominous sound of Vish's words. How long did she have before every Jarada in the complex succumbed to the insanity that was preying upon them? Would she be able to survive until the *Enterprise* located her and beamed her and her back to the ship?

Vish bobbed its head, its antennae drooping mournfully. "The more people who are affected, the more likely it is that the rest of us will also go mad. Each new victim rips a wider hole in our group mind, making it harder for the rest of us to resist. You are our last hope."

How do you say "Gee, thanks," in Jarada? she wondered. Even though she recognized how Vish was manipulating her, it was difficult to refuse. Somewhere on the planet was an outstanding reference on human psychology and Vish had studied it thoroughly. "If I am your last hope," Crusher answered with a trace of acid in her tone, "then the very least you can do is provide me with the necessary tools. And that includes people who can operate the equipment and translate the results into a language I can understand."

Vish pushed itself away from the table and started for the door, dragging its claws against the tiled floor. "It shall be as you wish."

The laboratory was spacious and well-equipped, with everything she could have wanted and several things she hadn't thought to ask for. Lab benches filled the center of the room, providing working space for a dozen researchers. The protein analyzer, the gene sequencer, and the medical examination scanner all shone with the unmistakable gloss of new equipment, their fresh-from-the-factory patina unmarred by time and the brush of countless claw-hands. One entire wall was covered with computer screens and control panels, each component looking slightly mis-shapen or oddly sized to Crusher. Everything was ready for her, was waiting for her to set in motion the research that would justify this laboratory.

Crusher shivered, wondering what would have happened if she had refused to help. *I'd probably be here anyway*, she grumbled to herself. The Jarada had been entirely too confident about her acceptance and entirely too casual about obtaining what they wanted by any means. For now she didn't see any options beyond cooperating, but she decided to make the process as unpleasant for them as it was for her. "I want complete bioscans of everyone in this complex," she ordered. "And I want those scans compared with every previous bioscan made of that individual."

"That will take an enormous amount of time, Honored Bev-er-ly." Vish's antennae wiggled in distress. "I do not see why you need new bioscans, when all of us had complete scans taken just before we were assigned here. Unlike your people, our bioscans do not change unless an individual is about to molt."

"Permit me to doubt." Crusher sat on one of the lab benches, letting her legs swing free. She stared at Vish, her arms folded across her chest. "You ordered me to do this job and I—reluctantly—agreed. However, I insist on doing it my way, without any kibitzing from you. If you want my expertise, you will allow me to conduct the research in any way my human intuition suggests to me."

"But I assure you, our bioscans do not change."

Deeply distressed, Vish shifted its weight from one strong-leg to the other. "This has been proven over thousands of generations. The only time a Jarada's bioscan changes is when it is preparing to molt. None of the individuals who have become unbalanced have been approaching their molting time."

Crusher drummed her boot heel against the bench's leg. "In other words, you haven't checked anyone's bioscans to see if the insanity produces any measurable changes in the body chemistry?"

"Of course not," Vish curled its strong-arms to its shoulders. "Why should we waste our time on a useless experiment we all conducted in our first biology class?"

Crusher glared at Vish. "In that case, I particularly want to see the current scans for the individual who attacked me. If you don't like the direction my research is going, then send me back to the *Enterprise* and do the work yourself?"

"Very well." Vish's tone was so reluctant that Crusher almost broke into laughter. Whether she was on the right track or not, her first hunch was leading her down a path the Jarada had not considered. "If you will watch, we will show you how the bioscanners work so that you can operate them on your own."

Vish beckoned to another researcher and that Jarada stepped into the orange-gold cone of the scanner field. In response to Vish's commands, the lights on the control console flashed and winked in time to the scanning procedures, and columns of the oddly shaped Jaradan characters rolled across the screen. Crusher activated her tricorder, using it to record both the operating procedure and her own readings of the Jarada's biochemistry. The tricorder's capabilities as an analytical instrument were severely limited without access to the *Enterprise*'s main computer, but if she lost her Jaradan assistants, she would need every tool at her disposal.

A soft chime marked the end of the scan. The Jarada stepped out of the field, chittering softly in its own language. One at a time, the other Jarada submitted to the procedure while the first Jarada left to relay Crusher's request to the other workers in the complex. By twos and threes the workers filed in and waited their turn. Crusher thought they seemed oddly subdued, as if the threat of madness rested on each of them as heavily as the mass of the building that surrounded them.

After half an hour Crusher was beginning to wonder if her hunch had been wrong. So far, the scans had seemed amazingly uniform, reflecting both the physiological conformity of the Jarada and the genetic uniformity of the individuals within a given caste. Before her doubts could solidify, a small tan-colored insectoid near the head of the line began twitching its head. The smell of sage, overpowering in its intensity, swept over Crusher.

"Quick! Get that one in the scanner!" she ordered. After a moment's hesitation, the four nearest Jarada converged on their afflicted associate. The small Jarada fought with surprising ferocity but no finesse. Eventually it was forced into the bioscan field, biting and clawing the entire time. Vish slapped a hot pink button, and blue lines of force surrounded the tan Jarada, immobilizing it while the bioscanner did its work.

Crusher watched the readings scroll across her tricorder with mounting excitement. Even without running a comparison, she could see the differences. The activity levels of several key enzymes were skewed far beyond every other reading she had obtained so far. Three of the readings were below five percent of the values for the other Jarada, while one enzyme registered almost eight times the next highest concentration she had found. Although Crusher did not yet understand the function of those enzymes, she *knew* the insanity was somehow linked to the readings. The question was—which enzyme was responsible? Or were all four linked to the problem?

"This is not possible." Vish's tone was subdued. "All the best medical researchers for millennia have proven that our physiology is stable."

Resisting the urge to say "I told you so," Crusher scrolled through the data on her tricorder before she answered. "There are many races in the galaxy that show a strong correlation between insanity and biochemistry. In most cases, a disruption in an individual's biochemistry causes the abnormal behavior, but in a few races, insanity disrupts the physiology. Once we have determined cause and effect here, we can begin to solve your problem."

"We are the Jarada." There was a tone of finality in Vish's voice. "We are not like other beings."

Closing her eyes, Crusher counted to ten before she answered the insectoid. "There are certain universal rules that govern ninety-nine percent of all life-forms in the galaxy. It would be exceedingly unusual if your physiology were *not* governed by the same general principles as every other intelligent race. I grant that there are differences in function, that in detail Jarada physiology is uniquely different from every other race. However, unless the same underlying rules apply, unless your bodies are composed of amino acids and proteins and water and minerals and organic molecules which obey the laws I learned in my biochemistry classes, there's no point in my being here."

She drew a deep breath to emphasize her final salvo, even though she already knew what Vish would say. "If your physiology is really so unique that my knowledge doesn't apply to you, then let me return to the *Enterprise*, because there's nothing at all I can do for you."

"You will stay." Vish drew itself up to its full height, but for once, its air of command faltered. "What do you need from us to accomplish your task?"

"First, I will need scans of everyone affected by this madness. And I still need baseline data to compare the new scans with. After that, I require co-operation and assistance." Crusher ran a hand through her red hair, stalling for time. There had to be a way to handle the stubborn Jarada, but what it was remained a mystery. Their racial intolerance made reasoning with them almost impossible. She was beginning to think an insane Jarada was only marginally less rational than a supposedly sane one. "I can do nothing for you if I am constantly fighting with you about the appropriate direction for my research. If you want my help, you must let me do this in what I judge to be the best possible way. Is that clear?"

Vish curled its true-arms to touch its shoulders with its claws. "If that is what you require, we will obtain it for you. In addition, I sense the approach of someone who will serve as a better assistant to you than the ones I have at my disposal. He should arrive within the hour."

"What are you talking about?" She shook her head, trying to follow the abrupt shift in topic. "Have you been in contact with someone who is immune to this madness?"

"Those details are not important." Vish's tone said that the matter was closed. "We have much work to do. I will have our guardians bring the people for whom you have requested bioscans."

One at a time the guardians hauled the insane Jarada into the laboratory and forced them into the scanner field. Most of them were under restraint, their bodies twitching and jerking so much that Crusher had no trouble visualizing what would happen should the bindings work loose. A few were comatose, so far gone in their madness that they were no longer aware of their surroundings.

She studied each new set of readings with growing excitement, as the data confirmed her original guess. The biochemistry of the insane Jarada was severely distorted, with a clear correlation between the severity of the madness and the extremity of the imbalance.

Crusher was so busy searching for the underlying explanation for her findings that she forgot about the promised assistant until someone flung open the door and announced, "He's here." Battered, bruised, and muddy, Will Riker limped into the room.

Chapter Sixteen

AFTER AN HOUR that seemed more like twenty to Keiko, the Jarada quit throwing themselves at the tree trunk and wandered off. It was fully dark by then, and she was unable to tell what the insectoids were doing on the ground below. Even after fifteen minutes of quiet, she thought she saw several darker shadows stumbling through the forest in an erratic pattern. It was enough to discourage her from descending to the ground, but she didn't want to stay where she was either.

"Reggie?" she whispered, hoping her voice would carry only as far as the branch where he was sitting. "Reggie, are you all right?"

For several heartbeats, only silence answered her. Then, softly, Tanaka's voice floated out of the darkness, hoarse with pain. "My leg is pretty badly torn up. . . . I stopped the bleeding, I think, but I won't be able to run from them."

Keiko groaned as the sight of the maddened Jarada replayed itself before her eyes. She couldn't outrun the

Jarada either, and both her legs were uninjured. "We can't stay up here when all our supplies are back at camp."

The tree quivered and the branches below her rustled as Tanaka pulled himself to his feet. Slowly, he levered himself up to her level, guiding himself by touch more than sight. At last he eased himself into the crotch around the tree from Keiko. "I could stay here safely enough if I thought they wouldn't come back. But if you're not used to trees, you'd fall off when you went to sleep."

"And you wouldn't? Are you crazy?" Keiko shivered at the thought of the long drop to the ground. It was bad enough just *being* here, without having to think about *staying*.

"I grew up on Dulsinaray. I'm used to living in trees," He shifted position, the dark bulk of his body leaning over to probe his injured leg.

Keiko closed her eyes and hugged the rough trunk tighter. The sight of Tanaka casually ignoring the open air below him made her stomach roll. She took a deep breath and exhaled slowly, trying to exclude all other thoughts. Instead, the name Dulsinaray teased at the edge of her consciousness. Something in the news, something she had completely disregarded at the time but which had turned up later in one of her classes at the Academy.

Suddenly the memory clicked. About fifteen years ago a group of terrorists had seized the capital of Dulsinaray, taken the government hostage, and proceeded to execute the citizens until their demands were met. Most of the details had faded from her memory, but she still remembered the manner of the killings. Dulsinaray's population was arboreal, living in spacious tree houses far above the swampy, carnivore-infested surface of the planet. The terrorists had exterminated their hostages by setting fire to their tree-homes and stunning anyone who tried to escape to the adjoining trees. The people had either burned to death or had fallen into the swamps below, where their bodies were devoured by the ravenous predators. If Tanaka had been in Dulsinaray City during that brief reign of terror, it explained his reaction to the thought of being held hostage again.

"Dulsinaray?" Keiko asked finally. "Are you from the capital?"

"Yes." He clipped the word so short, she could barely understand it. Then, as if to compensate for his rudeness, he added, "I lost all my family. Can we change the subject?"

"Sure," she agreed, too quickly. The thought of the blazing trees reminded her too much of their current predicament. All they needed was one crazed Jarada to stumble through the woods with a torch lit from the bonfire to make their precarious situation worse. They couldn't outrun the insectoids on the ground, and an uncontrolled fire would turn the forest into a deadly inferno. "How are we going to get out of here?"

Tanaka shifted uncomfortably on his branch and Keiko realized he had been having similar thoughts. She heard him give a deep sigh. "For myself, I'd go through the canopy. I was studying the limb structure earlier this afternoon, while you were asleep. All the trees go up to about the same height, and the branches on the upper levels are firmly interlaced. Skipping from one limb to another in a forest like this is child's play."

"And you don't think I can do it?" Keiko's stomach knotted at the thought of traversing the forest canopy in the dark. Tanaka might think it was easy to stroll along a tree limb using other branches as handholds and to change from one branch to another while the rounded surface beneath his feet bounced in response to his movements, but Keiko found the idea terrifying. However, she was even more afraid of staying where she was.

"Then let's go." He pulled himself to his feet, grunting with pain when he put his weight on the injured leg. "I for one want to be a long way from here when those lunatic bugs come back for us."

Keiko swallowed hard, forcing her stomach back under control. She had, after all, volunteered to try Tanaka's chosen method of escape. Perspiration sprung out on her palms at the thought of following him through the treetops. She wiped one hand and then the other against her uniform, trying to remove the dangerous slipperiness. Reluctantly, she pulled herself to her feet, keeping one hand locked around a branch at all times.

Anything he can do, I can do better, she told herself over and over as she started up the tree after Tanaka. It wasn't that she doubted her abilities exactly, but tree-climbing was not high on her list of job skills. She followed him slowly, glad he was setting a careful and deliberate pace.

As they reached the canopy level and started to work their way across the forest, the reflected glow from the gas giant gave them more light. Even so, Keiko found she was relying on touch rather than on sight to settle her feet on the springy, rough-barked limbs. Her hands were slick with perspiration before they had been moving five minutes.

Fighting her nervousness, Keiko made sure she was grasping one branch before she released her previous handhold. After she adjusted to the idea, she realized she was glad they were doing this in semidarkness. That made it easier for her to convince herself that she was barely above the ground, that if she slipped, the worst thing that would happen to her was a skinned knee or a sprained ankle. Somehow, false as it was, she found comfort in the illusion.

Three hours and a dozen near falls later, Keiko was less reassured by her pretense. She felt dirty and sweaty, her arms were shaking from the constant effort of holding and lifting and balancing her body, and, worst of all, her stomach was seesawing between hunger and nausea with alarming regularity. All she wanted was to crawl into her tent and sleep until the *Enterprise* found them.

"Look. There's the road." Tanaka pointed to a narrow break in the trees.

Keiko shook herself, wondering how he knew it was the road and why it had taken them so long to cover the distance. She was afraid she knew the answer, that her inexperience—more than Tanaka's injured leg or the darkness—had been the reason for their slow pace.

As they reached the row of trees bordering the road, Tanaka told her to hold her position and went on by himself. Part of her protested at being left behind while he scouted out their course, but she was so tired from the unaccustomed mode of travel that she wedged herself into a secure perch on a forked branch. Wrapping her arms tightly around the trunk, she surrendered to her exhaustion. She could not remember when she had felt so sweaty, so thirsty, and so downright miserable in her life.

Fifteen minutes later Tanaka swung onto the branch opposite her. His approach had been so quiet that she jumped in surprise as his hand closed on her shoulder.

"Easy," he murmured, keeping his hold on her. "I didn't realize you were so tired."

"I'm not tired," she protested, her words sounding like a spoiled child. "I'm just not used to this."

"Uh-huh." His tone was noncommittal, refusing the argument. "We've got to go down to the ground now. There's no other way to cross the road."

"Do we need to cross it?" All at once she realized that descending from the trees frightened her as much as climbing through them. Why couldn't they stay where they were until the *Enterprise* got a fix on them? How much longer could it possibly be before the ship located them? Surely her husband was in the transporter room, waiting for the sensors to give him their coordinates.

"I'm afraid we do. My leg needs treatment soon, and the only first aid kit around is in my tent." He squeezed her shoulder for a moment longer. "Besides, we both need sleep, and first-timers should be roped into their perches. I didn't think to bring any rope. Did you?"

Keiko forced a weak grin, although she knew he couldn't see her face. "Not even a millimeter. But is it safe to go down?"

Tanaka sighed. "I think so. At least I didn't see anyone around and the campsite seems deserted. If we cross the road here, circle around through the trees, and approach our tents from the other side, I think we'll be safe. I don't know what else to do."

"Then let's do it now, before I think of some other reason why you're wrong." She took a deep breath, trying to gather up the courage to match her brave words. If nothing else, they should collect their water bottles, first aid kit, and remaining ration bars from their camp. After that, returning to the trees might be their best course of action, but then they would be equipped to handle a long siege.

"That's the spirit!" Tanaka's cheer seemed forced, but Keiko decided not to examine it too closely. "Follow my lead down, since you've picked the best tree for it already."

The limbs were closely spaced, making it easy for her to lower herself from one branch to the next without falling. Only the last stretch was bad, with a gap of twice her height between the bottom limbs and the ground.

Tanaka dropped first, swinging from the lowest branch and then releasing it. He grunted when his weight landed on his injured leg. Before Keiko could ask if he was all right, he whispered up at her, "Wrap your legs around the trunk and let yourself slide down. I'll catch you."

For a moment she clung to the last branch. Finally she released her hold and slid downward toward Tanaka. He caught her at waist height, where she could stand without sprawling in an undignified heap.

It was a pleasure to feel the solid ground beneath her boots, to not sway and bounce with every gust of wind or shift of weight. Keiko leaned against the tree, savoring the feeling of terra firma while the small night noises drifted around her. A squirrellike animal jumped from tree to tree above her head while the hunting cry of a nocturnal bird-analog echoed through the forest. Everything seemed quiet, peaceful, undisturbed. She heard nothing to indicate the presence of a group of crazed Jarada anywhere nearby.

"Come!" Tanaka whispered, tugging on her sleeve.

He started for the road, limping heavily on his injured leg. In spite of that, he slipped through the undergrowth as though he belonged there, barely making any noise. Keiko was hard pressed to keep her movements as quiet.

When they reached the road, they paused to look for Jarada. Everything seemed quiet, and Keiko could only hope that no one was waiting to ambush them. It seemed unlikely, given the irrational behavior the Jarada had shown earlier, but neither of them wanted to gamble unnecessarily. Finally, they took the chance, scooting across the road as fast as Tanaka's injured leg would let them.

On the other side, safely screened by the underbrush, Keiko sagged against a tree, limp with relief. More than anything, the tension was getting to her, draining her of what strength she had left. Tanaka, too, seemed to be losing his edge, his energy and enthusiasm waning with each step. He started off, keeping just inside the forest until he reached the closest approach to their tents.

From the protective shadows, the meadow was a vast and dangerous expanse that offered no shelter or escape from potential attackers. Thirty meters of waist-high grass separated them from the edge of the lake. Nothing moved, no bird-analogs or potential prey, predators, no small grazers or larger gently nodding blades were. Overhead, the rusty ball of Bel-Major glared down on the scene like a bloodshot eye. She shivered, unable to shake the image of an angry god watching her.

"We'll have to crawl," she whispered at last, voicing the thought they both had been avoiding. She had known all along they would have to risk it, but she had hoped a miracle would alter things.

"You lead," Tanaka answered. "I'll be rear guard. If they surprise us, head for the water. I don't think they can swim."

"Right." Keiko crouched low and darted from the trees to the edge of the tall grass. She threw herself flat, holding her breath until Tanaka joined her. They lay still, listening for the uproar that would indicate they had been discovered. The silence enfolded them like a blanket, thick and soft, and after a bit Keiko began inching forward.

The grass was spiky and rough, scraping at her

exposed skin with serrated blades. It was an effort to keep down and keep moving, but somehow she did. Behind her she heard Tanaka's slither and pause, carefully timed to sound random to any but the most discerning listener. Keiko had forgotten how uncomfortable crawling was, how the damp earth clung to her uniform and how every pebble in the entire field gouged her knees and elbows. She was grateful to finally see the silvered expanse of sand through the last clumps of grass.

Keiko looked out cautiously, checking both directions, but the beach was deserted. Wiggling up beside her, Tanaka gave a groan of dismay. At first she didn't see what had caught his attention, but when she did, she had to bite her lip to keep from crying in frustration. Where Tanaka had pitched his tent, the ground was littered with shredded cloth and scattered bits of destroyed equipment. She felt sick, thinking about the effort it had taken to get back here.

After the first shock had passed, Keiko studied the campsite more carefully. Tanaka's tent, programmed the gaudy orange that no one could miss, was destroyed, his sleeping bag and other equipment trampled into the sand by their crazed hosts. However, Keiko's tent survived and a faint line of shadow marked its camouflaged edge. Against all odds the Jarada who had trashed the campsite had missed the second tent. Or had they?

Keiko shivered, wondering if the Jarada were waiting for them inside, hoping that the humans would assume they had missed the tent. She sketched the outline of shadow for Tanaka and then leaned close, whispering in his ear, "Is it a trap?"

He drew a deep breath, testing the air. Keiko copied him and smelled only the damp soil beneath her body. Tanaka's shoulder moved against hers as he shrugged, telling her that he couldn't determine whether any Jarada were still in the area. "I'll go first. If anyone jumps me, head for the water."

Rolling over the pile of boulders that separated the meadow from the beach, Tanaka slithered across the sand to the tent. For the first time, in the ruddy light reflected from Bel-Major, Keiko got a clear look at the gash on his leg. It ran nearly from knee to ankle and went deep into the muscle, although apparently no major blood vessels had been hit. He had stopped the bleeding with a makeshift tourniquet fashioned from his shredded pants leg. The binding was still loosely wrapped around his thigh, although Tanaka had long since released the pressure. However, the reason the wound had stopped bleeding was that Tanaka's calf was swollen nearly double its normal size. Keiko shuddered, wondering how much longer the leg could go untreated. Even with the Enterprise's advanced medical technology, such an injury could cause him to lose the leg if he did not get proper care soon.

Tanaka reached the tent and lifted the edge of the flap. No one attacked at the movement, and he eased himself inside. Keiko watched, but except for a brief jiggle the tent remained motionless. Taking a deep breath, she slipped from the cover of the grass. She felt terribly exposed, as if she were standing naked before the entire crew of the Enterprise, but she forced herself to dash to the tent.

Quickly, she searched the remains of Tanaka's tent until she located his undamaged canteen and the nearly indestructible box of the first aid kit, half buried in the sand. She freed both objects and hurried inside, hoping no hostile observers had seen her. Logic told her that they were safe, that the Jarada would not expect to find them here after their possessions had been destroyed, but Keiko did not want to take any chances. At least if she was in the tent, she was hidden from view; she hoped that would be enough to protect her from further attacks.

Tanaka had collapsed across her sleeping bag, his breathing shallow and feverish. She tried to get him to move, but he didn't respond. After a second attempt she decided he was unconscious and likely to stay that way. Under the circumstances it seemed unwise to make him too comfortable, so she left his boots on but tugged the sleeping bag out from under him to use as a blanket for both of them.

Before she slept, though, Keiko knew that Tanaka's leg needed as much care as she could give it. She draped the sleeping bag over herself and pulled out the flashlight to examine the injury. Dried blood caked the wound and streaked the leg. The edges of the cut were yellowish-white and crusted with dried pus, but most of the calf was a dark purplish-red and hot to the touch. Keiko shuddered, thinking she had never seen a wound become so badly infected so rapidly. Most likely, the Jarada's claws exuded something toxic to humans.

She cleaned the gash as best she could, unwilling to disturb the scabs, and slathered antibiotic ointment into the wound. Looking at the leg, she knew her treatment was completely inadequate, but their first aid supplies were an emergency stopgap, intended to patch someone up before beaming back to the ship. Nothing in the kit was intended for situations like this. Tanaka shivered, his body burning with fever. For good measure, Keiko dug out the hypo and injected him with a double dose of broad-spectrum antibiotics and an antivenom shot.

Then, with nothing more she could do, she stretched out on the air mattress beside Tanaka and pulled the sleeping bag over both of them. *Miles will find us soon,* she promised herself, trying to hold her apprehension at bay. She had intended to keep watch, but in spite of her best intentions, exhaustion claimed her and she drifted off into an uneasy sleep filled with nightmares of friendly insectoid beings that changed into enemies when she turned her back on them.

Sometime much later Keiko drifted back to consciousness, awakened by the sound of several Jarada talking outside the tent.

Chapter Seventeen

THE DANK, MOLDY TUNNEL seemed to go on forever, with no cross-tunnels or intersecting shafts that offered any hope of escape. The thick mud squelched under Worf's boots, a constant reminder of how far underground he was. After ten minutes the corridor ended in a T-shaped intersection. He started to the right, but found his way blocked by a cave-in before he had gone more than fifty meters.

He reversed his course and tried the other direction, but found that the builders had stopped their excavation just beyond the intersection. That left him with two options, neither good. He could return the way he had come, hoping to find another escape route before his pursuers found him. Or he could try to worm his way through the cave-in and hope that an exit lay beyond it.

It didn't take Worf long to decide. Clearly, he had to get back to the captain to warn him of what was happening to the Jarada. His chances of fighting off the overwhelming odds he would face if he retraced his steps were slim. Although a warrior's greatest ambition was to die in battle, death should count for something. To deliberately court suicidal odds when he had other options, however distasteful, was not the warrior's way. With a growl of frustration Worf headed back for the cave-in.

He studied the pile of mud and rubble, trying to make sense of the chaos. Rotting timbers sagged from the ceiling and jutted from the dirt at drunken angles. He prodded a two-decimeter beam, wiggling it until he discovered that it had once been anchored in the tunnel wall. Apparently the builders had tried to shore up the roof at that point, with little success. From somewhere within or beyond the collapsed section he heard the trickle of running water, a constant drip and gurgle that added to his uneasiness. There was too much water in these tunnels, so much that he felt as though an entire lake were poised over his head waiting to sluice over him.

Worf climbed halfway up the mound and prodded at the gap near the ceiling, looking for a hole big enough to crawl through. At first the spaces he found were barely large enough to accommodate a human child. He was almost ready to give up, when the rotting beam again caught his attention. It was wedged between two large boulders and half buried under the mud, but if he could pull the end free, Worf thought he could just barely wiggle through the hole.

Planting his boots into the slippery muck, he shoved against one of the boulders. At first it would not budge, but finally, with a revolting sucking noise, it came free of its muddy cocoon and rolled down the incline.

The second boulder was more difficult. Even when he braced himself against the side of the tunnel and shoved with all his strength, Worf could not get enough leverage to force it loose. Finally, he realized he was not going to budge the rock, so he turned his attention to removing the beam.

Lying flat on his back in the cold, slimy mud, Worf kicked upward, aiming at the unsupported middle of the obstruction. The rotten wood gave a tortured groan and cracked under the impact. Three more powerful kicks widened the break. Worf scrambled to his feet and wrapped his arms around the beam. Throwing his weight backward, he jerked against the weakened section. It yielded slowly, creaking and groaning in protest. Worf continued the pressure until the beam snapped. Overbalanced from the effort, he tumbled backward down the slope and fetched up against the boulder he had managed to move. The impact knocked his breath from his body.

Grunting from the shock, Worf climbed to his feet and crawled up the mound to examine his handiwork, slithering half a step backward for every step he took. A bristly, ragged break separated the two sections of the beam. By tugging the broken ends aside, Worf was able to create a hole that could just accommodate a Klingon. He poked his head into the opening beyond.

The trickle of running water was louder, and it echoed in the empty space. He could see nothing in the darkness, even after he let his eyes adjust to the minimal light that leaked in from the corridor behind him. He felt around with his hands, but encountered only emptiness overhead. A vertical wall rose above him, its surface unnaturally smooth.

Worf slid backward until he regained his footing. To get anywhere, he needed a light. If he had a phaser, he could dry out the rotten wood and use it for a torch. On the other hand, if he had a phaser, he wouldn't be in this mess. The stun setting would easily have eliminated the threat from the crazed Jarada, and he could have rejoined the captain long before.

He started back along the corridor, studying each of

the glowstrips. Most were in such poor condition that it wasn't worth the effort to remove them from their brackets. Finally, he found one strip that still put out a consistent, if weak, glow. It was firmly attached to the wall and it took Worf several tries to break it loose from its fasteners. Bearing his prize, he returned to the cave-in.

In the feeble light from the glowstrip, the opening extended upward into darkness. Worf examined the walls carefully, confirming his guess that the builders had intended to put an enclosed ramp here. The sides of the shaft were smooth as far up as he could see, although the far wall was buried under a mass of mud and debris that filled the bottom of the shaft and spilled out into the corridor beyond. Water slicked the walls and pooled in the low places near the perimeter of the shaft.

A steel rod, about three centimeters in diameter and with a rust-streaked surface, jutted upward in the center of the opening. Worf climbed up to its level and pushed against it, testing its strength. With one hand clamped around the rod, the other hand just reached the wall. The rod flexed slightly but seemed sound and well anchored, and Worf guessed that its upper end was still anchored to the construction bolts. Apparently the cave-in had halted all work on this part of the complex. He just hoped the shaft opened out on another level before it ended.

Wedging the glowstrip under the edge of his sash, Worf started to climb up the slippery pile of mud. His progress was slow, with each step carrying him back downhill almost as fast as he could pull his boots free for the next step. After fifteen minutes of slithering and sliding he reached the top of the mound of waterlogged dirt. Smooth walls extended upward on all sides of the shaft.

Muttering with frustration, Worf held the glowstrip

over his head, trying to see what lay farther up the shaft. The mud under his feet had come from somewhere, and he had been gambling that it had fallen from a hole that he could use for an escape route. At first he thought he had lost his bet, but then he saw a darker shadow on the wall just at the limit of his vision. It was difficult to estimate distances in the uncertain light, but he guessed that the darker spot was about seven meters above his head, which put it two levels above the corridor where he had started. If he was right, the upper corridor had crumbled into the shaft when the construction crews connected the two. All he had to do was get to that upper tunnel.

Holding on to the central rod for support, Worf played the glowstrip over the sides of the shaft. The finish was smooth, almost polished, and showed no signs of obvious deterioration. Briefly, he wondered why the Jarada had not used the same coating on all these lower tunnels to exclude the moisture rather than foolishly building kilometers of corridors that fast became unusable. The mud beneath his feet shifted, forcing him to take two steps to regain his position. That triggered another train of thought, suggesting that perhaps the moisture buildup behind the coating was what had caused the cave-in.

Such speculations did not solve his immediate problem, however. The shaft was too wide for him to jackknife his way up it and the surface was too slick to provide any handholds. That left only the central rod. He shook it again, listening to the hum of the vibrating metal and wondering how strong its anchoring bolts were. Given the condition of these tunnels, he was reluctant to bet his life on the sturdiness of the fastening. Still, if he could not escape by climbing up the rod, he would be forced to return the way he had come.

His decision made, Worf tucked the glowstrip back

under his sash and started up the steel rod, hand over hand. The damp, rusty surface of the metal bit into his hands, alternately aiding and hindering him. He tried to keep his movements slow and deliberate to avoid excess stress on the upper end, but he could feel the metal flexing under his unbalanced weight. Worf decided to move faster, trying to shinny up the rod before it broke loose.

Three meters. Four meters. Five. He was beginning to hope he could make it when the ominous screech of a bolt pulling loose from rock echoed down the shaft. The rod shuddered and started to sag toward the wall. Worf grabbed another handhold higher on the rod, abandoning all caution and trying to climb high enough while he still had time.

A second bolt shrieked and a rain of mud and small pebbles pelted Worf. He lunged upward again, bringing himself to the level of the dark shadow he had noticed from below. He twisted his head to look over his shoulder, confirming that this spot was the scar where the tunnel had collapsed into the shaft.

The edge looked crumbly and weak, and Worf doubted that it would hold his weight. The bar shimmied beneath him, and Worf didn't need to see the anchors to know that only one bolt was left. He made another grab, hoping to get the last bit of height he needed just as the remaining fastener pulled loose.

The steel rod snapped against the side of the shaft with a deafening clang. Worf hung on with desperate strength, hoping his weight would dampen the rebound. The glowstrip slipped loose from his sash and tumbled away, quickly swallowed by the darkness beneath his feet. His knuckles scraped against the rock, but the rest of his body encountered only air.

Worf loosened his legs from around the rod and pushed off, trying to swing himself as far into the opening as he could. Trusting to luck, he released the bar and dropped to the mud, throwing himself backward to get the maximum body area in contact with the floor. Even so, he slid downward and, despite his efforts, arrested his descent only after his boots were hanging out into thin air.

Carefully, Worf rolled over onto his stomach and wiggled uphill. The mud sloped upward toward the ceiling, again blocking his way. Without the glowstrip he had to explore by touch alone, probing with his fingers to find any openings. At first it seemed like he was out of luck, with the mud blocking this tunnel completely. Finally, he located a gap that was just too narrow for his shoulders.

Muttering under his breath, Worf began clawing at the damp, clayey soil. It gooped through his fingers and clung to his hands as if it were glued there, cold and slimy and repulsive, but slowly he forced his way through it. After three meters of squirming on his belly like a snake, the passageway became wider and drier. Phosphorescent patches, possibly bacteria released from broken glowstrips, shed faint, patchy light into the tunnel.

Getting to his hands and knees, Worf began crawling, eager to escape the cramped passageway. It seemed to go on and on, an endless nightmare of cold and wet and mud. He was in so much of a hurry that he didn't notice the subdued buzz of Jarada voices until he almost fell on the two guardians.

Suddenly aware of his danger, Worf froze, berating himself for his lack of caution. The dirt that clogged the tunnel ended abruptly against a wooden retaining wall. A short distance away, a similar barricade closed off the tunnel from a brightly lit corridor beyond. In the space between the barriers, two Jarada were clutching each other and writhing on the ground.

More insanity? Or simply illicit behavior such as drugs or forbidden dueling? Worf decided he didn't want to know.

Creeping back from the edge, he reversed his position. Feetfirst, he dropped over the wall. Grabbing the Jarada by their necks, he cracked their heads together with his full strength. Both sagged to the ground, unconscious. Leaving them, Worf crossed to the second barricade and looked over it. He was in a well-lit, *dry* corridor that ended a few meters to the right at a well-marked door. As he watched, it opened and a dozen guardians marched out, moving at double time. Worf ducked below the barrier and waited until the clatter of their claws faded into the distance.

When he was sure the corridor was deserted, he climbed over the barricade and headed for the door. Much to his surprise, it responded to the same sequence as the others: 1-1-3-2-1-2-3-3-1. He entered the shaft and started up, counting doorways. If he was right, he needed to climb four levels to reach the ground floor.

Once, halfway to his goal, Worf heard another troupe of guardians enter below him. However, his luck held and they went down, the clatter of their claws receding as they descended. The shaft ended in a flat landing at what Worf thought was ground level. For a moment, thinking that the shaft's entrance might be public, Worf considered retreating one level. If he did that, he would have to find another way out of the building, and he had seen more than enough of the underground tunnels.

He entered the lock code one last time and waited for the door to open. The mechanism was sluggish, jerking the door a moment before pulling it back into the wall. Worf stepped into the deserted corridor and saw the most welcome sight of his life. A broad, arched door that opened onto a wide avenue was opposite him. In three long strides Worf crossed the space and shoved the door open.

It was dark outside, with the huge rusty ball of Bel-Major casting an amber half-light across everything. Worf looked around, trying to get his bearings. Through a gap in the bushes he saw a broad, swift-moving river flowing beside the building he had just left. He started toward the water with a sinking feeling in his gut. Almost certainly, if his sense of direction had not completely betrayed him, the Governance Complex—and Captain Picard—was on the far side of the river.

The road turned to the left and dipped downward through a dense wall of bushes. Following his instincts, he started toward the river. From the other side of the hedge Worf saw the spidery strands of a bridge stretching across the water and the globular architecture of the Governance Complex on the far bank. He started toward the bridge, wondering if things could really be so easy.

He studied the layout from the cover of the bushes, looking for concealed obstacles. The deck of the bridge was broad and unguarded, inviting him to cross. No one moved on either side of the river. Their information on the Jarada had not said when the insectoids slept or how long their sleep cycle was, but Worf decided he would not have a better opportunity than now.

He was nearing the middle of the bridge, keeping to the shadows as much as he could, when he heard the hum of a vehicle behind him. He broke into a jog, trying to reach one of the support pylons before he was spotted. Several of the deck plates were missing on the far side of the road, and the edges of the holes were warped. In his haste Worf failed to notice the loose plate ahead of him. His foot landed on its edge and knocked it free.

Worf felt his footing drop out from under him and grabbed for the rim of the hole, a moment too late. His fingers slipped off the metal decking and he dropped toward the river, fifty meters below.

Chapter Eighteen

THE INTERCOM ROUSED PICARD from a fitful sleep. "Go ahead," he told the computer as he swung his feet to the floor and tugged his uniform into place. Sleeping in his clothes was not something he usually did anymore, but the events of the last few hours had revived old habits. Far too often in the old days, patrolling the Neutral Zone, the entire command crew of the *Stargazer* had been forced to sleep as they were and when they could for days at a stretch. The continual alerts were one thing he certainly did not miss in his current assignment aboard the *Enterprise.*

"Selar, here," the speaker announced. "I have preliminary results on the Jarada pilots, if you would come to sickbay."

"I'll be there as soon as possible, Doctor." He tapped his communicator as he stood. "Mr. Data, meet me and Dr. Selar in sickbay in five minutes."

"Yes, Captain," the android answered.

Data arrived from the bridge just as the turbolift deposited Picard outside sickbay. They entered together, threading their way through the complex of treatment rooms and laboratories to the security area where the Jarada were being held. The tall Vulcan doctor greeted them with a brief nod and activated her monitor.

"What did you find, Doctor?" Picard skimmed the columns of data, but the information made no sense to him. That was not really a surprise, since he knew only enough biochemistry to realize how complex the field was. He glanced at Data and was surprised to see a puzzled frown creasing the android's face. Selar's results must be unusual, if the readout could produce that reaction from Data.

"Preliminary results are that both Jarada pilots are suffering a form of insanity due to biochemical imbalance." Selar's voice was calm and level, as though she were reporting the status of inventories in the medical storage locker. "They appear to be suffering from intense paranoid delusions, particularly the delusion that everyone they meet is attempting to destroy their world. Unless they are kept drugged and under restraints, they press home ferocious attacks against any individual who comes within reach. Unfortunately, the levels of sedation that we have been forced to use distort their biochemistry further and interfere with some of our tests."

"Doctor, do you have any explanation for the cause of this biochemical imbalance?" Even as he asked the question, Picard had a sinking feeling that he already knew the answer. The Federation had so little information about *normal* Jarada that it would be virtually impossible for Selar to explain abnormal Jarada.

"We have taken scans of all their biological functions. Unfortunately, I was unable to locate any records of normal Jaradan physiology to use for comparison purposes. All the readings transmitted by the away team from the planet must be considered

228

suspect, until we understand the underlying cause of this aberration." A hint of frustration flickered across Selar's face before she resumed her impassive Vulcan mask. "Without baseline information I will be forced to conduct a random search until I can determine what the problem is."

Data stepped closer, examining the readings before turning to face Picard. "Captain, may I make a suggestion? My positronic brain contains the bio-chemical specifications for one thousand seven hundred and twenty intelligent and semi-intelligent species. With Dr. Selar's help I could compare the structure of the various Jaradan enzymes with those for other races. If I can spot any comparable structures, we should be able to shorten the search process considerably."

Picard glanced at Selar for her reaction. She lifted both her eyebrows to indicate she had no objections. "If Commander Data is willing to help me locating the necessary information, I shall be grateful for the assistance."

"In that case, make it so. Contact me as soon as you have something to report."

"Yes, Captain."

The Vulcan doctor and the android turned to their task, with Selar calling up the descriptions of each enzyme while Data searched his memory for analogs. Picard watched for long enough to realize just how tedious the process would be and then left, unheeded. Their discussion followed him until the door closed.

With all thought of sleep driven from his head, Picard headed for the bridge. He could have called in his request for a progress report on the search just as easily, but he suddenly felt an urge to check things in person. It was the type of hunch a commander ignored at his own peril.

When Picard stepped out of the turbolift, Geordi

looked up from the engineering console, his face registering surprise. "Captain!"

Picard crossed to Geordi's side to see what he was doing. "Mr. La Forge, I didn't think this was your shift."

Geordi gave an apologetic shrug. "Data showed me his latest simulations on how the Jarada might be disrupting our sensors and the patterns kept running through my head. I couldn't sleep, so I decided to try adjusting the sensors to compensate for the hypothetical interference. It beats worrying about it half the night."

The captain leaned over to study the display more carefully. Geordi was working with a theoretical model for the jamming signal, trying to guess the wave frequency and interference characteristics of the radiation the Jarada *might* be using to distort the *Enterprise*'s sensor readings. Half a dozen waveforms of varying frequencies twisted across on the screen, adding and subtracting from each other to create a tangled composite. *"Hypothetical* interference? Can't our sensors at least tell us if someone is disrupting our scan?"

The chief engineer shook his head. "No, Captain. That's one of our main problems. The background radiation in this system has been giving us problems from the word go. As we orbit around Bel-Major, we pass in and out of its radiation tail, which further complicates the readings. Also, Data has virtually proven that the Jarada stole most of the specs for our system when they scanned us at Torona IV. So—*if* these Jarada have that information, and *if* they really are scrambling our scans, they're keying their interference off all the natural problems we'd be having anyway. In fact, we were getting similar results earlier when we ran simulations on how to maintain the transporter lock, and I think we're supposed to believe that it's natural. Of course, the only way we'll know for sure that they're jamming our equipment is when we succeed in breaking through."

"Are you having any luck with it?"

"Not yet." Geordi adjusted a control and entered some numbers in the console. After a moment the pattern on the screen developed two sharp spikes where there had been a broader curve before. "But I've tried only about a dozen combinations so far."

"Carry on, Mr. La Forge." Picard turned away, measuring off the descent to his command chair with even strides. If he was going to spend the next couple of hours trying to figure out his next move, he might as well do it here on the bridge. That way, if anything happened, he would know immediately.

Two hours later the monotony of the planet rotating beneath the *Enterprise* finally began to lull Picard from the hyperalertness that had followed Selar's page. He was even starting to think he had misinterpreted the warning prickle that had sent him to the bridge when he heard Geordi give a short grunt. The captain rose to his feet and circled back to the engineering console. "Find anything, Commander?"

"I think so. Just a minute." Geordi entered a correction into the console, checked the display for the results, and modified his settings yet again. The readout began flashing the words DATA MATCH and a set of coordinates. "We've got someone!" Geordi's voice was exultant.

"Beam the person up immediately," Picard ordered even as Geordi was relaying the coordinates and the jamming pattern to the transporter room. The environmental-status report, the chirps of the various monitors, and the muted buzz of the lights filled the tense silence. The murmur of the air circulation system crescendoed until its oppressive hum echoed from every corner of the bridge. *You never realize how many background sounds there are on this ship,* Picard thought, *until all the foreground noises disappear.*

"Captain, we've beamed Lieutenant Worf aboard and he's fighting mad. Do you want his report now, or should he change into a dry uniform first?" came O'Brien's voice over the intercom. Picard raised an eyebrow, wondering if everyone on the ship was standing extra watches because they couldn't sleep.

Before Picard could answer, Worf's familiar growl ended the discussion. "I will tell the captain *now* of how disgracefully those creatures treated me. They have no honor whatsoever!"

"Send Mr. Worf to my ready room as soon as he's had a chance to see to his immediate needs." Picard started in that direction himself. He had just reached the door when the turbolift opened.

Worf was soaked to the skin, his uniform plastered to his body. Water dripped from his hair and from the points of his dark beard. Despite looking as though he had gone swimming in his clothes, the ends of his fingers were caked with mud, and patches of wet clay were plastered to his uniform. A murmur went around the bridge as everyone caught sight of him. The Klingon strode down the ramp to the ready room, apparently oblivious to the stir his appearance was causing.

Picard led Worf inside. "I could have waited for you to change," he said when the door closed behind them. "You will do me little good if you let yourself die of pneumonia."

"Begging the captain's pardon, but my first duty is to report the treachery of our hosts. You must recall anyone left on the planet before it is too late." Worf grasped the back of the chair Picard indicated but remained standing, dripping water on the floor. After a moment the captain sat anyway.

"We're aware of the problem." Picard studied Worf. Although the Klingon needed dry clothes soon, the captain guessed that he would get little cooperation from him until Worf had told his story. As a stopgap, he ordered hot tea for both of them so that the security chief could have something to counteract the chill of his unplanned swim. "Give me your report, Mr. Worf. Then I expect you to get some dry clothes and some hot food before doing anything else."

"Yes, Captain." Worf described his adventures in the succinct, pithy way that only a Klingon could master. His sparse account of the attacks and his escapes left much to the imagination, but Picard had no trouble visualizing an entire society suddenly gone as crazy as the pilots that had attacked the *Enterprise* earlier. They had to find the rest of the away team and beam them up immediately.

"Thank you, Lieutenant." Picard noticed that Worf's tea was untouched. "Go change into a dry uniform while I see if Commander La Forge can use any of this information to aid in his search. And have someone take a look at your communicator. It isn't registering on the ship's sensors."

"Yes, Captain."

Picard was still mulling over Worf's report, trying to decide what it meant and how to confront Zelfreetrollan with the information, when the door buzzer interrupted his thoughts. "Come."

Data entered, pausing beside the table but not sitting. "Captain, Dr. Selar and I have determined several possible abnormalities in the Jaradan biochemistry. All are related to trace element deficiencies within the enzymatic structures. She is attempting to determine the precise biochemical function of these compounds in the Jaradan body while I run additional sensor scans of this solar system to ascertain if any of the suspected elements occur in amounts considerably below the expected norms."

"May I inquire which elements you will be looking for?"

"Certainly, Captain." Data clasped his hands behind his back and shifted his weight from one foot to the other, reminding Picard of a lecturer he had had at the Academy. He wondered if Data had also sat through Rohner's deplorable lectures on military tactics in the prespace flight era.

"Our best extrapolations suggest iodine, barium, or one of the lanthanide series of rare-earth elements. It may not be easy to determine which element is actually causing the problem, since we expect these elements to occur only in extremely small amounts in any system. However, I have a few ideas that may help narrow the possibilities, once I get the appropriate geochemical information for this solar system."

"Make it so, Commander." Picard pushed himself to his feet and left the room with Data, wanting to observe the results of the scan for himself.

Worf, in a dry uniform, had joined Geordi at the engineering station and they were both hunched over the screen, debating the best way to speed up the search. "I still say we have a better chance if we start from the Governance Complex and then move outward to every major building in the area," Geordi said. "They were invited to attend functions with important dignitaries. We are most likely to find them if we concentrate our search around the primary structures."

"I disagree. The Jarada have connected their city with a network of tunnels leading in every direction," Worf straightened when he noticed Picard's approach. "If Dr. Crusher or Commander Riker encountered difficulties with their hosts, they are likely to have escaped into the tunnels, just as I did. They could be anywhere and moving in any direction, depending on the nature of the obstacles they encounter."

"What about Ms. Ishikawa and Ensign Tanaka?" Picard directed the question to Worf, even though he had stopped beside Geordi to study the display.

"Since we believe Ms. Ishikawa and Ensign Tanaka are some distance beyond the city limits, we will have to institute a standard spiral search pattern centered on the city in order to locate them." Worf zoomed his display to show the area he was talking about. The amount of the territory to be searched was daunting when one considered the difficulty of locating two humans stranded without communicators. "At this time it would seem a better use of our resources to attempt to locate Dr. Crusher and Commander Riker."

"Make it so, Lieutenant." Picard left them to work out their search pattern and settled himself into his command chair. He had just found the correct position for maintaining alertness despite the late hour, when Data's voice broke the silence.

"Captain, I am picking up some unusual thermal readings about three hundred kilometers northwest of the city in an unpopulated sector."

Picard straightened in his seat, wondering what the android had found. "On screen, Mr. Data."

The reference image of deciduous woodlands mixed with scattered lakes and meadows, marked with various identification codes, appeared on the screen. Data adjusted the controls, overlaying the reference scan with his current readings. A gasp of dismay rippled through the bridge like the first breath of a storm. The forest was ablaze, with greedy scarlet and yellow tongues of flame devouring everything within reach. "Wildfire," someone murmured, his tone a mixture of awe and horror.

235

After a moment Picard regained control of his voice. "Is there anyone in the area, Mr. Data?"

The silence stretched while the android attempted to get the answer from the sensors. "It's difficult to say, Captain. Unraveling the thermal signature of the fire from all other readings is a challenging problem in combinatorial mathematics. I am detecting sporadic readings of several large life-forms, but I am unable to determine whether they are Jarada or if they are indigenous animal life."

Picard drew in a deep breath, debating the decision. "Can you scan them well enough to get a transporter lock, Mr. Data?"

"I believe so, Captain." Data replied.

Picard turned toward Worf. "Take a group of your men and meet our 'guests' in the transporter room. Set your phasers to heavy stun."

"Aye, Captain." The Klingon relayed the order and then marched into the turbolift. His face wore a fierce grin, as if the thought of turning the tables on a few Jarada pleased him.

"Why security?" Data asked, puzzled. He realized he was the only person on the bridge who had not followed the logic of Picard's order.

"Because, Mr. Data," Picard answered in a grim voice, "anyone who sets a forest fire is probably as crazy as those pilots down in sickbay. Relay the coordinates to the transporter room and tell them to begin transport at their convenience."

"Aye, sir. Relaying first set of coordinates now."

Picard leaned back in his chair, watching on the viewscreen as the fire devoured its surroundings. He hoped he was doing the right thing, rescuing any Jarada trapped down there. At the moment he needed answers and he needed bargaining chips to get his ship and his crew out of this confusing and potentially lethal situation.

Chapter Nineteen

"WILL!" CRUSHER GASPED, her blue eyes widening in surprise. "How did you get here?"

"That's a good question. I wish I could answer it." Riker limped over to a bench and painfully levered himself up to sit sidesaddle on its top, his swollen knee swung around to rest on the counter. "Right now, though, I'd settle for knowing why."

Crusher slid to her feet and adjusted the tricorder for human physiology. "I can guess part of the reason anyway. I've been demanding an assistant ever since I got here. It looks like you're it." She ran the tricorder over his body, frowning at the readings.

For a moment Riker tried to see himself through her eyes and realized how awful he must look. His uniform was caked with mud and slime and, despite the toughness of the fabric, ripped in a dozen places besides. He'd lost track of the number of scrapes and bruises he'd collected and the nicks from Zarn's claws were starting to feel distinctly painful. A grin twisted the corners of his mouth as he pictured anyone in his

237

present condition, even Wesley, being allowed near Crusher's neat, tidy lab on the *Enterprise*.

"What are you laughing at?" Worry sharpened her tone more than she had intended. "In your condition you ought to be in bed, at least until the swelling in that knee goes down." She turned toward Vish, who was trying to herd the other Jarada from the room. "Is there somewhere Commander Riker can wash off and get something clean to wear?"

Vish jumped, its claws skittering nervously on the tile floor. "Of course, Honored Bev-er-ly. There is a washing trough in the room where you treated your arm. Do you not remember the way there was marked?"

Crusher sighed. "I'm afraid I don't. Would you please show us there again?"

"If that is your wish." The insectoid skittered between them and the door while Riker eased himself off the bench and back onto his feet. "Your time would be better spent in conducting the research you were brought here to do, rather than worrying about inconsequentials. There isn't much time left."

They left the laboratory and started down a corridor, with Vish dancing ahead impatiently and then backtracking to converse with Crusher. Riker's body had stiffened painfully during the ride to the complex, and he was barely able to match the slow pace Crusher was setting. "Truly, you should not spend this time polishing your assistant's carapace," Vish repeated as they turned into a side corridor. "You can worry about its esthetics after you have solved our problem."

"I'm not worried about esthetics," Crusher snapped, her temper starting to fray under the Jarada's chatter. "I'm worried about his ability to function at all in the condition he's in."

"In that case, we can throw this one out and get you one that works properly."

"No!" Riker and Crusher said in unison, their voices mixing like a Jarada's. After a moment Crusher continued without Riker, "I will take any others that you can locate, *in addition to this one,* but he will stay."

"Very well." In a human, Vish's tone would have been decidedly sulky. Riker wasn't sure how much of a human response he was projecting onto the Jarada, but he suspected that Vish's actions boded nothing good for them. He found himself wishing for Zarn, who had disappeared after they entered the complex. Vish's behavior was too irrational to reassure him about the Jarada's motives.

They rounded a final corner and Vish pushed open a plain wooden door. "Here is the place, Crusher-Doctor. I will bring you polishing cloths to dry your assistant's carapace and something to cover it with. But I beg of you to hurry with these inconsequential activities."

"I understand." Crusher's voice cracked with impatience. "I will use the time to inform my assistant of what I expect of him, if only you will quit harassing me!"

"It will be as you wish." Vish skittered away to fetch the promised towels while Crusher held the door aside for Riker.

He limped inside, feeling too drained to care what was happening. The room was small, with a low workbench and several shelves along one wall. Glass jars and small covered pots of various colors occupied most of the shelf space. Crusher pointed to the low arched door in the back wall. "The washing trough is in there. I'm sorry about the lack of privacy, but it doesn't seem to be a concept the Jarada understand."

The washing trough was exactly what its name suggested—a sunken, elongated tub with water flowing in at one end and out the other. Riker wiggled his fingers in the water, surprised to find it was tepid and not the icy chill he had expected. He wouldn't want to spend a lot of time immersed, but he could at least get most of the grime off his body without suffering from hypothermia. The trough was a little small for a human, but again, he thought he could make do. He stripped and eased his body into the tub, wincing as the water touched the raw scrapes on his legs.

He looked around for soap, but all he could find was a bucket of sand. No doubt the gritty stuff would work fine on the Jarada, but just now his skin didn't need any more abrasion. With a sigh Riker began working his fingers through his toes to remove the mud that had oozed into his boots. In the other room he heard Crusher talking to someone, but he didn't pay any attention until he heard her boots moving toward him.

A wadded ball of fabric sailed over his head and dropped into the water in front of him. "Here. A polishing cloth," she said. "There's some more behind you to dry off with, and a couple of sheets that will have to do for clothing." Her footsteps retreated into the other room and he heard her fussing with something on the workbench.

Riker unrolled the cloth, soaked it in the water, and began washing the rest of his body. "What's going on here anyway?" he asked, needing the answers as much as he needed anything else.

"I'm not entirely sure," her voice came back to him. "Vish told me that I was brought here to solve a form of planetwide insanity that's destroying their people. However, they expect me to do it with their equipment and their databases—and without contacting the *Enterprise* for help. What happened to you?"

He gave her a shortened version of his adventures, concentrating on the behavior of the Jarada he had met in hopes that she could find some clue in his descriptions. By the time he finished his story he was clean and dry, with one of the sheets tied around his waist like an Indian dhoti.

"Before you do anything more, let me take a look at your back," Crusher said as he started to drape the other sheet over his shoulders.

"Why? It's just a couple of cuts, isn't it?" Nevertheless, Riker tossed the sheet over his arm and joined her by the workbench.

Crusher activated her tricorder and scanned the cuts on his back. Each of the places where Zarn's claws had broken the skin was surrounded by a purplish-red welt, as though the wounds had been poisoned. By contrast, the deep gash on her arm was still painful and had spotted the bandage with blood, but when she eased the gauze aside, she saw no unusual discoloration. Either the ointment Vish had given her was the antidote for a toxin on the Jarada's claws, or Riker had gotten something into the cuts that had poisoned them.

Since none of the scrapes on his legs showed any abnormal inflammation, Crusher decided on the first hypothesis. She worked the ointment, a pungent mixture of herbs in a tarry base, into each cut and then, for good measure, slathered it on every other wound she could find.

"How much of that stuff do I need?" Riker protested as she smeared it over a scrape on his swollen knee. "It smells horrible."

Crusher stood, wiping the excess off her fingers with a spare rag. Pointing the tricorder at the ointment, she ran a duplicate analysis on it before she capped the jar and returned it to the shelf. "It may smell horrible, but you've got several badly inflamed cuts on your back. Similar injuries on my arm show no signs of infection, so I'm not taking any chances. Until we get back to the ship, that ointment's the best game in town."

"Whatever you say, Doctor." Riker wrapped the second sheet around his upper body and tied it over one shoulder, toga-style. "What's our next move?"

"There's one set of experiments they showed me earlier that I would like to check again. Something about trace elements determining the colors of a plant's flowers. But after that—," Crusher shook her head in frustration, flipping her hair across her face like a red curtain. Raking it out of the way, she shrugged. "I've got tricorder readings on fairly normal to completely unbalanced Jarada, and I've recorded what their bioscanners reported for each individual. But if Vish thinks I can use their computers to make sense of the data, it needs to reconsider."

"Personally, I didn't think Vish was acting all that stable." Riker grimaced, remembering the ochre Jarada's impatient dance as it led them from the lab.

Crusher rubbed a muscle in her neck, frowning in thought. "You're right. In fact, Vish has been acting less and less normal since we got here. I think this insanity is beginning to affect its stability too."

"In that case, I suggest we check out those plants you want to study, then barricade ourselves in that lab with all the equipment. We may not be able to understand it well enough to get any science out of it, but I'm willing to bet we can find something that will attract the *Enterprise*'s attention."

"As long as you're the one who's rewiring things. I'll have you know that I can use any device that comes with a halfway decent operator's manual, but I can't replace the codecard on a door lock." Crusher holstered her tricorder and poked her head into the hall, checking for Jarada. When she saw the corridor was deserted, she stepped through the door and motioned for Riker to follow.

He picked up the bundle that held his wet uniform and limped after her. The textured tile floor was cold against the soles of his feet. For no good reason Riker shivered, wishing his socks and boots had not been too wet to wear. Even more than the rest of his strange costume, his bare feet made him feel vulnerable. As they walked, he continued their conversation. "When it comes to electronics, I have to admit that I flunked the course—twice. I kept cross-circuiting my experiments so that they never worked the way they were supposed to."

"And you're telling me this to build my confidence?" The twinkle in Crusher's eye belied the skepticism in her voice.

"Actually, yes." He paused while she shot him an outraged glare. "If you really want to know, I'm hoping my old skills are still working. If we just tell ourselves we're trying to reconfigure the medical scanners for human operation, I should have a functioning emergency beacon in no time."

Crusher snorted with laughter. Usually she spotted Riker's tall tales before he could spring the last line. For some reason, it made her feel better to know that his sense of the inappropriate was still functioning at peak efficiency.

After returning to the medical lab the doctor paused, searching her memory. She had been taken from the lab where she had been attacked directly to the room they had just left. At the time she had been too distracted to consciously memorize the route, so she had to think a moment, recalling the turns and cross-corridors by kinesthesis rather than by visual clues. The complex seemed deserted, and they met no one on their way to the botany lab.

When they got to the right hallway, Crusher tried

three doors before she found the one she wanted. The room was unchanged, with broken glassware and crushed plants still marking the place where the young researcher had attacked her. Glancing at Riker's bare feet, Crusher told him to wait near the door. She pulled out the tricorder and began walking along each aisle, recording the characteristics of each group of plants.

"What are you looking for?" Riker asked. From where he stood he could see the rows of glass tanks, each containing low bushes covered with different-colored blossoms, but could not tell why these particular plants were significant.

"These are all the same plant. Genetically identical. In most plants the color difference would be caused by variations in the genetic coding for the flower pigments."

"You're saying these plants *don't* have different genes for the different colors?" Riker shook his head, wondering if the insanity was affecting Crusher as well. Somehow the connection between these plants and their current predicament seemed extremely tenuous.

"Apparently not." Crusher shifted her tricorder to scan the next row, walking back toward Riker as she did. "Vish told me there was a link between the trace elements in the soil and the color of the flowers. What caught my attention was the fact that they had not been able to reproduce the color Vish said was the most common on their homeworld."

"Oh." Suddenly Riker felt the light go on in his head. "You think there's a connection between a trace element deficiency and their insanity."

"I'm sure of it. The crazy Jarada that I examined have readings that are well outside the parameters for the rest of their race. Unfortunately, if we're dealing with a biochemical imbalance, I have to *guess* where the deficiency is because I don't have any completely normal Jarada to compare my readings with. I wish we knew more about them."

Riker snorted. "From what I've seen, I'm afraid I know a little more than I would like. So far they haven't exactly been the most relaxing people I've ever been around."

"Yes, there is that." Crusher snapped the tricorder closed and returned it to its holster. Pausing by the counter with the smashed containers, she separated several broken stems from the tangle of crushed plants. "If you tuck these in with your uniform, they should keep well enough for me to do some cell workups when we get back to the ship."

"If you say so." Riker slipped the shoots into his bundle. "Is that all you needed here?"

Crusher nodded. "Let's get back to the other lab and try to get a signal to the ship before someone decides to check on us."

They retraced their steps, still meeting no one. Riker felt a prickle of uneasiness dance along his spine. He didn't know how many Jarada worked in this complex, but if humans had designed it, there would have been hundreds of people here. The solitude made him wonder where all the Jarada were. Had the facility ever been fully staffed or had something happened to the researchers after they were assigned here? Either set of possibilities was further proof of how things were deteriorating for the Jarada on this planet.

When they reached the lab, Riker began studying the equipment. To his surprise, the examination field for the bioscanner had an adjustable focus and could be adapted for what he had in mind. It took him two hours to reorient the components and to rip out the safety regulators, but in the end he had a device that could throw a signal far enough for the *Enterprise's* sensors to detect it. Crossing his fingers and hoping the ship would find them before the Jarada realized what he had done, Riker activated his beacon.

Chapter Twenty

KEIKO BIT HER LIP to keep from crying out at the nightmare sound of the Jarada voices humming and buzzing and clicking outside the tent. After the last few hours she was no longer sure how she should respond to them. All the students they had come here with were clearly crazy, their behavior unbalanced in the extreme. What she had seen of the teachers' disciplinary methods—killing deranged students instead of restraining them—inspired little confidence that the teachers were any more rational than their pupils. But was the insanity only temporary? Or, perhaps, cyclical? Or could a new group of Jarada have arrived to rescue them? As little as she wanted to admit it, the only way she and Tanaka were going to get back to the city was if the Jarada provided transportation. The question was—should they take a chance on trusting the Jarada or would they be better off waiting until the *Enterprise* spread its search pattern far enough to detect the two lone humans in this wilderness? She would have liked to discuss the

247

options with Tanaka, but he was still unconscious. Besides, with the Jarada outside their tent, any noise they made would attract the insectoids' attention.

Tension wound itself tighter around her belly, twisting her insides into a tight knot of fear, and cold sweat trickled down her back. It would be different if she had some means of defending herself. A phaser would be welcome since she was so badly outnumbered. Then she could protect Tanaka, stunning any attackers before they got close enough to injure either of the humans again. Still, given how deadly the Jarada claws were, she would have settled for a well-made staff or even a sturdy tree branch long enough to land a solid blow without putting her within reach of her opponents. It was the waiting, the huddling in the tent and *knowing* she had no way of defending herself, that got on her nerves.

She suppressed a shudder, thinking what would happen if the Jarada outside were as crazed as the ones that had chased her and Tanaka into the forest. No, it wouldn't do to attract their attention unless she was positive they were friendly. And as long as they were speaking their own language, she had no way to tell what they were up to. She reached for the Jaradan translator, but stopped with her hand on the switch. The sound would attract attention from the insectoids outside, and she wasn't sure she should trust the Jaradan device. Tears of frustration burned her eyes as she thought of the damaged communicators. With a functional communicator she would have access to the ship's Universal Translator and she would *know* whether these Jarada were friends or foes. More to the point, she wouldn't even *be* in this mess. At the first sign of trouble, Miles could have beamed them back to the *Enterprise*, Tanaka would not have had his leg injured, and she wouldn't be lying in the darkness with several potentially insane Jarada outside her tent. To keep her panic at bay, she let her mind dwell on Miles and on how she would apologize to him when she got back to the ship. He *had* been right about this assignment, although she still could not fathom the logic behind his conclusion.

After what seemed like forever, the voices faded away as the Jarada wandered off down the beach. Keiko didn't know if they were following the trail she and Tanaka had left—was it only a few hours earlier? —when they had walked along the lake after setting up their camp, or if the Jarada had just drifted that way by chance. Either way, she and Tanaka were safe for the moment.

Her body went limp, sagging against Tanaka's as the tension drained out of her. She shivered, unpleasantly cold where the air touched her sweat-slicked skin, and tried to pull the sleeping bag over herself. The far edge was folded under Tanaka's fever-hot body, and she couldn't free it without moving him. Nor could she raise the temperature to a more comfortable level for her exhausted body. The tent's controller, concealed in its pocket outside the door, might as well have been on the *Enterprise* for all her chances of reaching it.

After a brief struggle she gave up and wiggled as close to Tanaka as she could, thinking, *If Miles hears of this, he'll never stop screaming about it.* Still, it wasn't as if she had a lot of choices. If she kept a decorous separation between herself and Tanaka, she would become thoroughly chilled and the chattering of her teeth would probably bring down an attack by marauding Jarada. And it wasn't as if they were *doing* anything. With Tanaka in the condition he was in, Keiko wasn't even sure he knew where he was or whom he was with.

As if her thoughts had penetrated his delirium, Tanaka stirred and murmured something. Keiko put her fingers to his lips, hoping the gesture would quiet him. Instead, it seemed to have the opposite effect. He thrashed harder, jabbing an elbow into her ribs. She groaned and rolled away, fighting the sudden return of her nausea. It would *not* do to get sick inside the tent, and she dared not crawl outside for fear of attracting attention from any hostile Jarada still in the area. For that matter, wherever she got sick, it would be like a beacon to a race that used scent as extensively as the Jarada. Jamming her hand across her mouth and swallowing rapidly, Keiko fought to keep her body from betraying them to the danger outside.

Finally the queasiness receded and Keiko crept back to check on Tanaka. His breathing was shallow and rapid, and he felt as if he were burning up from the fever. Gritting her teeth, Keiko examined the leg, although the sight of it and the putrid smell of the infection made her stomach lurch. It was worse, much worse, with the swelling and redness stretching upward well past his knee and the yellowish-white rim extending over a centimeter back from the edge of the wound.

Although she knew it was futile, she injected him with the last of the antibiotics and squeezed the remainder of the ointment into the gash before replacing the bandage. Surprisingly, after his earlier restlessness, he was still while she treated him, although she didn't think he was conscious. The job finished, Keiko sat back on her heels, shaking with reaction. She did not need any medical training to know that, unless they were rescued soon, Tanaka was going to die from the toxins in his leg.

He started to thrash again, muttering in his delirium. *What if he makes enough noise to attract the Jarada?* Keiko thought, not liking the direction that thought led. They would both be trapped, since Tanaka was unable to go anywhere and she could not escape into the trees without his help. She crawled under the sleeping bag and held him, stroking his back and murmuring nonsense words to him. For a wonder, it worked and he quieted, lapsing again into sleep.

Keiko lay in the darkness, all desire for sleep driven from her. To keep the dogs of panic at bay, she went over their meager inventory of equipment in her mind, searching for items that could be adapted to broadcast a signal strong enough for the *Enterprise* to pick up. She tried to remember what she had seen in Tanaka's electronics kit, although she feared all the tools had been trampled into the sand by the Jarada who destroyed his tent. Still, if there was anything she could use, if she could recall just one object that might help her, she would brave being caught by the Jarada to find it.

Twice while she lay there she heard the sound of Jarada voices. Once a group, possibly the ones who woke her earlier, passed along the beach headed for the Jarada encampment. Later she heard loud yelling and the thunder of running claw-feet on hard ground as a group of the insectoids charged through the meadow. Keiko did not need to see those Jarada to know that they, at least, were insane.

Fifteen minutes later Keiko noticed that one side of her tent seemed lighter than the others. Frowning, she shook her head to dispel the illusion, but the effect intensified. She glanced at her chronometer, even though she knew it was many, many hours to sunrise. The brightness couldn't be moonrise, because Bel-Minor's small moons were too inconsequential to give much light. The only illumination should have been the ruddy glow of the gas giant, now almost directly overhead, but that would not cause the sudden glow she had noticed.

A sudden gust of wind, heavy with smoke, shook the tent walls. Unable to help herself, Keiko began coughing. She had been trying to ignore the possibility, hoping that if she didn't think about a forest fire, the trees wouldn't burn. When she recovered her breath, she decided that she might as well look outside. If any Jarada were in the area, her coughing had already alerted them to her presence.

Once outside, she saw the extent of the disaster. To the north, where the road entered the area from the highway, the forest was a smoldering ruin. Keiko shuddered, realizing what would have happened if she and Tanaka had stayed in the trees near the road. As it was, the breeze off the lake had blown the fire north, away from their camp, while she and Tanaka had slept. Now, however, the wind had shifted direction, pushing the flames back toward the lake. One tongue had raced ahead, spearheading the onslaught, although most of the nearby forest was as yet untouched. At the edge of the meadow a tree exploded in flames, shooting sparks and smoldering brands in every direction. Satellite fires blossomed in the meadow, dancing among the stalks of grass.

Keiko checked the distance from the edge of the meadow to her tent. It was nowhere near adequate, even if she had had sufficient warning to soak down the fabric beforehand. In fact, she wasn't sure if the entire beach was wide enough, especially when her life was at stake. She stared at the lake, chewing her lip thoughtfully. The water offered their only refuge from the fire, but she wasn't sure how long she could keep them both afloat. Still, they didn't have any other options.

Tanaka was heavier than she had thought, his unconscious body dragging like so much dead weight. She hauled him outside, straining with the effort. Once he was clear, she retrieved their canteens for the purified water they contained and collapsed the tent, hoping against hope that it might escape the fire. By then, all but the fringe of trees nearest the meadow were in flames, and the crackle and roar of the fire almost deafened her.

Summoning strength she didn't know she had, Keiko grabbed Tanaka and lunged for the water. Once she got him moving, the sand made it easier, slipping under his boot heels instead of grabbing at them. She staggered into the water, shivering as the cold soaked into her uniform. Tanaka thrashed and fought, splashing them both thoroughly, but couldn't free himself from Keiko's hold around his shoulders. When the water reached up to her waist, she knelt, submerging herself to the neck and letting Tanaka's legs trail to the bottom.

A ring of flames marked the edge of the meadow, little dancing, spinning orange and yellow demons that mocked her with their cheerfulness. Beyond the grass fires the trees were a solid wall of flames too intense to look at. Even at this distance she could feel the heat blistering her face.

A loud explosion boomed across the meadow. Cascades of sparks fountained into the air, shooting in every direction. Slowly, a huge tree toppled toward the lake, its crown aimed straight at Keiko and Tanaka, flames streaming upward from every limb. Guessing its height and trajectory, Keiko scrambled to her feet. Gulping a deep breath, she pushed off on a diagonal, away from the shore. Tanaka hung in the water, his weight a drag on her movements, but at least he offered no resistance. Perhaps the cold water had shocked him to enough wakefulness that he would let her do the work.

She risked one glance toward the shore, just as a large, blazing limb landed across the tent. Unable to withstand direct contact with that much burning wood, the fire-resistant tent melted and its contents smoldered into flames. The falling tree hit the ground, bounced, and shattered into blazing fragments. One chunk arched out over the water, falling toward Keiko. She kicked desperately, trying to pull Tanaka out of the danger zone, but she knew she didn't have the strength to move both of them that fast.

Gulping a deep breath, she dived, pulling Tanaka down with her. The orange reflections in the water over her head spread farther and farther as the burning log fell toward them. The mirror splintered and the water erupted into a boiling froth. A red-hot chunk of wood seared her arm, and Tanaka jerked as another piece hit him. Then, at the moment when Keiko felt the last hope abandon her, the familiar tingle of the transporter wrapped itself around her and lifted her from the water.

Chapter Twenty-one

WORF COULDN'T DECIDE which was the greater pleasure —frog-marching the sane Jarada to sickbay for Dr. Selar to examine, or stunning the insane Jarada as they boiled off the transporter pads and charged anything that moved. Either way, it felt good to be the one in control.

By ones and twos O'Brien locked on to the insectoids near the forest fire and beamed them to safety. So far they had rescued almost thirty Jarada in varying conditions, and Worf felt admiration for Data's skill retrieving them. It was a difficult task, separating out the insectoids' life-form readings from the thermal background noise and from any creature that belonged in that forest. He had expected at least one large predator to get beamed up despite their precautions, but so far only Jarada had materialized on the pad.

"Why don't we just let them fry?" O'Brien muttered during a brief lull in the work. "They've made off with our people and I say we don't owe them anything."

Worf grunted. "I believe the captain wishes to question them. A wise commander uses all available sources of intelligence."

"This lot doesn't know anything," O'Brien's scowl deepened. "Why should we waste our time rescuing them when they turn around and attack us?"

"Because the captain ordered it," Worf's tone rejected any possibility of disputing Picard's wisdom in the matter.

"These are the last two," Data's voice said over the intercom. "And they seem to be moving."

O'Brien adjusted the controls, tweaked one of the levers against Data's readings, marginally, and energized. Two drenched humans and several gallons of water materialized on the pads. Keiko was clutching Tanaka as though her life—or perhaps his—depended upon the strength of her grip. Worf did not understand much about human relationships, but he knew instantly that in his present mood O'Brien would find the worst possible misinterpretation for this scene.

"Keiko! What the hell do you think you're doing?" O'Brien, his face flushed a brick red, stared at her as if he could not believe what he was seeing.

For a moment Keiko stared back at O'Brien, her expression starting at confusion and shifting in visible steps toward anger. Then Tanaka gasped, struggling for air. Keiko tore her attention away from her husband and lowered Tanaka to the floor, laying him on his stomach and turning his head to the side. When she hit his back with her hands, water gushed from his mouth.

Worf tapped his communicator. "Medical emergency! Doctor to the transporter room!" He glanced at O'Brien, but the transporter chief was still locked in mortal combat with his temper, so Worf started over to help Keiko.

Her second blow shoved more water from Tanaka's lungs. She was preparing for a third try, when he started coughing. That forced out more liquid and Tanaka lay on the transporter pad, gasping. Worf frowned, wondering how a human could recover so quickly from inhaling that much water.

Keiko started to stand, but swayed dizzily from the sudden change in position. Before Worf could steady her, she had slumped to the floor, retching. With clinical detachment he noticed that she had not eaten anything recently.

The medical team charged through the door and descended upon their patients. Wisely, Worf executed a tactical retreat. It was never wise to get between a doctor and her patients. Selar ran her tricorder over both Tanaka and Keiko, then ordered them taken to sickbay. As Tanaka was lifted onto the stretcher, Worf got a clear look at the gash on his leg. The Klingon suppressed a growl, wondering what had caused that wound and why he had not known of such a threat on the planet's surface. The security chief was *supposed* to prevent dangerous aliens from attacking the ship's crew.

Keiko recovered enough to argue with Selar's orders, but the doctor was adamant. Even so, Keiko refused to get on the stretcher and, instead, walked from the room with unsteady strides. O'Brien watched her, furious now because Keiko had ignored him after his angry greeting. *Humans!* Worf thought in disgust. They always seemed to go out of their way to cause trouble for themselves. To avoid getting drawn into this particular family row, he headed for the bridge to report this latest development.

"Ms. Ishikawa and Ensign Tanaka?" Picard repeated Worf's words for confirmation.

"Yes, sir," the Klingon replied, straightening his

shoulders to rigid attention. Behind him the image of the burning forest still occupied the bridge's main viewscreen. "They have been taken to sickbay for examination. Ensign Tanaka has a bad wound on his leg, but Ms. Ishikawa appears uninjured."

"Thank you, Worf. Carry on with your arrangements for our other—guests," *While I decide how we're going to get out of this mess,* Picard told himself. By now he had to have all the answers at his fingertips, but it felt as though one of the key pieces to the puzzle was still lying facedown, where he couldn't see the vital clue.

"Captain, we are receiving another message from Commissioner T'Zen." Data's voice was flat, a perfect study in boredom. "It is the same as all the previous ones, requesting to know if you have transmitted the draft agreement yet."

Picard suppressed a grin, thinking that the monotonous repetition of T'Zen's message had finally given the android a handle on why humans resented tedium so much. Had it really been only twelve hours since they had forwarded the agreement to the Federation Council? Thinking of everything that had happened since then, Picard was tempted to slap a quarantine on the Beltaxiyan system and leave. If Riker and Crusher weren't still on the surface, unaccounted for, and if they hadn't just rescued twenty-nine Jarada from the fire zone, the temptation would have been even greater.

Before he left the system, though, Picard wanted to know *why* things had gone so wrong. Clearly, his first hunch, that he and the *Enterprise*—and the Federation—had been set up, was correct. For his own peace of mind he needed the answers to the mystery. With a shake of his head he pulled his attention back to the android's statement. "Mr. Data, tell Commissioner T'Zen yet again that she should already have received the draft agreement, and that we cannot answer for the validity of the translation or the sincerity of the Jarada."

Data's hands flew over his board as he sent the message. "Captain, do you believe this repetition will in any way influence Commissioner T'Zen's actions in the future?"

Picard stood, unable to resist the desire to pace the deck any longer. "Probably not, Mr. Data. The commissioner seems remarkably impervious to our opinions." He circled the bridge, stopping beside the android to study the sensor readings. Data was far more capable than he was of interpreting the information, but on occasion Picard still liked to see the reports as they came in.

After a few moments the captain resumed his circuit of the bridge, stopping again between the forward stations. "Open a channel to the planet. Let's see if Zelfreetrollan will speak to me *this* time."

The viewscreen shifted to blank, waiting for the Jarada's reply. As Picard expected, it remained dark. "No response on any channel," Data said finally. "I have repeated the message five times on all frequencies."

"In that case, record a message that we have thirty-one Jarada aboard the *Enterprise* and wish to speak to the Council concerning their—disposition. And repeat it at five-minute intervals until further notice."

"Aye, Captain."

Picard started back for his chair, wondering what to do next. Judging from Worf's expression when he had returned from the planet, Picard was sure his security chief would like nothing better than to take an armed force into the Council Chambers and "persuade" Zelfreetrollan at phaser point to give them the answers. The problem with Worf's method was that it was a little too blunt to work with anyone who did not view things in the same stark light as a Klingon.

Data's voice interrupted Picard's thoughts. "Captain, I am picking up an anomalous burst of energy from a location in the mountains a hundred and fifty kilometers south of the city." The android's fingers danced over his board, adjusting the settings. "And, Captain"—he paused again to confirm the readings—"I am scanning two humans in close proximity to the signal."

A sigh of relief and of triumph washed through the bridge. Data had found both Riker and Crusher! "Relay the coordinates to the transporter room, Mr. Data. Tell Mr. O'Brien to beam them home."

"I don't understand his reaction!" Keiko's voice was shrill with indignation. She shifted her shoulders, as if trying to find a comfortable position on the diagnostic bed. After a moment she turned her head toward Troi, her mouth compressing into a stubborn line. "And I don't see why I need to be here either."

"Your husband has been very worried about you," Troi said in a gentle voice. "Men often react with anger to cover the fact that they are relieved."

"Damn stupid reaction! Why couldn't he have just said he was glad to see me?" She changed position again, and this time Troi sensed that her discomfort was mostly emotional. "And why is the doctor keeping me here anyway? I'm not sick."

Troi debated what she should tell Keiko. Anything close to the truth would probably be unwelcome, she decided after a few moments. That left Troi with the option of trying to devise a plausible lie. "That burn on your arm is not trivial. Besides, Dr. Selar wishes to examine you thoroughly, in case you brought any unknown diseases back from the planet. We know so little about this system that every bit of information is useful."

"If there was anything harmful on the planet, the transporter would have filtered it out." Keiko's voice slipped into the didactic tone of someone who doesn't like children but is trying to reason with a four-year-old. "I feel fine. I don't need to stay here."

Troi glanced at the monitors behind Keiko, reading the confirmation for what she had already sensed. No, Dr. Selar did not intend to release this patient until someone, preferably a human doctor, had a long talk with her. Summoning her best professional smile, Troi patted Keiko on the shoulder. "Consider it an unexpected vacation while your husband is getting control of his temper." *And you, of yours,* Troi added to herself. "Besides, given the shape Ensign Tanaka is in, I think the doctor would like you to stay here for now."

"I don't want to!" Despite the defiant words, Keiko's face suddenly went pale and she clamped her hand over her mouth. She swallowed several times, fast and hard.

A commotion at the door interrupted Troi's reply. With relief she broke off the argument as Beverly Crusher herded a limping Will Riker into the room. Troi gasped as she got a good look at them. Crusher's left arm was bandaged from wrist to elbow in heavy gauze, the dressing a textbook example of emergency field care on a primitive planet. Riker had two off-white sheets tied around his body. They were adequate to protect his modesty but did little to hide the numerous scrapes and bruises that covered almost every inch of his body.

"I won't take any more arguments from you, Will." Crusher pointed him toward an empty bed with a gentle push on the shoulder. "You are on the sick list until the swelling goes down in that knee."

"What about you, Beverly? Are you going to relieve yourself of duty until your arm heals?" He paused, but not long enough for her to interrupt him. "The captain needs me on the bridge to help sort all this out."

"Wrong! What information the captain needs he can ask you for shortly. But you're not going anywhere. There's too much risk of serious complications from bruises as severe as yours, particularly since they weren't treated promptly."

"Complications?" To take the weight off his swollen knee, Riker sat on the edge of the surgical bed, but he showed no signs of being ready to lie down. "Hardly anything more severe than would happen to your arm if it started bleeding again, I should think."

"Practicing medicine without a license, aren't you, Commander?" Suddenly, hands gripped him from behind and Selar guided him backward onto the bed. Crusher swung the biomedical unit into position over his torso and locked it in place while Selar brought a smaller unit for his knee. "To answer your question— yes, those bruises are more dangerous because blood clots could develop and then break loose into your bloodstream. The quicker we take care of you, the better I like it."

Riker rolled his eyes, his expression telling her that he still thought she was overreacting. "And what about your arm?"

Crusher snorted at his persistence. "I will *gladly* let Dr. Selar treat it as soon as I take care of you." She checked the readings on his monitors and adjusted the biomedical units slightly. "There. That should do it."

Selar had been watching her, noticing in particular how little trouble she had using her injured arm. "Dr. Crusher, may I ask what happened to your arm?" Reflexively, Crusher brought the arm up against her torso. "One of the Jarada went berserk and clawed me."

"May I examine the injury?" Selar unwrapped the gauze and ran a scanner over the long, clean cut on Crusher's arm. Under the heavy coating of ointment the wound showed no signs of swelling or inflammation. "This is most peculiar."

"I don't see anything wrong." Crusher's tone was defensive. Hearing herself made her realize how tired she was.

"No, but Ensign Tanaka received a similar wound." Selar led Crusher over to Tanaka's bed, where the full-body biomedical unit was struggling to keep his condition stable. "We surmise that the wound was poisoned, but so far we have been unable to isolate the specific toxin."

Crusher handed her tricorder to Selar. "I ran two separate analyses of the ointment the Jarada gave me to treat my arm. You should be able to isolate the active ingredients and administer them in a concentrated form."

"Yes, Doctor." Selar took the tricorder and scrolled through Crusher's information. After a moment she went over to the computer and ordered the lab to make the appropriate medication.

Crusher's communicator chirped, reminding her she had responsibilities beyond her duties in sickbay. She tapped the device to acknowledge the page.

"Doctor, when will you and Commander Riker be ready to give me your reports on what happened on the planet?" Picard asked.

"I'll be able to give you my report in about ten minutes, Captain." *If I remain awake so long,* she added to herself. "However, Commander Riker is confined to sickbay and you will have to come here if you want his report."

"In that case I'll be there in ten minutes, Doctor. Picard, out."

Crusher shrugged and gave Selar an apologetic look. "It sounds like you'd better fix up my arm fast. I think things are about to get a whole lot busier."

Selar glanced around the room, then nodded significantly toward the security area, where the crazed Jarada, under restraints, were being monitored. "I was not aware that we needed any more business to occupy our time to the fullest."

Crusher followed Selar's look, for the first time realizing how many Jarada were in her sickbay. A relieved grin spread across her face. "You've been running tests on them, of course." When Selar nodded, Crusher's grin widened even further. "With those scans and the data I collected on the planet, we should have the answers to this entire mess."

"I sincerely hope you are right." Selar's tone was restrained, but Crusher could see the hope that blazed in her eyes for the brief moment before the Vulcan turned to get the anabolic protoplaser to repair her arm.

O'Brien stood awkwardly just inside the door to sickbay, trying to work up enough nerve to face his wife. He knew he shouldn't have blown up at her, but after the long hours of worrying, seeing her hanging on to Tanaka had been too much for his frayed nerves. Keiko squirmed uncomfortably on the bed, as if held by invisible restraints. Finally, knowing he had postponed his apology too long, O'Brien crossed to her bed.

"I'm sorry, sweetheart," he said as soon as she saw him. "I shouldn't have yelled at you."

"If you'd just looked, you would have seen we were in trouble." Her tone was resentful, but less so than he had feared. She shifted again, trying to find a comfortable spot for her shoulders. No matter how many advances were made in designing hospital beds, no one had ever found one that satisfied an unwilling patient.

O'Brien took her hand. "I know. I was just so worried that I wasn't thinking straight. Will you forgive me?"

For a moment her expression remained so serious that he thought she would refuse. She studied him carefully, and then a brilliant smile spread across her beautiful face. "Of course, Miles. We can talk about it later." The smile shifted to a grimace of intense frustration. "If you'll tell the doctor to let me out of here! I keep telling them there's nothing wrong with me!"

He looked around, trying to find any of the doctors. As if by magic, they had all disappeared. O'Brien squeezed her fingers. "I'll do my best, but it doesn't look like they're going to make it easy. Why haven't they let you go?"

She shook her head. "Dr. Selar said something about routine tests, but they finished all of those. I want out of here!"

O'Brien leaned over and kissed her. "I'll see what I can do." He wanted Keiko out of sickbay as much as she wanted out. He could not give her a decent apology, with a romantic dinner and soft music, while the doctors had her connected to so many monitors.

Chapter Twenty-two

It WAS AMAZING how much clearer everything seemed after a good night's sleep, Picard thought as he surveyed the group around the table in his ready room. Riker was present, certified fit for duty although his stiff movements proclaimed that he was not yet fully recovered. Worf, at the far end of the table, glowered at his shiny reflection with more than usual intensity. Picard didn't need to ask for recommendations to know that his security chief desired a rematch with the Jarada, this time on more equal terms. Even Troi's face wore an unaccustomed grimness, as though she blamed herself for not sensing the Jarada's insanity before so many people were jeopardized.

Picard shifted his attention to the other two officers in the room. Data, he knew, was eager to share the results of his geochemical surveys of the Beltaxiyan system with anyone who would listen. Crusher, although her eyes were dark-shadowed from lack of sleep, appeared almost as eager as Data to report her findings. Between those two reports, Picard hoped, he would have the information to plan their next moves. Mentally, he flipped a coin to decide who should go first.

"Dr. Crusher, would you give us your medical report?"

"Dr. Selar's preliminary tests linked the mental instability with enzyme malfunctions and showed the biochemical imbalances were related to trace element deficiencies in the diet of the Jarada on Bel-Minor. When we compared her results with the scans I made of various Jarada on the planet, we were able to pinpoint the problem. Problems, actually." Brushing a lock of hair off her forehead, Crusher gave a sigh of frustration. "The biochemistry is very complicated, and we're only beginning to understand it."

"Can you give us a brief summary, Doctor?"

"The extreme aggression is caused by *overproduction* of the hormone that functions in their bodies the way adrenaline works in ours. The feedback loop that controls this depends on an enzyme that contains an iodine atom. When the iodine levels fall below a critical value, the system produces the adrenaline-analog continuously. It simply won't shut off." She grimaced, thinking of what a human with a similar condition would be like. "At the same time, the intense delusions are caused by the malfunctioning of another set of enzymes. We haven't completely worked out their proper function yet, but we do know that shortages of three of the rare-earth elements disrupt the secondary and tertiary folding structure of these proteins. At the moment Dr. Selar is administering the deficient elements to several of our guests and observing the results. Her preliminary reports are encouraging."

"Mr. Data, how do your findings correlate with Dr.

Crusher's?" The physical parameters of the system would tell them the absolute limits imposed on any solution.

"The correlation is very strong, Captain. My surveys indicate that when the Beltaxiyan system formed, a number of the heavier elements were preferentially partitioned into Bel-Major. In particular, Bel-Minor shows a strong depletion in all the rare-earth elements and in the heavier of the gaseous elements, such as iodine, which are the elements that Dr. Crusher reports are deficient in the Jaradan enzymes. Of course, it will take further study to determine the exact nature of the geochemical partitioning that occurred when this system formed."

"Thank you, Mr. Data. Please consider the information you need to gather about this system, providing its owners give us permission." Picard doubted that the Jarada would want them around much longer, but if his hunch was wrong, they could start working immediately.

Riker drummed his fingers thoughtfully against the mirror-smooth tabletop. "What do the element deficiencies mean in terms of our mission, Doctor? Will the Jarada you are treating recover completely?"

Crusher shrugged. "It's too early to tell yet, but my hunch is—yes. All our simulations showed that the effects were completely reversible. In fact, Dr. Selar found some tantalizing evidence to suggest that this condition might have survival value if a hive were severely threatened. Crazed fighters, such as the Jarada we've encountered, would be harder to stop than normal individuals."

"Ritual diets or fasting are part of the warrior tradition in many societies," Troi frowned, searching her impressions of the Jarada for supporting evidence. "The carvings and mosaics we saw around the Governance Complex suggest a strong martial element to their culture."

"As did the actions of their guardians," Worf added. "However, we are not talking about their warriors now."

Riker nodded in agreement. "We are talking about an entire society that is being warped by external forces."

"The question is—do we offer them the doctor's findings now?" Picard looked at each of his officers, checking for any final recommendations before reaching his decision. Only Crusher had anything to add.

"This problem completely baffled their best minds, Captain. Any hope we can offer them is better than what they have now."

Riker shifted uncomfortably in his chair, trying to ease a sore muscle. "Besides, by the time they answer our message, Dr. Crusher's results may be conclusive. Unless they have finally responded, all we can do is add this to our broadcast and wait."

Picard nodded. "Mr. Data, make it so."

O'Brien was waiting in her office when Crusher got back to sickbay. "Doctor, is anything wrong with Keiko? Dr. Selar won't let me even see her."

"Keiko!" Crusher slapped her forehead with her palm. Selar had insisted on keeping Keiko overnight, but all the test results had fallen within the normal range. "In all the excitement, I forgot about her."

Lines of tension carved themselves deeper into his face. "I really didn't mean to yell at her when she got back, but— She is all right, isn't she, Doctor?"

"She's fine, Miles," Crusher fought to keep the grin off her face. "But you're going to have to be a little more understanding for a while. She's going to need your help."

"What?" O'Brien blinked, his face gone blank with confusion. "I don't understand."

"I shouldn't be telling you this first, but—you're going to be a father," Crusher watched the proud, bemused grin spread over his face and was glad she had told him. She suspected that she would get little gratitude from the other prospective parent. However, that didn't mean she could put off talking to Keiko any longer.

"I'm what?" Keiko gasped when Crusher told her the news. Her shock made Crusher wonder how she had managed to ignore all the symptoms so far.

Crusher leaned against the bed, watching Keiko with an amused expression on her face. The look was feigned, because she knew *exactly* what Keiko was feeling. She could still remember that horrible sinking sensation when her doctor had given her similar news halfway through her last semester of residency. In the long run, it had meant only that Wesley appeared a year earlier than she and Jack had planned, but in the short term, morning sickness and medical school had been a stressful combination. Still, the experience had taught her that sympathy was the last thing Keiko needed.

"What are you laughing at?" Keiko demanded, turning her anger from her husband to her doctor. "I suppose you think it's funny or something!"

"Actually, I was thinking about myself." Crusher allowed the corner of her mouth to lift in a self-mocking grin. "You sound exactly like I did when I found out I was going to have Wesley."

"You didn't want to have Wesley?" Keiko's anger vanished as she considered this interesting puzzle. "I always thought you were the perfect mother."

"Yeah, well—" Deliberately, Crusher looked down at the floor, as if weighing a heavy confession. When she judged her timing was right, she looked up with an embarrassed shrug. "Jack got an unexpected leave and—well, it happens to the best of us. I've set up a reading program for you so you'll understand what's happening with your body. And, please, come in to talk anytime you need to. I'll be glad to listen."

Keiko took a deep breath. "Does this mean I can get out of here now?" she asked in a calm tone.

"Yes." Crusher stepped aside to let her swing her feet off the bed. Keiko swept out of sickbay, pausing only to glare at O'Brien, who was still waiting in Crusher's office.

Looking crestfallen, O'Brien came up to the doctor. "Does she really hate me that much? I mean, if two people really love each other, shouldn't they be happy to have a baby?"

Crusher sighed. "Which answer do you want for that question?"

"Which?" O'Brien shook his head, looking more puzzled than ever. "I don't understand."

"You want me to tell you, 'Yes, the baby will make her happy because she loves you.' And it probably will, eventually." She gave him an apologetic grin. "Then there's the other answer, the one that isn't so easy. For every woman, pregnancy is a little different. Some become every bit as irrational as our Jarada guests—and for about the same reasons. When you put a woman's body through the changes that go with pregnancy, the mind is affected by the hormones too. Whether you want it to be or not."

"But, Doctor—how long is she going to keep hating me for this? I mean, I've got six younger brothers and sisters and my mother was always so happy when another one was coming."

Crusher shook her head. "Remember, I told you every woman is different?" When he nodded reluctantly, she gave his shoulder a reassuring squeeze.

271

"Your job is to help Keiko as much as possible. That's all you can do right now. While I"—she glanced significantly toward the security area—"have to try getting a different set of biological parameters back to normal."

"Dr. Crusher, can I ask—I mean, I couldn't help but hear what you told Keiko." O'Brien shifted his weight from one foot to the other. "How long did it take for you to quit being mad at your husband?"

She gave him a speculative look, trying to guess how much reassurance he needed. There were times when she could use Troi's empathy! "Oh, about the time I quit being morning sick." *But he doesn't need to know I was one of the unlucky few who was morning sick for eight of the nine months.*

"Thank you, Doctor." His look of relief told her she had guessed right. Now, if only their solution to the Jaradan problem worked so quickly and so well! She stopped for a moment to check Tanaka's leg, which was (at last) well on the road to recovery, before moving on to administer the next round of treatments to the Jarada.

Once more Picard and his senior officers were gathered in the ready room to discuss the Jaradan problem. They had a guest, a Jarada pilot rescued from one of the attacking ships. The russet-colored insectoid stood in the corner of the room, its legs tucked under its body in a resting position. It watched its hosts with great interest, its head moving back and forth as each person spoke. "Still no response to our message, Mr. Data?" the captain asked, just to confirm what they already knew.

"No, sir. There has been absolutely no indication that the transmitter is receiving our signal."

"Dr. Crusher, what is your report?"

Crusher glanced toward her guest before speaking. "The first Jarada to receive injections of the deficient trace minerals have fully recovered. Based on this, we are administering the therapy to all the Jarada on board. We estimate that even the worst cases will be fully recovered by tomorrow morning at the latest."

Picard nodded. "Now that we have the answers to the questions, what's our next step?"

Again Crusher glanced toward her guest. The russet-colored Jarada bobbed its head at her. "I've checked the ship's stores and we can easily spare a three month supply of the necessary elements for every Jarada on the planet. That will give them time to locate their own supplies, even if they have to mine Bel-Major to get them. As far as contacting the Council of Elders, Zelk'helvk'veltran has some thoughts on the matter."

Picard bowed his head to the Jarada. "We would be honored, Zelk'helvk'veltran, if you would share those thoughts with us."

The Jarada stepped forward until its claws rested on the table. "In all probability, the transmitter has been taken off line or has been damaged by unbalanced individuals. I predict that most of the Council of Elders are still capable of dealing rationally with your people, if you can locate them. However, they will not be readily accessible, because they will not wish to be harmed by the insane members of our own society."

"Could you take us to Zelfreetrollan?" Picard asked, leaning forward in his chair to pin the Jarada with his command look.

The Jarada curled its arms upward toward its shoulders. "I believe I can, but I have no guarantees that he will be in the location I predict."

Yes or no? It wasn't a question to ask aloud with their guest in the room. Looking at each of his officers in turn, Picard waited for the fractional nods that indicated they felt the gamble was worth taking. "Mr. Worf, assemble your team in the transporter room in twenty minutes. Dr. Crusher, Counselor Troi, and I

273

will accompany you, as will any of our guests that the doctor feels are in fit condition to return home."

Riker, straightening abruptly to attention, winced involuntarily as a bruised muscle protested. "May I remind the captain that his duty is to remain on the ship in cases of potential danger?"

"Objection overruled, Commander." After a moment Picard let a smile lift the corners of his mouth. "For one, you're in no condition to move fast if it becomes necessary. But more to the point—I've got the authority to conduct this diplomatic mission. And unless I miss my guess, we're about to enter the last round of the negotiations."

"Very well, Captain." Riker looked unhappy, but Picard had effectively shot down his best arguments.

"In that case—we'll beam down in twenty minutes. Meeting adjourned."

They materialized in a deserted corridor in the center of the Governance Complex. Zelk'helvk'veltran pointed to a door near the end of the corridor. "The transmitters are in that room," it said.

Worf moved forward, phaser at the ready position and flanked by two of his men. Cautiously, he pushed at the door. At first it wouldn't budge, but with a little more pressure it swung inward. One of the security guards, crouched to make a smaller target, scuttled inside. After a minute he stepped out again, gesturing to Picard. "Captain, come see this."

The equipment was in ruins, the consoles so thoroughly battered that Picard couldn't begin to tell which device was which. Broken glass, wires, and fragments of chip matrices covered everything. Of the Jarada who had vandalized the room, there was not a trace.

Troi joined Picard. "That explains why they didn't

answer our message," she said as she surveyed the wreckage. "There is no way they could have received it."

"Indeed." Picard turned toward Zelk'helvk'veltran. "You said you could take us to Zelfreetrollan."

The Jarada bobbed its head. "There is a high probability that I know where he is hiding. However, we may not be lucky enough to find him there."

"Show us the way."

Zelk'helvk'veltran started down the corridor, its claws clicking against the tiled mosaics. The *Enterprise* security men fell in behind it, phasers ready to stun any Jarada who challenged them. At first their course seemed random, and Picard was unable to tell where they were heading. After five minutes they reached a sloping ramp and began descending. From then on, every time they reached a split in the corridor, Zelk'helvk'veltran chose the downward route.

Twice they met groups of Jarada, crazed individuals who charged them with bone-jarring shrieks. With great glee Worf cut through their ranks with his phaser, leaving mounds of stunned Jarada to clog the tunnels. Picard felt himself grinning as he watched the enthusiasm the Klingon put into protecting his captain.

The corridors twisted and turned, going first in one direction and then another, but always heading downward. It took Picard several minutes to figure out the pattern and realize that they were heading for a location deep beneath the heart of the Governance Complex.

On the lowest level Zelk'helvk'veltran stopped before an unmarked section of the wall. The Jarada tapped against it, its claws beating a complex rhythm against the rough plaster. Nothing happened, and Zelk'helvk'veltran repeated the sequence. Suddenly every light in the corridor went out and Picard heard the grinding of security doors closing behind them. A heavy, sweet scent filled the air, and then he lost consciousness.

Picard groaned and tried to open his eyes. The light was like twin spikes jabbing through his head. He slapped his hands over his eyes to block out the painful brilliance. Heat singed the backs of his hands briefly, then unaccountably lessened. Perhaps he wouldn't be roasted to death today after all.

"Forgive the manner of our bringing you here, Honored Picard-Captain." Zelfreetrollan's voice was apologetic. "You have seen the nature of the affliction that troubles our people, and we had to be sure that no one could learn of the entrance to this place."

"A simple 'Please don't tell' would have been sufficient." Picard removed his hands from his eyes and was relieved to discover that the light had been reduced to a bearable level. He and Zelfreetrollan were alone in what appeared to be a private sitting room. Half a dozen Jarada-shaped chairs and a few low tables, one of which held a pitcher and some glasses, were the only furniture.

"That technique might work for your people, but it would not have been sufficient for those of my hive who were with you." He paused, watching Picard examine his surroundings. "Please do not concern yourself for your companions. They are receiving refreshments in an adjoining area while we conclude our business."

"I take it, then, that you have some proposals that you wish to discuss." Picard shook his head to clear it. Somehow, his words seemed backward, although he could find no other sensible explanation for Zelfreetrollan's actions. The Jarada must have something new he wanted to talk about, or he would not have admitted them to his sanctuary.

"Yes. I was told that your doctor has solved the problem that baffled our best minds." Zelfreetrollan reached for the pitcher and poured two glasses of fruit nectar.

Picard accepted a glass. "Actually, it was a group effort. My people are not that different from yours. They rarely work in isolation."

Zelfreetrollan waved one claw in a gesture that dismissed Picard's words as irrelevant. "It is of little importance. I was originally going to trade you back your hive workers as payment in full for that knowledge, as is usually done in these matters. Now, I suppose I will have to convince your next in command that he must release this information in exchange for your lives."

Ransom? Picard touched his chest, feeling the blank spot where his communicator should have been. With the Jaradan transmitter out of commission, Zelfreetrollan needed their communicators to contact the *Enterprise* with his demands. The devices were probably somewhere nearby, well protected against any attempt to reclaim them.

Suddenly Picard felt the answers click into place. The Jarada, for whatever reason, could not accept a gift of the medical knowledge and the trace element supplements that Dr. Crusher had prepared for them. They had to have something to trade for them and, he guessed, such hostage exchanges were a standardized ritual among themselves.

Remembering the carvings on the Audience Chamber doors, Picard decided he was on the right track. If their honor would be satisfied by accepting the information and the supplements as a payment to release him and his security team—well, it was without doubt one of the more bizarre transactions of his career. He drew in a deep breath and began speaking.

"First Among Council, as commander of the *Enter-*

prise, I will order Commander Riker to give you that information." He paused, trying to guess how the Jarada was reacting to his words. When Zelfreetrollan said nothing, Picard moved to press home whatever advantage he might have. "In addition, if you will return our weapons and communicators to us, we are prepared to give you three months' supply of the necessary mineral supplements and our geochemical surveys of this planetary system. With that information you will be able to obtain what you need by your own efforts."

Zelfreetrollan studied him for so long, nervous sweat started crawling down Picard's back. If he had guessed wrong, if the Jarada were playing by a different set of rules, they were all doomed. Finally, the Jarada nodded its head. "There is one final condition to which you must agree. This is the most important condition of all."

Picard clenched his hands on his thighs, fighting not to show any reaction to seeing defeat loom again after he had gotten this far. "And what is this condition, First Among Council?"

The Jarada sipped his nectar while he looked Picard up and down, much as he would have examined a laboratory slide of an unpleasant disease organism. "After due consideration, my people have decided that we do not wish to be involved with your people or your Federation. You must promise that you will leave our planet and that your Federation will not disturb us again."

"If that is your wish." Picard let out a huge sigh. "My superiors will expect me to ask you to reconsider your decision, but I think we both know how effective that will be."

"Indeed we do." Zelfreetrollan hummed a minor chord. He stood and held out a hand toward Picard. Opening his claws, he offered Picard his communicator. "I have come to respect you, Picard-Captain, but my people have no desire to associate with outsiders. If you will request delivery of the items you promised, I will permit you to return to your ship."

"As you wish." Picard activated the communicator and relayed his orders to Riker.

"There. That's the last survey." Riker shifted the screen so Zarn could read the file header. "Now we have delivered everything that the captain promised."

The Jarada bobbed his head. "Yes. All the terms of your agreement have been fulfilled."

Riker leaned back in his chair, moving carefully to avoid aggravating his bruised muscles. "Does it have to end this way?" he asked. "Your people and mine could learn so much from each other."

Zarn emitted a high-pitched, whistling sigh. "I, too, believe this would be good, but that opinion is not held by the majority of my people. I am bound to serve according to the wishes of my Hive, until such time as their ideas change. That is the way it has always been."

"If they change their minds, give me a call. I'd like to have a rematch with your musicians when I'm a little better prepared."

The Jarada clacked his claws together in amusement. "I think they would appreciate that as well. I am glad we were able to rescue your instrument for you from all that confusion."

Riker stood and reached for the trombone case.

"Thank you, my friend. I am grateful for your thoughtfulness." He bowed, his gesture matching the formality of his words.

"And farewell to you, my friend." Zarn gave Riker a deep crouch, holding the position until the transporter beam took Riker.

* * *

* *

Six hours later the *Enterprise* headed out of the Beltaxiyan system after delivering the last of the recovered Jarada to Bel-Minor. Picard relaxed in the embrace of his command chair, grateful to be back where he belonged.

"Do you think we did the right thing?" Riker asked, watching the image of the system dwindle on the viewscreen.

Picard shrugged. "It was what they wanted. It's not Federation policy to force people to join us if they don't want to."

"Still, I imagine Commissioner T'Zen will have something to say about all this when she gets our final report. Kind of makes you glad we're this far out, doesn't it?"

Picard groaned. "I'm *sure* she'll have plenty to say." After a moment a smug grin spread across his face. "Which was why I recommended that she be the next person to try negotiating with the Jarada. I'm sure they will appreciate her almost as much as we do."

Riker chuckled. "That sounds just about perfect."

"Coming up on safety point for initiating warp drive," Chang said from the conn.

"Warp factor two. Engage," Picard ordered with relief. "Take us to our next assignment."